SHE RODE WEST

SADDLEBAG DISPATCHES AND W🌼MEN WRITING THE WEST PRESENT

SHE RODE WEST

TALES OF COURAGE, DUST, AND DESTINY

EDITED BY

RACHEL SANTINO

Saddlebag Dispatches, LCC
A Subsidiary of Oghma Communications
Bentonville, Arkansas
www.saddlebagdispatches.com

She Rode West: Tales of Courage, Dust, and Destiny
Description: First Edition | Bentonville: Saddlebag Dispatches, 2025
Identifiers: ISBN: 979-8-89299-060-8 (trade paperback)| ISBN: 979-8-89299-061-5 (eBook)
FICTION/Westerns | FICTION/Action & Adventure |
FICTION/Women

Trade Paperback edition June, 2025

Cover Design and Interior Design by Casey W. Cowan
Cover art by W.H.D. Koerner (1878-1938)
Riding the Range, 1909, Oil on canvas
Interior Art by Charles Marion Russell (1864-1926)
Lady Buckaroo, 1920, Watercolor & pen and ink on paper
Editing by Rachel Santino

For Velda Brotherton—
mentor, matriarch, trailblazer, and friend.

You taught us to write with courage, to live with grit, and
to laugh loud enough to get kicked out of a saloon or three.
You believed in strong women, in truth told plain, and in
stories that could outlast hardship.

You lit the fire in so many of us and kept it burning
through kindness, mischief, wisdom, and the fiercest
kind of love. This book is for you and the women you
championed, the voices you uplifted, and the stories you
knew were worth telling.

The West may be darker without you,
but we carry your light with every word.

Godspeed, Velda.
This ride's for you.

CONTENTS

$\mathcal{J}$NTRODUCTION

WHEN WE THINK of the American Old West, we picture dusty trails, saloons, stagecoaches, and shootouts. Cowboys, outlaws, and gold miners fill the legends of the West—but behind that weathered frontier mythology lies a quieter, often forgotten story. A story of women. Pioneers, ranchers, doctors, teachers, madams, and mothers who shaped the land with determination just as fierce as any gunslinger's draw. This book is about them.

In the 1800s, as settlers moved west in pursuit of land, gold, and a new life, women moved with them—sometimes by choice, sometimes by circumstance. Whether married to a homesteader, seeking work in a new boomtown, or striking out alone in search of opportunity, women brought strength and structure to a land known for lawlessness and uncertainty. They did more than endure the West—they helped build it.

They raised families in sod houses and canvas tents. They established the first schools, opened boardinghouses, published newspapers, and operated general stores. Some stood by their partners through brutal winters and lean harvests. Others defied gender norms entirely—owning land in their names, running cattle outfits, or defending their homes with rifles slung across their shoulders.

The West tested everyone, but for women, survival came with unique challenges. Frontier women navigated isolation, childbirth without medical care, and the constant threat of violence—not only from nature and war but also from men who underestimated or exploited them. And still, they persisted. They carved out roles in towns, tribes, mining camps, and remote homesteads. They brought law, order, healing, education, and sometimes rebellion to the growing West.

Not every story comes with a famous name. For every celebrated figure, thousands of women worked the soil, taught the children, tended the sick, and held families together with little recognition. Writers and historians have too often reduced Western women to caricatures—the schoolmarm, the saloon girl, the outlaw's long-suffering wife. But real frontier life defied such simple roles. Women moved in and out of social categories depending on the demands placed upon them. A widow might run a ranch. A prostitute might save enough to open a hotel. A miner's daughter might become the first female mayor of a frontier town. Their names may be lost to history, but their impact endures.

Many women had to be both nurturing and ruthless, practical and visionary. They didn't have the luxury of being just one thing. In a world where survival demanded flexibility, they became experts in adaptation.

They also resisted—and reshaped—the rigid norms of the 19th century. The frontier gave them chances they wouldn't have had in the East, like the right to own land, to vote in local elections, to work for themselves, and even to reinvent their identities. The hardships were immense, but so were the possibilities. Their resilience continues to inspire. And their legacy—hidden in the records of towns, prairie cemeteries, oral histories, and diaries—is a vital part of the American story.

This book is a tribute to women of the Old West, a reminder that history is richer, wilder, and often surprising when we look beyond the legends and listen to the voices that were always there—just harder to hear. The story of the West is incomplete without them. I hope you'll find inspiration in these stories that capture the hopes, hardships, and triumphs of frontier women.

—**Rachel Santino**
Editor
June 12, 2025

$\mathscr{F}OREWORD$

IT IS MY honor to introduce this eclectic group of women writers in *She Rode West: Tales of Courage, Dust, and Destiny.* The fiction and historical fiction works herein feature remarkable women who helped shape the American West. Stories selected for inclusion in this first-ever anthology span historical to modern times, illuminating diverse women who, by their very existence, colored the world with feminine flair while nurturing their families and communities.

As a retired Oklahoma State Trooper and former U.S. Army Reserves drill sergeant, I speak with some authority on the struggles women have faced and continue to face—often in predominantly male-dominated careers—as we carve out our place in the Western world.

Women on the American frontier encountered difficulties and dangers I can't even fathom. But through these diverse stories, we hear their unique voices. We see the landscapes of their lives. We feel their heartbreak, joy, and love. Their depth, drive, and determination enrich our lives—not only through their survival in harsh conditions but also through their remarkable ability to thrive and blossom despite their circumstances. Even when they were regarded as property, deemed second-class, and dismissed as lesser, they persevered—and prevailed.

She Rode West: Tales of Courage, Dust, and Destiny brings to life historical and fictional characters, showcasing the grit required of women who were—and are—more than soiled doves, dance hall girls, house-wives, or broodmares. These are stories of resilient women who demon-strated their vigor in everyday life in their uncommon occupations and in their unfailing love of the uncharted American West.

—**Betsy Randolph**
U.S. Army Military Police (Ret.)
Oklahoma State Trooper (Ret.)
June 18, 2025

ACKNOWLEDGMENTS

>—·····—≫⫶≪—·····—≺

THIS BOOK RIDES on the strength of many. It was born of passion, carried forward by community, and shaped by those who believe the Western isn't just a genre—it's a living, breathing legacy of story, song, brushstroke, and grit. We are deeply grateful to our partner organizations who continue to keep the spirit of the West alive.

First among them, our presenting sponsor, Women Writing the West—a vibrant, generous, and fiercely committed organization championing women's voices in the genre. Their support turned an idea into a mission. Special thanks to current president Vicki Felmlee, past presidents Gayle Gresham, Lynn Downey, and Betsy Randolph, and board members Alice Trego and Ann Edall Robson—each of whom embodies the strength and vision this collection celebrates.

To the Will Rogers Medallion Awards, thank you for raising the standard. Under the leadership of Executive Director Chris Enss, Secretary Laurie Cockerell, and founder Charles Williams, WRMA has become *the* premier organization recognizing Western storytellers across words, verse, and film in America today. Their tireless work ensures that the old trails never grow cold.

We would also like to tip our hats to the Cowboy Artists of America and their current president, C. Michael Dudash, whose work continues to breathe life into the Western image. In an age when art is too often diluted or disposable, their commitment to truth, beauty, and heritage stands tall.

To Rachel Santino, the editor of *She Rode West*, you are the steady hand and sharp eye behind every page. You brought these stories together with clarity, compassion, and an unwavering sense of purpose. Your mark is on every word, and this collection would not exist without you. You had the backing of our team at *Saddlebag Dispatches*, including Publisher Dennis Doty, Managing Editor Anthony Wood, Copy Editor Don Money, Associate Editor Ben Bailey, and Business Manager Amy Cowan—each one part of the engine that makes the journey possible.

We extend heartfelt thanks to every writer who submitted work. Though only a fraction could be included due to space, your voices matter. Your stories matter.

The soul of this book reaches back more than a decade, to the Northwest Arkansas Writers Workshop—a group of kindred spirits and determined writers, led by two towering figures in Western literature: Dusty Richards and Velda Brotherton. Their belief in storytelling as a shared craft—not a solitary struggle—shaped the ethos of *Saddlebag Dispatches*, Roan & Weatherford Publishing, and our parent company, Oghma Communications. Dusty taught us to write with heart. Velda taught us to write with fire. Together, they mentored hundreds of writers, always with generosity, always with grit. This book, and everything we do, is rooted in their legacy. It is dedicated to Velda specifically, whose spirit remains in every story we share.

We also honor a group of remarkable women writers—trailblazers from both inside and beyond the Western genre—whose work, tenacity, and unwavering dedication continue to inspire us. Some are contributors to this collection. Others are guiding lights who helped shape our path. Some are old friends, and some are new. But all have left their mark. Their words push us forward. Their example reminds us why we do this. Jodi Thomas, Pamela Foster, Patty Stith, Linda Apple, Ruth Weeks, Chris Enss, Sherry Monahan, Betsy Randolph, Linda Sartin, Margot Abbott, Barbara Clouse, Regina McLemore, Kimberly Burns,

Staci Troilo, Dani Nichols, Sharon Frame Gay, Michelle Ferrer, Lindsay Flanagan, and Patty Rusten. Each of them has shown what it means to write with courage and conviction—and to lift others as they climb.

For too long, the Old West has been told through a narrow lens—its women too often cast as background, caricature, or conquest. But the truth is this: they were just as tough, just as brave, just as essential as any cowboy who ever saddled up. They faced the wilderness with children on their hips and grief in their bones. They made homes from nothing and held ground that tried to break them. This book is a testament to their stories, their struggles, their victories, and their fire.

They rode west, too.

And we remember.

—Casey W. Cowan
President & CEO, Oghma Communications
Executive Director, *Saddlebag Dispatches*
June 18, 2025

SADDLEBAG DISPATCHES AND W⚘MEN WRITING THE WEST PRESENT

SHE RODE WEST

TALES OF COURAGE, DUST, AND DESTINY

Until Next Time

KIMBERLY KAYE BACHMAN

WIPING HER JAW, she gazed at her dirty forehand. Blood. She laid a hand to her mouth, running her fingers across her teeth to check. Yep, just as she suspected. She finished pulling the tooth that was hanging on by a thread. Examining its bloody roots, she cussed as she threw it. Hattie lamented that it was a front tooth, which was visible when she flashed a smile.

"Well, I reckon I'll not smile for a while," she mumbled.

Pulling herself to her knees in the dusty street, Hattie Malone attempted to stop the world from spinning. Once she got her bearings, she stood on her feet. She didn't make eye contact with those watching. Instead, Hattie proudly straightened her jacket and then situated the belt that snugged it in close. Adjusting her hat, she wiped her bloody jaw one last time for good measure.

Knight and Lula, the mercantile owners, watched the entire scene unfold... again. Lula had fought the urge to intervene. The last time Lula tried to help, she received a hard blow to the back of the head. It took her three days and a visit to Doc Williams for pain medications. Knight wouldn't have it again. Lula dared not ever step out of the mercantile to arbitrate again.

Hattie winced with every step. She was getting too old for this.

Swinging the saloon door wide, Hattie pulled both pistols. Shooting them in the air, she made her presence known by shouting.

"I'm Hattie Malone, and I aim to run hell on Tieg. Tell me where he is now—save your own skin."

The day drinkers barely stopped to listen to her demand. They, too, had witnessed this scene a time or two.

A man from the back of the saloon shouted, "He went out the back. Hold your fire on us, Hattie. We ain't got no quarrel with you."

Running for the back door, Hattie carefully kept her pistols at the ready. She wasn't about to be ambushed by that yellowbelly weasel again. She stepped cautiously out the door, looking left then right. The sun was starting its descent, blinding her as she searched west.

The whistle of a bullet stung the air, missing Hattie's right ear by mere inches. It infuriated her.

"That's enough," grumbled Hattie as she stepped away from cover and unloaded her pistol in the direction the shots originated. A shout from a lone wagon packed with supplies just a few feet away confirmed a hit, and a dirty hat was flung into the dusty street.

"All right. God damn it. Hold yer fire. I'm coming out."

Hattie held her fire but kept her pistols cocked. Out walked the man who had bloodied her face. She noticed the black eye she planted on him just minutes ago—a good trade, she supposed.

She knew this scoundrel well. He was tall and slim, with piercing blue eyes and predominant cheekbones well seated above a strong jawline. His dark, almost black hair was much like hers, straight and thick. Many women would sell their mama's china for that beautiful hair. He hadn't cut it for years. It hung below his shoulders now.

"Hattie Malone, you shot me, and I swear...." he said, fading off while wiping his surface wound.

With no intention of hitting him, Hattie shot one more off.

He danced a bit while holding his hands in the air.

"Dagnabbit, girl! Put those pistols down."

Hattie laughed and then holstered her weapons.

"Get yourself over here and sit a spell," said Hattie as she plopped down on the wooden step. Pulling her pipe and tobaccy from her jacket, she began to load it.

She heard him shuffle in and plop down on the step next to her. Not wanting to be distracted from tapping her spill, she ignored his loud sigh. In her peripheral, Hattie saw him remove his hat, lean back, and cross his legs. He gingerly tossed it in the air, catching it with the toe of his boot, a natural hat hanger on this sweltering hot afternoon.

She drew from her pipe and handed it to him. He inhaled, then coughed like a beginner.

"You never was a smoke man, was ya?" Hattie, half teasing, half perturbed with his insufficiency in smoking, promptly took her pipe back.

"Hattie Malone," he waved and coughed, "we've got to stop meeting like this."

"It ain't the meeting up that troubles me," she retorted. "It's the behavior that the meeting up instigates that's got me troubled. You knocked my dang tooth out. Look at this," she said as she pointed to her missing tooth.

Tieg made no acknowledgment even though he clearly saw the result of his works.

"It's always been that way."

"And it ain't gonna change," said Hattie.

Both stared into the horizon. The heat waves danced across the prairie just above the grasses, blowing gently in the wind. It created a wave effect rolling up and down. It had a real chance of making one seasick should they watch it steady for any length of time.

"Tieg," she addressed him directly, "you didn't fall in with the horse thieving in the past few months, did you?"

Tieg sat up straight and threw his hat on the ground, angered by her line of questioning.

"I don't take kindly to your accusations, and I ain't gonna respond," he half shouted.

"Then I reckon I just got my answer," said Hattie slowly. "I'd sure hate to see you hang."

"Word has it you got yourself into some less-than-profitable card games lately, Hattie Malone," pushed Tieg.

"In your own words, I don't take kindly to that accusation, and I ain't gonna respond," said Hattie, half caring.

"And in your words, I reckon I just got my answer," Tieg fired back.

Hattie smiled. He always was quick-witted.

The two sat out back for a long spell, not a word between them. It was their way. Words were merely a necessity at most. The fewer spoken, the better their conversation. They drew on each other's violence and reciprocated peace. Both had a restless spirit conjured up by the least amount of turmoil. They were always the first to ride in, the last to ride away, as predictable as they were unpredictable. Folks liked them except for the few that did not. Tieg and Hattie did not let the latter dominate their thoughts.

Hattie Malone finally spoke. "I reckon we're in town for the same reason, Tieg."

"It's that time," Tieg breathed out.

"It's a hard walk," Hattie said thoughtfully. "We best get started before the sun goes down. She's expecting us for damn sure."

Standing up, Tieg reached down, extending a hand to Hattie Malone.

She accepted and let him pull her to her feet. He turned to wipe some bloodstains from her mouth. Hattie never made this walk looking less than respectable.

She let him tug at her face until she couldn't stand it.

"Tieg, you're about to wipe the skin right off my jaw. What ain't coming off, ain't coming off. Let it be. She won't mind."

Before she finished barking orders, she reached for Tieg's collar, straightened it, and patted his dirty jacket down. Dust flew, causing them both to cough and sneeze.

"By God, I'm a bit dirtier than I thought," laughed Tieg. "Been a spell since I've had a long, hot bath."

"You ain't telling me nothing I ain't noticed," retorted Hattie Malone. "Let's get started."

The two walked side by side as they approached the front of the building. Although townsfolk were in the streets and on the boardwalk, only a few noticed them.

"Looks like they're heading up there," said one man to another standing near.

"It's that time again," came the response. "She'll be glad to see them, I reckon."

Hattie Malone and Tieg continued their saunter through the street. It was dusk—the sun glowed on the horizon.

Perfect timing, thought Tieg.

Dust kicked up in small swirls. Spurs jingled in accompaniment.

Hattie pondered the countryside. It was lush in its own way. Cattle grazed on ground so rich it smiled a profit. She grew up in the muddy gumbo that wouldn't sprout a tree, a vegetable garden, or a weed, to be truthful. The sun would beat down so fiercely it created rock-hard soil that wouldn't care to absorb a drop of rain… if it ever had a mind to rain. This particular piece of ground was a bit of an oasis, and Hattie decidedly liked its looks when she returned every year.

Tieg strolled step after step with Hattie, having much the same thoughts. He admired the stirrup-high grasses blowing across the prairie. Cattle grazing in the far pasture were as content as any he'd ever seen. If he weren't such a rambler, this town would be his choice to lay down some roots. Won't happen. He wasn't the settling down sort of man.

Always the saddest walk, thought Hattie with every step they took.

For the life of her, she could not figure out why she and Tieg had to damn near kill each other every single time they came into the same territory. They had shot each other up, torn each other off their horses, and one time, Hattie Malone bit off the tip of Tieg's ear in a raging scramble of a fight. Every fight ended with a shot of whiskey and a reinforced bond that perplexed them and everyone who watched.

Approaching the far end of town, they stopped momentarily at the church. Gazing up, both, in their own awkward way, they paid respects to the higher power of God himself. They were rough as cobs but fully believed God paved their path.

Tieg turned to Hattie Malone.

"Ya ready?" he asked.

"Reckon I'm ready as I ever was," she spoke.

Tieg pulled his hat off his head, then opened the gate, motioning to Hattie with a polite gesture to enter before him. They entered the cemetery in silence. Walking slowly, they approached the grave. Standing in front of the stone, they read the epitaph. It was short, pointed, and strong. Each stood before her, lost in their memories, painful and lovely as they were.

As with every visit, they stood longer than they intended.

Hattie moved first. Tieg followed.

The glow on the horizon was now a bit fickle, having second thoughts on its departure. It would retreat, then rise again as if to say this has been a good day—let it never end. Then, in slow regret, it finally retreated, leaving Tieg and Hattie caught in its mystical grip.

"Well, Tieg, we have done what we came to do. I have no cause for regret in our visit this year."

"I reckon this is it then, until next time," responded Tieg, tugging on his hat.

"Next time I swear you shoot that close to my head, I'll take your whole ear off," said Hattie, grinning.

"I'll be a bit more particular next time," said Tieg, smiling.

She watched as he walked away. Tough as he was, she knew different. Tieg knew the same of her. They would meet again, at the same time, at the same place next year. It was a tradition expected not to be missed.

Tieg reached his dark bay horse and swung on. He loped out with a slap of the reins, waving his hands high for a good show.

"So long, Hattie Malone, until next time!"

Hattie smiled. While wiping a tear, she waved big.

"God be with you until next time, Tieg Malone!"

…and she watched her brother ride away.

—*Kimberly Kaye makes her home out on the sprawling prairie along the Wyoming border of South Dakota. Raised in the flatlands of rural Iowa on a working farm, she is no stranger to driving equipment, tending livestock, and throwing bales. Her rural background, time in the saddle, and infectious sense of humor connect seamlessly with her music, writing, and storytelling. She recently retired from a successful music career. Over the past decade, she has consistently traveled eight states a year. She is an award-winning multi-instrumental singer-songwriter who has played the stages with names you know and love. Her book* Circle Back *was a top-five nominee for Western Poetry Book of the Year in 2022 with the International Western Music Association. Her Western historical fiction novel* 70 Days *was released in July of 2023. Its sequel,* The Next Few Years, *was released in October of 2023.* We Lived It, *the final book in the trilogy, was released in the spring of 2024.*

WRANGLERS WANTED

NATALIE BRIGHT

FORT WORTH
1875

CRISTINA ROSE CHESSER stood near the entrance to the Rusty Nail Saloon staring at a poster.

Wranglers Earn $30 Per Month
Cattle Drive
Central Texas to
Montana Territory
Able to endure harsh weather, hostile Comanches.
Dehorning and animal doctoring most helpful.
We do not care about a man's past but require a good attitude.
Drink, gambling, and cussing will not be tolerated on trail.
Inquire Within
Slaughter Land & Cattle Company

She read the help wanted poster at least five times. Thirty dollars was more money than she had ever seen in her seventeen years. That was enough money to buy Mr. Robertson's gray foal. On the days she rode to town, she had seen the little roan horse in their neighbor's corral, kicking and running circles around his mother. She could train him to be really something.

The batwing doors swung open and a clump of cowboy hats passed by and spilled into the street, their voices full of excitement and energy.

"I'm sure ready to hit the trail. Did he say we were staying on the Chisholm all the way?"

"Stay with me when we get to Kansas, boys. Let's go all the way to Montana."

"I lost my good cow pony last year. He stepped in a badger hole."

Cristina moved aside to let them pass. They never noticed her. "Going up the trail" is all everyone talked about these days. Four months in the saddle pushing lanky, wild Texas longhorns north to the railheads in Kansas would turn any boy into a man. Her brothers bragged about going, a fact they only mentioned when their mother wasn't within hearing distance. Her grandfather had made several trips in the late 1860s, just as the main routes were getting established. She had heard the stories too many times to count.

"Cristina Rose!"

She squinted her eyes at the sound of her mother's voice. She'd been found. Eilene Chesser stopped beside her, the scent of rose water brought a pleasant relief to the odors coming out of the batwing doors of the Rusty Nail. The saloon's name was supposedly related to the method used to create the amber color in the watered-down whiskey served here.

"Cristina Rose," Eilene said again through gritted teeth. "Stop dawdling. Let's get home. Your grandfather is joining us for dinner."

"I'd like a drink of whiskey first," she said with a giggle. Her mother was not amused.

Cristina loved and admired Grandpa but that meant the talk around the table would be an endless repeat of stories about the dangers of the cattle trails. With a sigh she turned to follow her mother along the crowded boardwalk. She watched the purple plume on her mother's hat bob back and forth between town ladies, cowpunchers, store-suited businessmen, and ruffians.

"Cristina Rose Chesser, stop dawdling!"

"Thank goodness you keep reminding me of my name because I might forget it," whispered Cristina under her breath as she hurried to her mother's side and then felt instant guilt for being insolent. It was a character flaw according to her parents. She needed to work on her attitude.

Standing next to their buckboard was her brother, Chet, talking to Roper Jackson, his best friend.

"Good day, gentlemen." Her mother handed Chet her packages.

"Hello, Missus Chesser. Miss Chesser," Roper said as he tipped his hat.

Cristina rolled her eyes. She had known Roper since he was in short pants. She had followed him and her brothers around since she could walk. What was he up to by calling her Miss? She stared at him, but he only grinned back.

"Roper. Please join us for dinner, if you can." Eilene smiled at the boy as he offered a hand to help her in the wagon.

"Yes, ma'am. Thank you, ma'am."

Cristina put the basket in the back, walked around the buckboard, and climbed up in the seat by herself.

Chet clicked his tongue and slapped the reins. "Git up now."

It was market day. The streets were as crowded as the sidewalk, with wagons and carts of every size loaded with chickens, pigs, lambs, lumber, and hay bales. Carriages were parked without the livestock that had pulled them, and teams of horses stood patiently in their collars with no carts attached.

Roper soon caught up with them on his Paint horse named Paint— the boy had no imagination. Cristina admired the way he and his horse moved as one through the crowded streets of the city. He always rode top horses.

They arrived at the Bar C Ranch as the sun rested on the horizon painting the cloudless sky with a golden orange that faded above into a dull blue. In a few moments the light would disappear completely.

"Set the table, please," Mrs. Chesser said. "The day linen napkins will be fine, and then you can slice this bread."

"Yes, ma'am." Cristina stayed busy until Chet and Roper sat down. Her grandfather sat at the head of the table.

By the time her mother had the food served, her father was the last to arrive and sat at the opposite end of the table. Grandpa was already in the middle of a story before they had even blessed the food.

"And then one-eyed Gus yelled, 'Stampede!' The static from the thunderstorm was so thick, it made your hair stand on end. And when the cow's horns touched as they ran, sparks ignited. It looked like a swarm of lightning bugs was flying along with us. Never seen anything like it."

AFTER DINNER, CRISTINA cleared the table in record time and hurried to the porch where the men had gathered.

"I may sign on this year," said Roper.

"Me too," said Chet.

"No, you're not!" Both her father and Grandpa said in unison.

Cristina hid a smile behind her hand when she noticed the pitiful look on her brother's face. At fourteen he thought he was invincible, and that could get him in trouble.

"I could sure use that thirty dollars," she said. "I want to buy Mister Robertson's new foal."

"First of all, girls could never survive a herd of Texas longhorns," said Chet as he stood and leaned next to her ear. "And secondly, that is way more horse than you could ever handle, big sister. Stick to the kitchen. Oh wait, you can't do that either." He sniggered. In a louder voice he said, "Mother! Do you have any more apple pie?"

Cristina's blood boiled as she watched Chet and Roper disappear inside. She could ride a horse as good as any boy, and she was working on her roping. When she turned her head, she noticed that her grandfather was watching her with an intensity that made her nervous. She met his gaze. It was as if he wanted to say something but then held his tongue. After a few more moments he just winked at her and gave her a big toothy grin.

Then an idea took root and almost made her shout out loud. Before she could change her mind, she ran upstairs to her brother's room and found a dirty pair of pants and a shirt. She could still hear the boys in the dining room. Grabbing a sweaty, stained hat from a hook by the back door, she tucked her hair up and slipped out unseen. Before walking into the stable, she peeked around the corner to make sure no one was around. Saddling her mare in record time, she galloped all the way to town.

THE RUSTY NAIL Saloon was in full hoedown mode by the time she stepped through the batwing doors. The piano player and fiddler were sweating, and the dance floor was packed. Several men who dressed like they might be important sat behind a table spread with papers. Cristina backed against the wall to watch the room and get her bearings.

A bowlegged cowboy sauntered up to the table. "Are you still taking on punchers to go up the trail?"

"We sure are. Sign your name here. This is a map of where we'll meet up with the herd. Thank you, sir."

With her heart thudding in her chest, Cristina pulled her hat low and strolled up to the table.

"You look a mite young, son, for a trail hand. We still need a horse wrangler. Does that suit you?"

She cleared her throat. "It sure does," she answered in a low, husky tone but shakier than she would have liked. She signed the paper. For the remainder of the summer, she would be the horse wrangler for the Mitchel and Dickson outfit who answered to the name of Cris Chesser.

As she turned away from the table, she had a panicked thought. She should have used a different last name, but it was too late.

On the road home she worried about how to tell her mother. Maybe she could say that she was spending the summer at a friend's ranch. She could work for the family. She had an aunt and uncle who ran a herd of cattle near Fort Sumner, New Mexico, but her mother would never let her travel that far by herself. She did not want to lie. Chessers were people of their word. Maybe she could leave during the night and not tell anyone about what she was doing. Saying nothing wasn't really a lie.

After a sleepless night, Cris stumbled downstairs to breakfast. Ignoring her little brother who leaned against the counter sipping coffee, she picked up a piece of bacon. Looking around, she noticed that the kitchen was too quiet.

"Where's Mother?" she asked.

"How should I know."

"I'm leaving for a few days," Eilene said as she passed through the kitchen carrying a canvas bag. "Your Aunt Ginnie got bucked off a horse. The telegram did not say when it happened, but I have to see about her. Your father is taking me to the train station. You two behave."

She kissed her son's forehead and then turned to look at Cristina. "Why are you smiling? Your aunt could be in serious pain."

"Sorry, Mother. Of course I am sad to hear about Aunt Ginnie. Do be safe on your travels."

"I considered taking you with me, but you can stay here and help your father. Make coffee. Boil some potatoes." She leaned closer and gave her daughter a kiss on the cheek. "Take this opportunity to work on your cooking skills, Cristina Rose."

"Yes, ma'am."

AT THE END of the week Cristina got out of bed before sunrise. Her bedroll contained a spare shirt, pants, and two pairs of socks. Her brother's old hat was big enough that she could wind a tight braid on the top of her head and pull the hat down low past her ears. She thought about leaving a note but then decided against it. Her father stayed busy this time of year with spring calving, it might be a few days before he realized that she was gone. She saddled her mare and took off toward the gathering place arriving just after midday.

A herd of grazing cattle covered the shallow valley bottom as far as she could see. She cut through the beeves toward a bunch of mounted cowboys.

"I am Mister Brown, the trail boss," said a man on a solid black horse. The distinguished-looking boss spoke with a voice that held authority and a calm confidence. He wore a black hat and black vest with a bright red wild rag around his neck.

She eased her mare to the back of the new hires, trying not to attract attention. They were a hardened-looking bunch, obviously not the first trail drive for many. Most of them were not much older than she was.

"No cussing, no whiskey, no gambling. Every drover takes a turn at night shift. No exceptions," Mr. Brown continued. "You'll need to pick out a good string of horses, with at least one that is surefooted enough for night riding. Where's my horse wrangler at?"

Cris slumped down in her saddle to hide behind the group of punchers but then thought better of it, so she kneed her horse closer to the front and raised her hand.

"Cris as I recall. Report to Cookie right now."

She reined her horse around and almost collided with Roper who paid her no mind. Cristina ducked her head and headed toward the chuck wagon.

Grandpa used to tell her that no good cowboy would ever work as a chuck wagon cook unless they got kicked in the head. Cookie was no exception. A stained apron covered his wiry frame, hair hung down to his shoulders, and on top of his head was the most sweat-stained and misshapen hat she had ever seen.

"No horses next to my wagon!" he yelled and pointed at the pasture. Cris backed up her mare and dismounted. For a skinny man he sure had a booming voice.

"Are you the wrangler? No cussing. No gambling. No whiskey and no sleeping when you're supposed to be working in my cow camp. Keep the remuda together and healthy. Can you do that?"

Cris nodded that she understood and almost asked what a horse wrangler did beyond that but held her tongue. She should have asked Grandpa before leaving the ranch.

"The mules are yours too," he said. "Now, help me load these supplies."

Boxes and crates surrounded the chuck wagon. Cris carried the items Cookie asked for. A slab of beef wrapped in a tarp went on the very bottom. Large sacks of salt and pepper, a stack of tin plates, eating irons, a giant box of soda, matches, and a sack of cornmeal and flour—all went in the drawers at one end of the wagon. A shovel, rope, and other tools were arranged at the back of the wagon.

"Lay these under the bench seat." Cookie handed her a wire basket of eggs. She lifted the wagon seat to see that the space beneath was filled with oats for the mule team. She nestled the eggs one by one into the feed.

Cookie handed her a shovel and told her to dig a fire pit, and then he showed her how to pile the wood and set the irons over the fire for holding the coffeepot.

The trail driving crew began to ride up and dismount and toss their bedrolls into the back of the wagon. Some of them brought extra mounts, which they handed off to her.

"This is my morning horse," one cowboy said as he slipped the bridle and reins off before slapping the horse on the rump so that it could join the others. There were so many cowboy names and horse names, she would never remember.

The afternoon passed fast and in no time the entire outfit were sitting on the ground and leaning against their saddles around the campfire with a plate of beans and a hot sourdough biscuit. Cris had never tasted any bread as good as this.

"I got more sinkers if ya want 'em," said Cookie as he served the men another sourdough.

"Man at the pot," someone shouted. That cowboy picked up the five-gallon coffeepot and filled everyone's tin cup.

"We leave at first light," said Mr. Brown as he rode up and dismounted. Cris noticed that he tied his horse to the wagon wheel and Cookie ignored it.

After the mules had their oats, the dishes were done, and the men were bedded down, Cris finally had a chance to find her bedroll in the back of the wagon.

"My spot is under the wagon. You can spread out wherever you'd like," said Cookie. "And keep your boots close or under your blanket, otherwise the coyotes will run off with them."

Cris's head had just hit the pillow before a soft kick to her shoulder brought her out of a restless sleep.

"Rise and shine. I need firewood."

She hustled out into the gray of a predawn morning and returned with an armload of firewood. Tonight, she would gather the wood before going to sleep.

The cowboys rolled up their beds and sipped coffee until Cookie gave the word. "I made it fer ya special, but don't start thinking that I like any of ya."

Cris's empty stomach felt like it touched the back of her spine. She was so hungry, but she waited until the punchers had filled their plates. A large Dutch oven held rice. What a strange breakfast, but she dished it out and took a bite. The most delicious flavors swirled together in her mouth. Bits of raisins and the harsh sweetness of dark molasses blended with the soft rice. She cleaned her plate in no time.

"I need water for the barrel and the wreck pan," said Cookie.

Cris hauled bucket after bucket of water from the stream until the barrel attached to the side of the wagon was full. Then she filled an old metal washtub for the cowboys to dump their empty plates. She hid her face when Roper brought his plate.

"Let's move 'em out!" shouted Mr. Brown from his horse a few yards away.

It was like a fire lit under those punchers. Cris had never seen anyone that could saddle a horse that fast, and in the dim light too. They swarmed into the remuda with their bridles hanging from one arm and their saddle in the other hand. In a few short motions they were mounted and trotting in a single line around the back of the herd.

"Stop gawking and start packing," said Cookie. "Here. You're gonna need this." He tossed a square of blue calico toward her.

In no time the air filled with dust and moans as over a thousand beeves began moving north. The cowboys whistled and shouted and slapped their thighs with their hats. The lanky longhorns tossed their heads in defiance, some challenging the men on horseback, but those ranch horses never back down.

Cris tied the wild rag over her face as she noticed the other riders had done and moved back and forth behind the extra horses on her mare, easing them forward to follow the chuck wagon.

Just like that she was a trail hand on the Chisholm Trail. She couldn't still the beating of her heart or wipe the grin from her face.

DAYS TURNED INTO nights which turned into more long days as the work began before sunup and ended after the sun had disappeared below the horizon. She began to learn the horses' names and personalities. They were always frisky and stubborn in the early morning and hard to catch.

The cowboys would call out their preferences.

"Bring me Pablo."

"Catch Major for me."

"I want that buckskin with the one white sock."

As they filled their plates and coffee mugs, Cris tried her level best to have the horse bridled by the time the rider approached with his saddle.

One evening, Cookie was in a good mood and told her that he was making the boys some fluff duff.

"Candy just like Mama made it, God rest her soul," he said as a tear ran down his cheek.

At supper Cookie proudly passed around a tin plate of dark-colored candy. When they put a piece in their mouths, a look of surprise formed on their faces. Cris had to stifle a giggle. She tried to bite into the treat but hurt her jaw. It was like biting into a rock, so she let it set on her tongue instead. Molasses and cinnamon.

"I jus' broke a tooth," whispered one man. The other cowboys gave him a frown and told him to shush. Grandpa always said only a fool argues with a skunk, a mule, or the doughbelly.

Cris watched as they helped themselves every time the tin plate was passed around. Cookie grinned and puffed his chest out, pleased as punch that the boys had enjoyed his mama's candy so much.

Under a full moon Cris silently slipped out of cow camp to take care of personal business. The prairie was silent except for Roper's scratchy voice as he rode night watch. When she tiptoed between two mesquite trees, she stumbled on a pile of rocks. She squinted at the ground and stopped because those rocks looked awfully familiar. She picked one up and sniffed. There was no mistaking Cookie's candy. The boys had emptied their pockets, and someone had hidden the evidence. With a giggle, she took off her bandana and filled it up, tying all four corners together.

The next morning when she approached the remuda, she gave every horse that allowed her to rub his nose a piece of that candy. The others soon caught on. As the men called out which mount they preferred, she had them all bridled and waiting.

Mr. Brown rode up at about that time. "Good job, son."

IT TOOK A week for the herd to get trail broke. They traveled during the day and then they were thrown off the trail every evening to drink, graze, and bed down for the night.

Cris was able to avoid Roper because they kept so busy. By the second week it seemed that he was always near. She stayed on the opposite side of the wagon when he came around or she would leave to pick up cow chips or wood for the cook fire. She caught him staring at her several times.

"Don't I know you?"

Cris jumped out of her skin at the sound of that familiar voice as she resisted the urge to turn and look at Roper who stood just behind her. She ducked her head and focused on the washtub.

"No, sir," she replied.

He didn't force a conversation but left her with her heart hammering so hard in her chest she thought she might pass out.

When it was time to set up camp, Cookie called out as he pulled on the driving lines to stop the wagon. "Woah. That's not good."

Cris steered her mare up next to the chuck wagon and looked in the direction he was pointing.

Dark gray and black thunderclouds churned in the distance with streaks of blue rain shooting to the ground in some places on the horizon.

"That's going to be on us by nightfall. Let's get the fly staked and stretched over camp. Keep a horse close and saddled, and sleep with your boots on."

The rain started just as Cris snuggled down into her bedroll and covered her head with her slicker and the canvas. The rain gently pelted her bedroll and lulled her into a deep, exhausted sleep. She woke with a start. A crack of lightning made her jump and then the ground vibrated beneath her.

"Saddle up and do what you can to keep the horses together," Cookie said as he flew past her, heading for the mules.

Cris jumped to her feet and sprinted for her horse. She turned the mare toward the remuda, but the horses were gone except for a few that came toward them.

The static in the air made the hair on the back of her neck tingle. She froze as she watched the herd milling around in a circle. The clattering of their horns created tiny sparks over their heads. Lightning flashed again and she could see the men on their horses spread out in positions around the herd, doing their best to keep them in a tight circle. She spurred her horse to fill the closest hole.

With the next flash of lightning the circle broke and the herd surged forward. Two cowboys were caught in the middle of the frenzy, and she couldn't tell if they had been trampled.

Cris trusted her horse and gave her rein to run. They had to find the remuda. The rain pelted her face. Her fingers ached because she gripped the saddle horn so tight, but all she could think about was staying in the saddle. There was no time for fear.

The thundering noise of a thousand hooves pounding the ground surrounded her. Even the booms of thunder and cracks of lightning couldn't silence their panic.

How many hours had she been in the saddle? The predawn light surprised her, but the longhorns were still running and her horse with them. The light did bring a different perspective, and she could see the horses running together on the outside of the herd. If she could work her way closer, she might be able to slow them down.

And just like that the rain turned to a gentle drizzle and the black sky turned to a dull gray. She began calling out their names and worked her way to the front of the pack. She had to give credit to this little mare she rode, as they worked together.

Cris had always had a good sense of direction, and she knew about where the chuck wagon had been. So she whistled and called out their names again until she had the remuda slowed. The entire group was lathered and panting. She turned them toward Cookie and wondered if there were any cowboys alive to finish the drive.

The last thing she remembered is being hurled head over boots and landing hard on her side. A sharp pain shot through her arm and the world went dark.

"Cristina. Wake up. Where are you hurt?"

She opened her eyes and saw Roper and two horses standing over her.

"Is my horse all right?"

"Yes. Can you stand?"

With his help, she slowly rose to her feet and then realized that he had used her name.

"You have to swear that you will never tell anyone," Cris said as pain caused tears to flow down her cheeks.

He touched her shoulder, and she yelled out. Taking the bandana from around her throat, he gently wrapped it around her arm to create a sling and tied it behind her neck. "I am fairly certain it's broken. And I promise not to say a word. Can you ride?"

She nodded and he gave her a leg up.

"I have to go," he said.

"I know."

Every step the mare took shot a jolt of pain up her arm, into her shoulder, and across her back. She needed to throw up.

The chuck wagon finally came into view, and she rode straight toward the welcome sight with the remuda in tow.

"You're a sight for sore eyes," Cookie said, and then he frowned. "And it looks like this is the end of the trail drive for you, kid."

THE LONG, HOT summer passed, and Cristina was bored to tears for most of it. Her parents had never questioned the horse incident that had broken her arm, nor had her father bothered her about the several weeks that she went missing. Her arm healed fine, although on stormy nights her wrist would ache something awful and her thoughts drifted to that night in the rain and lightning. She completely understood how that kind of life could work its way under your skin. As her grandfather told them many times, a man who has had a hand in trailing longhorns and eaten chuck wagon food, is not quite the same ever again.

In the early fall, Grandpa volunteered to drive Cristina to pick up their supply order and her mother had told her to pick out a piece of calico for a new dress. Roper was back and had asked her to the Henderson's barn dance.

The wagon rolled to a stop in front of the general store. Air left Cristina's lungs and her stomach clinched when she noticed Mr. Brown, the trail boss, walking their way.

She climbed down from the buckboard.

"Chesser! You old dog, you. It's great seeing you. We really appreciate the help your grandson gave us in April. I can't say enough about how sorry I am over his broke arm."

"My grandson? You must have the wrong boy."

"Cris Chesser. He was my wrangler for a few weeks until that durned freak thunderstorm set off a stampede. He sure hung and rattled, though."

"His name was Cris, you say?"

"Stayed with the remuda all night. Even had a few longhorns in the bunch when we found him the next morning. Hell of a trail hand. Wish I'd had two or three just like him."

Grandpa cleared his throat and placed an arm around her shoulders. "Have you met my granddaughter, Cristina?"

The trail boss removed his hat and shook her hand and then didn't let go as he stared at her face. He shook the questioning look from his eyes. "Nice to meet you, ma'am." And then turned to her grandfather. "If you ever want to go up the trail again, it would be fantastic to have a Chesser riding in the crew. And tell that grandson of yours to call me about next year."

Cristina stood frozen in place as they watched Mr. Brown walk away. Her grandfather slowly turned and faced her. Her insides were shaking as she fought not to lose her breakfast. Whatever the punishment, she would face it. Even if it meant nothing but inside housework. Even if it meant never being allowed to ride a horse again or being forced to stay in the kitchen for the rest of her born days, heaven forbid. Those two weeks pushing Texas longhorns up the Chisholm Trail were worth it.

She slowly turned and met his gaze.

Grandpa gave her a wink and a broad smile. "I bet you have some stories of your own to tell."

"Yes, sir, I just might."

—*Natalie Bright is a blogger and author of over twenty novels for kids and adults. She is also the author of two Western-themed cookbooks for TwoDot Books, holds a BBA in business and marketing, and is the owner of a cattle ranch. She loves museums, used bookstores, and Texas sunsets.*

ᴛʜᴇ *Legend of Silver Heels*

KIMBERLY BURNS

BUCKSKIN JOE, COLORADO
SUMMER 1905

BUCKSKIN JOE WAS full of ghosts—heck, the whole town was a ghost. Billy wasn't scared, but it was just common sense to take care when walking past a cemetery. He quickened his steps and tried to whistle, but the ever-present South Park wind carried the tune away as soon as it left his lips.

For millennia, wind rushed through Kenosha Pass and across the broad expanse of the old Indian hunting grounds of South Park. It ruffled the shaggy manes of massive buffalo and whistled through the antlers of grazing elk. In the winter, it drove snow into drifts as high as men's heads and in summer it danced across swaying gramma grass. The wind howled. It shrieked. It moaned. This afternoon, as it tousled Billy's hair, he thought it sounded like weeping.

Checking over his shoulder as he hustled along the wrought iron fence, Billy saw a figure. In the graveyard, the wind tugged at the long black skirts of a veiled woman. She moved slowly between the headstones, pausing at those made of granite and marble as well as the humbler resting places marked with a crude wooden cross. A gust lifted the thin gauze of her veil. Fear grabbed Billy. There was no face behind the veil.

He ran all the way through Buckskin Joe, past the abandoned houses, shuttered storefronts, and empty saloons to Grandpa Tobias's cabin. The old man liked to spend his summers in the high country, prospecting, and recalling his younger days when both he and the town were full of life. Billy found him sitting in the sunshine whittling.

"Grandpa Tobias!" Billy was breathless from running in the thin mountain air. "There was a woman in the cemetery," he gasped.

"Well," the old man drawled, never looking up from the knife blade. "Folks like to visit their loved ones who've passed and laid to rest here. What better place than in the shadows of that beautiful peak?" He pointed at the thirteen-thousand-foot mountain in the distance, still topped with sparkling snow.

The boy was rattled. "But, Grandpa, she wore old-timey clothes and a veil like she was at a funeral." He shivered. "It was a ghost, I'm sure of it. Grandpa... I couldn't see her face."

Grandpa Tobias hesitated before he shaved another sliver from the wood. "It was probably just the sunlight playing tricks on your eyes."

"Her shoes," Billy gulped and said, "they were shiny."

Grandpa stopped whittling mid-stroke. "Like silver?"

NOVEMBER 1861

ALTHOUGH WINTER IN the high country started weeks ago, it was a beautiful day, and Buckskin Joe bustled with optimistic energy. Last year's gold strike drew thousands of hopeful fortune hunters to the area. The town now boasted of three hotels, two banks, fourteen stores, several saloons, and a post office. However, there had been no time to build a school and hire a teacher. The few youngsters in town kept busy with chores and odd jobs until they were big enough to work in the mines.

Ten-year-old Toby Henry hadn't felt the need for a coat when Mother shooed him from the cabin. She wanted to take advantage of the warm turn to do some washing and air out the mattress ticks. Farther down the gulch, Father worked his placer, trying to wash sand and grit from the next golden mother lode. While his younger brother and sister stayed close to Mother, Toby was left to his own devices. Perhaps Tabor's General Store needed sweeping. Mister Horace paid in penny candy.

As Toby made his way through the rutted streets of town, there among the chaos of wagons, stagecoaches, and grimy prospectors leading shaggy burros, he spotted the sweetheart of Buckskin Joe—Silver Heels.

Everyone agreed she was the best-looking gal in the whole town, the whole territory. Honey-colored curls cascaded down her back. Her flawless skin was the color of fresh milk, and her eyes were as blue as a cloudless Colorado sky. The heart of her beauty—the feature that drew even the most cantankerous old coots to her—was her ever-present smile. The rose-petal lips that framed straight white teeth cast happiness to all who met her. It was as if her gaiety was contagious.

The only name people knew her by was Silver Heels. Her past remained mysterious, and she never mentioned any family. But it seemed most people in the Colorado Territory were escaping from secret pasts or running to an unknown destiny, so the miners did not question her. The handful of respectable wives were less accepting, and the soiled doves were openly jealous, for every man in town was in love with Silver Heels. But her affection could not be purchased like a common upstairs girl. She was the premier act at the Johnson Variety Theatre. She roused the audiences with lively tunes and enchanted them with lithe twists, graceful jumps, high kicks, and energetic toe tapping. The silver heels of her specially made dancing shoes flashed in the stage lights.

Although Toby's mother disapproved of dancing girls with their display of bare arms and ankles, he planned to ask Silver Heels to marry him when he grew up. Today, however, she seemed preoccupied and failed to notice Toby and his eager grin.

"Good morning, ma'am." Toby tipped his cap.

"Oh, hello, Tobias."

The boy puffed with small pride. She remembered his name.

"How is your family? Is everyone at home feeling well?" Her beautiful smile faltered as concern wrinkled her forehead.

"Yes, ma'am. We're all fit as fiddles."

"Good, good." She nodded distractedly, then took hold of Toby's arm and firmly said, "You run home now and stay there. Tell your mother to keep the little ones away from town."

A few hours later, Father burst into the cabin with the horrifying news—smallpox!

Within days the disease had spread like wildfire. The mayor sent an urgent plea to Denver for nurses to tend the ailing miners. None ever came.

"CLIMB ABOARD, SILVER Heels," Mrs. Tabor ordered. "We have room in the wagon."

Toby scooted over, hoping she'd sit next to him. The handful of women and children living in Buckskin Joe were heading to Denver to escape the raging epidemic, but the miners refused to leave. Some were lonesome bachelors with no reason to go. Most believed they were close to hitting the mother lode and couldn't bear to be away from their claims. Toby's father was among those that would stick it out.

"Thank you, but I'm staying," Silver Heels said. "I have nowhere to go. Besides, these fellas are as dear to me as brothers. They're the only family I have."

She and a handful of men waved goodbye to the little group as the wagon rolled away.

"Well, time to get busy," Silver Heels said with a determined bob of her head. "I'm off to check on those that are ailing. Mister Tabor, I'll be by the store later to pick up supplies."

Silver Heels traded her flouncy dance dresses for a plain calico and an apron. In the following days she visited every house, cabin, shanty, and lean-to. She fed and nursed the sick miners. She chopped wood and hauled water to clean vomit and excrement from the helpless men, their faces burning with fever and shame.

"Mister Wilson, I've brought you some broth. You must eat in order to regain your strength."

"There, there, Benny. Let me put a cool cloth on your forehead."

"Mister Smythe, you cannot lay in the snow bare-chested. Come inside. Oh, you are burning up."

"Mister Tabor generously gave me all the headache powder in the store. Let me fix you a draft, Mister Davies."

"Oh, Jack, I know it's painful, but you must not touch the blisters. I'll get you some salve."

She would hum "I Dream of Jeannie with the Light Brown Hair" to calm those agitated with fever. She'd sing "Camptown Races" and "Oh, Susanna" to cheer those in the long last days of recovery. "The Wayfaring Stranger" was the last melody some men heard.

"There is no sickness, no toil, no danger

In that bright land to which I go.

I'm going there to see my father

And all my loved ones who've gone on."

"I'm afraid your brother has passed, Raymond. Help me carry him to the cemetery road. Old James will lay him to rest with the others."

By Christmas, it appeared the epidemic had run its course. There was talk of families returning to celebrate the holiday. But the men decided to err on the side of caution. The women and children would come home after the first of the year. Unfortunately, several fools celebrated the new year drinking and singing in the saloons. Within a week the pox had taken hold again.

MOTHER'S HAND SHOOK as she opened the letter from Buckskin

Joe. She hadn't received a letter from Father in nearly three weeks. The writing on the envelope was unfamiliar.

Toby leaned over Mother's shoulder as she read from the single lamp in the small boardinghouse room the family shared.

Mrs. Henry,

I am writing to put your mind at ease. Your husband came down with the pox around the start of the month. Do not fear, his fever has passed, and he is recovering. I see him daily. He can sit up in bed and take broth. Mr. Henry remains as weak as a kitten but appears to have few scars. His greatest concern is for you and his children—he knows you will be worried having received no communications these many days.

He misses you terribly, but please do not return yet. Smallpox remains a grim resident of this town. I estimate a full third of our little hamlet has perished. Bodies lie stacked like cordwood along the cemetery road. I wrap them in simple shrouds made of their own bedding as coffins cannot be made quickly enough. As men regain their health, they take turns burying the dead.

Wishing you well,
Silver Heels

>------- ⫸⫷ -------◄

IT WAS APRIL before the snow and the disease relented, allowing the women and children to return to Buckskin Joe.

Toby felt as proud as a returning hero riding on top of the stagecoach as it rolled into town. His little brother and sister had to ride inside the bouncing coach with Mother.

"Father," Toby called and waved from his high perch. Only his father and one other man were at Tabor's General Store, which served as the stagecoach station, post office, and bank.

Horace Tabor stepped out of the store and gave Toby a hardy wave. His wife was the first person off the stage, pulling along their son, Maxie, who she did not allow to ride atop the coach. "I want to see the ledgers," Mrs. Tabor said as she swept into the store. "You have been recording deliveries and sales, haven't you?" Tabor grinned and shrugged as he followed his wife into the establishment she had built.

"It is so good to see you," Father said with a catch in his voice. He hugged Mother in a rare display of public affection. He helped Toby down and exclaimed, "You've grown! Why I hardly knew you." He patted little brother's head and swung little sister into his arms.

Mother laid a hand on Father's face, gently caressing the few pock-marks that dotted his cheeks and forehead. He pulled away from her touch and turned his head. Tears filled her eyes. "You're still the most handsome man I know, my darling Mister Henry." She rose to her tiptoes to lightly kiss him.

Toby had imagined a grander reception for the returning women and children. An unusual hush settled like fine dust on the streets of Buckskin Joe. The men were hollow-eyed shadows with slumped shoulders as if their backs and spirits had both been broken. Pox scars marred faces that had shone with vitality only a few months before. Gone was not only the confidence that good fortune was within reach, but also the vigor to find that fortune.

"I'd like very much to see Silver Heels," Mother said. "I want to thank her for caring for you while you were sick and her thoughtful letters when you were too weak to write." Mother ducked her head in shame. "I was less hospitable to her than I should have been. I'd like to apologize for that."

Father slowly shook his head.

Fear rose in Toby's chest. "Did she catch the pox?" he blurted out.

"I'm afraid so."

"Oh no." Mother clutched at the embroidered hankie she held. "Did she... pass?"

"No." Father let out a long sigh. "I don't know how the Catholic

Church appoints their saints, but if given the chance the citizens of Buckskin Joe would nominate that little gal for sainthood. She ran from cabin to cabin nursing the sick, preparing meals, and washing sheets. She even helped bury the dead."

"Where is she?" Toby needed to know.

"It's a strange tale. Let's go home and I'll tell you after supper."

Later that evening, Father lit his pipe and began.

"A few weeks ago—about the time everyone started feeling better—Silver stopped making her rounds. Fellas were asking around when was the last time anyone had seen her? Several of us went to check on her."

"SILVER HEELS, WE'RE here to see you," called the assembled men.

No answer came from the little cabin, but a curtain in the window moved slightly.

"Are you all right? We're worried about you. Let us in."

"No, no, go away," came the weak voice. "I have the pox. Go. Go." The curtain fell back, and the men reluctantly turned and left.

"We need to care for her as she cared for us," said an old prospector.

"She brought me broth and headache powder," said another.

"She boiled my bedding and washed my clothes in strong lye soap."

"She bathed my fevered head and chest with cool water."

No one knew much about doing laundry and it would be highly improper for a gentleman to wash her chest. So, it was decided they would bring her what food they could quickly scrape together—venison jerky and hardtack—along with a bar of lilac soap from Tabor's store.

The next day the men visited the dancing girl's cabin again. When they called to her, a weak wave appeared in the window. They left their package at her door.

Young Simon made a hearty soup of ham and dried peas scrounged from various larders and a crock was placed on her step. The next day, when the crock was set out empty and washed, the miners took it as a good sign that she was up and eating.

The men cared for their beloved Silver Heels through a shut door for ten cloudy days. Even the sun seemed to miss her.

"Silver Heels, it's us," they called. "We brought some sweet cider. Why don't you let us in?"

"Oh, no, I can't let you in." Her voice wavered with tears. "Please go away."

"Are you feverish?"

"The fever is gone. I'm feeling better. But you must go. Leave me."

"But why? What is wrong?"

A sob came from behind the door. "The pox has scarred me. My face is so hideous that I can never show it again. I can no longer dance. My appearance would be too offensive to any audience. I am ruined."

The rough old miners began to sniffle and wipe their eyes. "Don't you fret about that. You'll always be the prettiest gal to us." They could not convince her that her beauty was deeper than the scars.

The next morning the men of Buckskin Joe assembled and went en masse to Silver Heels's cabin. A young fella had made a rose of red crepe paper, since the mountain wildflowers would not bloom until June. They would make her understand she'd won their hearts, their everlasting loyalty with her kindness.

"Silver Heels," they called, knocking at the door. There was no answer. "Silver." The curtain remained still in the window. They pounded at the door. "Silver!"

Panic gripped the men, and they forced open the door. The tiny cabin was spotless. Dishes had been washed and stacked on the shelf. The floor was swept. No dresses hung on the hooks. The room was empty. The most beautiful woman they had ever seen was never seen again.

$$\rightarrow\cdots\!\!-\!\!\gg\!\!\ll\!\!-\cdots\!\!\leftarrow$$

BILLY PULLED GRANDPA Tobias's hand, hurrying him along.

Mount Silverheels. Photo by Larry Lamsa.

When they arrived at the iron gates of the Buckskin Joe cemetery, only unattended grave markers silently stood in the tall grass. The woman was not there.

"She was here, I swear it, Grandpa." Billy didn't understand where the woman in black could have gone.

"I don't doubt she was," Grandpa Tobias replied. He turned and tipped his cowboy hat to the snow-covered peak in the distance. The wind that blew down from Mount Silverheels sounded like a song.

⊱┄┄ ⊰⊱ ┄┄⊰

AUTHOR'S NOTE

HISTORIANS BELIEVE THE story of Silver Heels is a myth as there is no record of her existence. Her given name is unknown so no birth or death records can be found. She is not mentioned in any census. However, old-timers swore she was a real person. They named a peak in her honor with gratitude for her selflessness.

⊱┄┄ ⊰⊱ ┄┄⊰

—*Kimberly Burns grew up in Colorado hearing stories about the colorful characters of the Old West. She has degrees from the University of Colorado and the University of Hartford. Kimberly is a member of the Historical Novel Society, Western Writers of America, and Women Writing the West.* Her debut novel, The Mrs. Tabor, *won numerous awards. Her latest release,* The Redemption of Mattie Silks, *is a finalist for the CIBA Laramie Book Award for American and Western Fiction, as well as a finalist for the Western Writers of America Spur Award.*

She lives with her husband and black Lab in Florida and Virginia where she enjoys writing and researching wild-willed women.

A FLOUR SACK FOR REBECCA

JOANN CONNER

REBECCA MORROW WALKED toward the hotel, carefully holding a bucket in her hands. The pretty blonde-haired girl was nervous but hid it with a smile pasted on her face. A pale blue ribbon that matched her eyes held her hair at the nape of her neck.

The slender young girl was fast approaching her full height but had not yet filled out. Thank heaven. She was excellent with a needle and thread and had been able to let out the seams and drop the hem in her only dress, but the fact remained—it was getting thin and too tight. She would be fourteen in a few months, and sometimes she worried if she stretched too much, the seams of her dress would burst.

A young man mounted the steps ahead of her, carrying a large bag of flour. As he reached the door, he shifted the flour and turned slightly to reach for the handle. His brown eyes widened at the sight of Rebecca and he stood for a second, mouth slightly open, before he regained his manners and opened the door for her. His dark brown hair was carefully trimmed, and his wiry frame was dressed in clean brown cloth pants and a green shirt. He smiled slightly as Rebecca climbed the steps and walked through the open door.

"Thank you," she said, striving to keep the hurt out of her voice.

She just knew he was laughing at her shabby, albeit clean, dress. She felt the color rise up her neck and into her cheeks and she took a deep breath to calm herself. At least, as big a breath as she dared in the tight dress.

The dress she wore now was the last one she had received two years ago from a traveling pastor's wife. The woman had clicked her tongue at the stockings showing on Rebecca's legs and gave her an old dress her own daughter had outgrown. It was worn when Rebecca got it and now, two years later, it was thin and too small. She said a silent prayer as she approached the high desk where a woman stood, greeting guests.

"Is Mister Simon here, please?" She tried her best to sound confident and strong.

"I'm sorry, young miss," said the woman behind the desk. "We don't need any more waitresses or dishwashers right now." She was an older woman, a widow Rebecca guessed by her dress, and her smile was kind.

"Oh no, ma'am, I have other business to discuss with him, if I may." Rebecca did not look as if she had an education, but in fact, her mother had been to girl's school and her father had some schooling too. They had taught her proper speech and manners and it served her well.

"May I ask what this is about?" The woman studied her carefully, obviously taking her duties seriously but also feeling sympathy for the young girl.

"Well," Rebecca said slowly, glancing around the dining room before bringing her eyes back to the woman. "People tell me my baked goods are very good, and I thought maybe…." She swallowed hard. "Maybe Mister Simon would like to buy some to serve to his guests." On impulse, she pulled back the cloth on the pail and extended it to the woman. "Take one, if you would like," she said. "I brought enough for you to have a sample as well."

The woman looked in the pail and raised her eyebrows. She put her hand in and carefully withdrew a cookie. She took a small bite, and her eyes grew wide with surprise.

"This is the best cookie I have ever eaten!" She looked at Rebecca with renewed interest. "Wait here," she said, as she turned and disappeared through a door behind her. Seconds later, she returned with a twinkle in her eyes. The man behind her had his shirtsleeves rolled up, with suspenders holding up his cloth pants instead of a belt. He peered over his glasses, a smile on his face.

"Missus McKane tells me you are interested in selling me some baked goods for my customers," he said.

"Yes, sir, I am," Rebecca said, trying to sound grown-up. "Please try my goods for yourself." She extended the bucket and he looked inside, reached in, and withdrew a small cake. It was lightly iced with a sugar, egg white, and a little raspberry juice concoction that was baked to a perfect glaze on the top of the cake. She had saved a raspberry for the top as well.

"Oh!" Mr. Simon looked at Mrs. McKane in surprise as he chewed. "This is delicious!" He finished the small cake and looked at the pail with hope. "May I please have another?"

"You may," Rebecca said, "and you can have all you want if you hire me to bake for you." She spoke boldly, keeping a calm outward appearance even though her stomach was twisting with nerves.

"I like your gumption, young lady." He laughed. "Please, step into my office and we will discuss details." He looked at her with a sly grin. "Bring that bucket." He held the door for her and she entered, sitting carefully on a chair in front of his desk as he held it for her. She leaned forward and set the pail in front of him.

They agreed on pricing and payment, then discussed a schedule of what he wanted to have and when. Rebecca looked at the floor and bit her lip. How was she going to do all that he wanted in her small stove?

"Where would you be baking the goods?" Mr. Simon searched her face and confirmed his suspicions. "I would prefer you bake in my kitchen. It would be much easier to serve the guests from there. Besides," he beamed, "the aroma of your baking may entice my customers to buy some of these delicious delights!"

"You would let me use your kitchen?" She spoke without thinking, then caught herself. "I mean, of course I could do that if you prefer."

"Let's go look at the kitchen," Mr. Simon said, rising from his chair.

Rebecca followed him into the kitchen and had to fight down a gasp. It was so big—more counter space than she had ever seen and a large stove with a big oven. He smiled as he took a pad of cloth and opened the door to the oven.

"I could put several things in that oven at once!" Rebecca said, beaming. The oven had a shelf! It would be so much easier than placing the iron plate in the bottom of the woodstove, with the dishes filled with cakes or biscuits sitting on the piece of iron that rested on the coals.

The young man she had seen in front of the hotel came into the kitchen carrying a pail of eggs and another of butter. He started toward the corner where he had already deposited the bag of flour but stopped when he saw them, staring at Rebecca briefly before he looked to Mr. Simon for directions.

"Thank you, Brody," Mr. Simon said. "Just put the eggs and butter near the shelf." He looked at Rebecca. "I was thinking it would be easier if I just had the ingredients you need delivered. You can tell me what you need and Brody can deliver them from the general store. That would be easier for you, I think, and save you some time. I could just deduct the ingredients from our agreed amount, and since I get a special rate, it would be less expensive for you." He smiled at Rebecca. "What do you think of that idea?"

"That sounds perfect!" Rebecca could hardly contain her joy. She had been worried that she would not have enough money to buy adequate supplies until she earned more money.

"It's a deal then," Mr. Simon said, extending his hand. Rebecca shook his hand, feeling very much like she was a real businesswoman now. "Make me a list of what you need to start tomorrow, and I'll make sure it is ready for you." Brody was still standing near the shelf, flicking his eyes between Mr. Simon and Rebecca. "Brody, when you come back with the rest of the order, I'll give you her list, is that okay?"

"Yes, sir." He smiled, his perfect white teeth making his face even more handsome. He turned and walked away, shooting one more look in Rebecca's direction on his way out.

"I know the treats you brought today were part of your sales pitch, but if I pay you may I keep the rest?" He smiled as he pulled a nickel out of his pocket and extended it to her.

"I'm sorry, I don't have any change," Rebecca said.

"It's all for you today. Call it my welcome gift to a new employee."

"Thank you!" she said, surprised and pleased that she would be paid for her samples.

"Leave your list with Missus McKane before you leave," he said. "The kitchen door will be unlocked for you early in the morning. I will have the stove stoked and ready for baking." He grinned. "I am looking forward to seeing what you have for us tomorrow." He chuckled and walked away, leaving Rebecca with a small piece of paper and a pencil.

She thought about her baking tomorrow, then wrote her small list on the paper. She smiled as she handed it to Mrs. McKane, then walked home with a spring in her step. Tonight, they would all eat bread and butter with dinner!

THE NEXT MORNING, Rebecca stepped into the warm kitchen of the hotel. She went right to work, and it wasn't long before she was wiping the sweat off her brow with the hem of her apron. It was cold outside, but with the stove stoked, it was hot in the kitchen.

As she worked, her thoughts strayed to the day she realized she had to do something or she was literally going to have nothing to wear. It wasn't Pa's fault. Both he and her brother Cory wore threadbare clothing too. The difference was that Pa had been able to give Cory one or two of his things to wear, but he had nothing Rebecca could use. Their clothes took a beating as they farmed all day, taking time out only to try to catch or shoot some game. By the time Cory outgrew the clothes, they were virtually rags hanging on his skinny frame. There were no pieces of material she could use to patch her own clothing.

Rebecca had only been ten when her mother died of a fever. They shared a love of baking for their family and neighbors. Her mother had a gift and taught Rebecca her secrets. She thought of her mother every time she baked or looked in a mirror.

Her pa told her she was the spitting image of her mother, and indeed, one day Rebecca was startled at the likeness staring back at her in the mirror. She did not own a mirror, and it had been at least a year since she had been in a shop that sold fine millinery and premade dresses. The woman who owned the shop had let her assist with hemming a dress for a custom order. Rebecca looked in the mirror to see how the back of the dress hung and caught a glimpse of her reflection. She thought for a moment she was seeing her mother's ghost as she stared open-mouthed at the picture that met her eyes.

Her heart felt a pang of sadness as she recalled Pa's reaction to her going to work. She knew her talents were baking and sewing.

"Pa, if I can do all my chores here, I would like to offer some of my baked goods for sale in town."

"I'm sorry, child," he said, tears glistening in his eyes. "I can't afford to buy the extra supplies you would need."

"I will not eat any bread or biscuits for a week," she said. "I will use that extra flour and butter to make a few samples and take them to town. If I can sell my goods, I will buy all my own supplies."

"Why do you want to make money?" Her father studied her carefully, fearful of what she would say. Did she want to leave home? He wasn't ready to let his little girl go out into a harsh world alone.

"I want," she hesitated, looking down at the floor. She did not want to hurt him, but she just didn't know how to say it in any way that would not cause him to feel bad. "I want to buy some material to make myself a new dress." She raised her head, afraid he would think she was vain or foolish.

Her father looked as if she had struck him and stepped back to fall into one of the simple wooden chairs at their small table. He sat down hard and rubbed both hands over his eyes but could not stop a few tears from falling on his shirt.

"Of course you can do that," he said. "I don't need bread or butter, either, so put my share toward your project." He stood and walked to the door. "Rebecca?" he said, pausing in the doorway as he stared outside, not looking at her.

"Yes, Pa?" Rebecca held her breath, afraid he would change his mind.

"I'm sorry, girl. I wish I could do better by you." With that, he was gone—off to hunt for some meat for dinner.

Tears streamed down her own face as she went to tend to their small garden. They sold or traded most of what they grew for things they could not make, like boots and oil for the lamp. She knew her Pa would be hungry without bread to fill his belly, but she hoped that would only be for a short time. She took a walk up the little hill and was rewarded with a few berries on a bush that grew wild. She picked them and carefully carried them home in a small pail she had brought along for the purpose. At least they could have berries with their game for dinner.

TWO WEEKS HAD passed since the owner of the restaurant had given her a chance to bake for his customers. She arrived early in the morning and used the supplies he let her store in the corner of the kitchen. She needed to order more flour when she was done today. She had come to count on the supplies just being there when she wanted them.

She checked the cake in the large oven at the restaurant and smiled. It was a velvet cake, and the chocolate aroma made her mouth water. She stepped back to mix the batter for the cookies she would put in the oven while the cake was cooling. She glanced out the window over the top of the curtain and frowned. She would have to hurry. The sky was turning gray, which meant dawn was approaching. The regular cook would be in soon to start preparing for the breakfast crowd.

"What smells so divine?" Mr. Simon came into the kitchen.

"It's the velvet cake." Rebecca laughed. "You requested I bake something special for your friend's birthday today."

"He will be delighted! In fact, he wants to meet the 'baking angel' as he calls you. He has been eating one of your delights every day for the past week!"

"He wants to meet me?" Rebecca could not hide her surprise. At first a small flush of pride washed over her, but it was quickly squelched by the realization that she had not yet earned enough money to buy all the material she needed to make herself a proper dress. "I don't know," she said, uncertain.

"Please, as a favor to me," Mr. Simon said. "He will be in for his celebration late this afternoon. If you could serve the cake while we watched, it would be a perfect celebration."

How could she say no to Mr. Simon? He had been so kind to her, and more than generous. She licked her lips and met his eyes.

"What time would you like the cake served?"

"Five o'clock would be perfect!" Mr. Simon was like a kid at Christmas, excitement dancing in his eyes. She could not refuse.

"I'll be here a little early to get it ready." She smiled.

Rebecca left the hotel that morning and decided she would allow herself a little time to dream. She walked across to the general store and stepped inside, going straight to the dry goods counter where the bolts of fabric lay. She stared at the choices of cloth, resting her hand briefly on the beautiful crimson silk. It was so soft! Someday, maybe she could afford a silk dress, but for now… she shifted her attention to the cheapest material—the calico print. She almost had enough money to buy the material to make a dress. Then maybe she could earn enough to make Pa and Cory each a new shirt. Their shirts were so thin, they surely could not provide much warmth. It had been so hard for all of them.

Two years ago, they had left her mother's grave and the burned-out cabin and started west. The crops had all been lost and there was precious little that was stored in the cellar.

It had been a long, hard trip in the wagon with the mule. The back of the wagon was loaded with some food, blankets, and clothes they had managed to salvage, although none of her mother's remained. It took almost a year of hard driving over rutted roads, but they had finally found a place to homestead with good soil.

A noise behind her startled her out of her reverie. She jumped and turned around to find herself almost face-to-face with Brody! She backed against the counter holding the fabric and stood, somehow embarrassed.

"Did you need some help with fabric?" He met her eyes, then looked behind her at the bolts of cloth.

"I was just looking," she said, a little more bite in her words than she intended.

"We are a little low, but a shipment should come in a few weeks. I can get my mother to help you, if you would like," Brody said, looking over his shoulder toward the back of the store. He shifted his gaze back to her, his brows knit together in a question.

"Why would I want your mother to come? Do you want to see her laugh at my old dress too?" She ran out of the store, leaving Brody staring after her, speechless.

Rebecca ran most of the way home, tears streaming down her face. She didn't ever want to see Brody again! She busied herself for the next several hours, setting dinner to simmer on the stove and baking a fresh loaf of bread for their evening meal. She had enough time to walk up to the berry bushes and was pleased to see there were a handful of sweet, ripe berries. She put them in the small pail to take when she went back to the hotel. She would arrange them on top of the cake to make the celebration a little more special.

By the time she returned to the hotel, she had pushed the encounter with Brody to the back of her mind. She had a job to do. She was just laying the berries on top in a decorative design when Mr. Simon came into the kitchen.

"Is it ready?" Mr. Simon said, coming through the door from the dining room.

"Yes, I just put the final touches on top." She turned around with the cake on a plate in her hands.

"Oh," Mr. Simon said, stopping to stare at the delectable concoction. His wide eyes came up to meet hers. "Don't be surprised if Mister Glasson gives you a little extra money tonight. I have never seen a cake so beautiful!" He held the kitchen door open. "Let's go." He beamed.

Once in the dining room, Mr. Simon led the way to a couple of tables pushed together in the back. A tall, well-dressed man sat at one end of the table, and a beautiful woman in a dark blue silk dress sat beside him. There was another person sitting with his back to her, but she was focused on the guest of honor. Mrs. McKane was seated at the tables, smiling at her, and Mr. Simon had obviously been a guest at the table as well, since his coat was on the back of one of the chairs. As she walked to the table, carefully holding the cake, they all began to clap and wish a happy birthday to Mr. Glasson.

Rebecca carefully set the cake in front of Mr. Glasson, then stepped back to wait until she was told what to do next. It was at that moment she realized the person sitting in the other chair was Brody. He turned his head to smile at her, looking very handsome in a suit made of dark brown cloth. She caught her breath, taking a step toward the kitchen when Mr. Glasson spoke.

"Young lady, what is your name," he asked, smiling.

"It's Rebecca, sir," she said. His eyes sparkled with happiness, setting her at ease. She felt herself relax.

"You have an amazing talent. Would you please do me the honor of serving this masterpiece?"

The waitress appeared with a long knife, small plates, and some extra forks. She gave Rebecca a look of admiration as she handed her the knife and set the forks and plates on the table. Rebecca cut the cake carefully, giving the first piece to Mr. Glasson, then a piece to each of the women, Mr. Simon, and finally, she cut one for Brody.

Her hand shook slightly as she moved the plate toward him. Suddenly, his hand was touching hers, holding the plate steady. She drew in a quick breath and raised her eyes in a panic. Soft brown eyes met hers and she suddenly felt like she couldn't breathe.

"Won't you have a piece of cake with us, Miss Morrow?" Brody said the words softly, so no one else would hear. "There is an empty chair next to me." The others were busy moaning over the delicious bites of cake, laughing as they consumed the dessert and drank coffee.

Rebecca froze. What was he doing? Did he want her to sit with them so they could all laugh at her? She wanted to drop the plate in his lap and run out of the dining room. She wanted to go home, where she felt loved and safe.

"Rebecca," Mr. Glasson said, "this is the most delicious cake I have ever tasted in my whole life!"

"It is true," Mrs. Glasson chimed in, laughing with a lilt that was so pleasant to the ear. "I was never much of a baker, so I do not mind my husband giving you such praise."

"I would like to give you an extra bit of money for this wondrous gift you have baked for my birthday," Mr. Glasson said.

"I don't know what to say," Rebecca said, turning and releasing the plate to Brody as she did so. She was overwhelmed with all the different thoughts running through her head.

"Say thank you and accept my gratitude to you," he said, taking one of her hands and pressing a dollar coin into it.

"Thank you," Rebecca said, stunned at the coin. She looked at Mr. Simon, who was nodding and smiling. Movement caught her eye, and she turned her head to see Brody had set the cake down and was staring at her again. "I'll see you in the morning," she blurted to Mr. Simon. "I need to get home."

She almost ran from the dining room. She grabbed her thin coat in the kitchen and went out the back door, running down the darkening path to home. She tried to sort her thoughts as she walked. There were so many things clashing in her head, she was still distracted when she got home.

It was not until later, when she was preparing for bed that she remembered the dollar Mr. Glasson had given her. Now she would have enough to buy the material for a new dress tomorrow! She felt warm and good for the first time in a long time. She would have rested easy if the memory of Brody's eyes had not come to her just as she was drifting to sleep. She hoped he would not be in the store tomorrow.

>····· ➤⃦⃥ ·····◄

REBECCA ARRIVED EVEN earlier than usual the next morning and quickly completed her list of baked goods for Mr. Simon. She could hardly contain her excitement as she walked to the general store and went straight to the counter with the bolts of fabric. Mrs. Glasson was just putting the bolt of calico back on the shelf when she turned to see Rebecca.

"Hello, Rebecca! I am still smiling at the thought of that delicious cake last night."

"Hello, Missus Glasson," Rebecca said. "I am happy you enjoyed the dessert."

"What can I do for you today?" Mrs. Glasson asked.

"I need two and a half yards of the calico please," Rebecca said, feeling elated at the idea of a new dress.

"Oh," Mrs. Glasson said, the smile leaving her face. She took the bolt down and rolled it out on the counter, measuring swiftly. "I'm afraid Missus Jorgenson just bought most of what I had. I only have two yards left, and I won't get another bolt in for at least three weeks." She studied Rebecca's face. "Will it do?"

"I'll take it," Rebecca said, using all her willpower to hold back her tears. It wasn't enough.

She had measured carefully and knew two yards would not allow her to put long sleeves on the dress, or she would have to make it too short for propriety. But at least she could get started. Maybe there was some part of her current dress that could be used as a ruffle on the bottom until more fabric arrived.

Mrs. Glasson wrapped the calico in brown paper and gave it to Rebecca with a sympathetic smile. Rebecca paid her, took the package, gave her a weak smile, and turned to walk out of the store.

She nearly bumped into Brody. She hadn't heard him come up behind her. He had seen the whole thing! She couldn't help it. As she looked up at him, her eyes betrayed her and tears ran down her cheeks almost as fast as she ran out the door.

———

THREE HOURS LATER, she had most of the dress cut out. She had decided to put sleeves on the dress and try to find some material to put on the bottom of the dress for length. The knock on the door surprised her. They never got visitors, who could it be? She opened the door and stood, mouth open.

"What are you doing here?" She was angry now. How dare he come to her home to laugh at her!

"My mother felt bad that she did not have enough material for you," Brody said. He shifted from foot to foot, clearly uncomfortable. "We got a new type of flour sack in our store," he said. "I told her you were very clever and asked if I could have this for you." He bit his lower lip as he held out a piece of linen.

Rebecca took it tentatively and unfolded it. It was a flour sack! She did not know whether to laugh or cry. It was enough to make a ruffle on the bottom of the dress!

"She sent some ribbon she had that was extra, too, the end of the spools." He looked at her shyly as he extended the pieces of ribbon. "Maybe you could use it somehow."

"Why would you do this?" Rebecca said, shaking her head. "You have laughed at me from the day we met!"

"Laughed at you? Never!" He looked truly crestfallen. "I think you are talented and beautiful!" he blurted, shifting his feet as he shoved his hands into his pockets. He shook his head and turned to leave.

"Brody," she called when he was several feet away. He turned, his face apprehensive. "Thank you," she said.

"You're welcome, Rebecca," he said, his smile bright now. "I'll see you tomorrow." He walked quickly away toward town.

REBECCA DID NOT see him for two days. Oddly, she found herself thinking about him and hoping each day that he would walk in with supplies. On the third day, she looked up as the door opened and Brody stepped into the kitchen. He stopped and stared, running his eyes up and down Rebecca's figure.

"Oh," he said, bright red flooding up his neck and into his cheeks as he realized what he had done. "I am so sorry. I did not mean to be disrespectful! It's just that the dress is so pretty!"

"Thank you," Rebecca said, letting out the breath she had been holding. She did not realize until that moment that she was waiting for his approval. She had spent every extra waking minute for the past two and a half days working on the dress.

"It looks so beautiful on you," he said. He looked at the floor, then at the door, obviously considering whether to stay or leave.

"Brody?" Rebecca said.

"Yes, Rebecca?" He spoke softly, meeting her eyes with uncertainty.

"Would you like a cookie?"

—JoAnn Conner is a former English and history teacher who has published multiple Western historical fiction and mystery novels. She worked as a stringer on three small newspapers and has taught writing classes for both adults and children. She has a background in public speaking and was a featured speaker at the National Library Association convention, where she spoke as the director of the Washoe Heritage Information Network

regarding gathering of Native American history, culture, and traditions. JoAnn Conner has been awarded a Townsend Press Award, the Write from the Heart Poetry Award, is an invited author in the California State Fair Authors Booth, is a member of Women Writing the West, and is a member of the Western Writers of America, where she serves on the board for the Homestead Foundation.

A WOMAN'S DREAM

DAWN DEBRAAL

REBA BOONE STUDIED the picture in her father's newspaper of a woman named "Prairie Rose." She was posed with her horse, captioned as the winner of the first Cheyenne Frontier Days sharpshooter competition, sporting her rifle.

Never in her life had Reba seen a woman dressed in a shortened skirt that had been tucked into tall boots with spurs. At that moment, she saw herself wanting to do the same. Reba, a good horseback rider, now wanted to learn how to trick ride and shoot like the woman in the picture. She dreamed of being famous, being noticed, especially being taken seriously for the first time in her life.

Henry Ray, a ranch hand on her father's farm, was semiretired. As an elderly gentleman, he was placed on light duty because the man worked for Carl Boone's father, and his loyalty to the family assured his position of employment and future retirement. Reba, seeking his knowledge, walked to the barn to talk to her trusted friend.

Mr. Ray had taught her how to ride her first pony and worked for years with her until she could ride just about any horse, instilling confidence in her ability. Reba carried the newspaper clipping with her to the barn, handing it to the elderly gentleman.

"My, she sure is pretty," Henry said, admiring the picture, holding the clipping far from his face to sharpen his view.

"Pretty brave!" Reba said. "I want to be like her."

The elderly man looked at Reba. She was his star student, but he didn't want to get in trouble with her father. "Reba, your father would tan my hide if I let you do tricks on Trixie. It's enough that you are one of the best riders in the area."

"I want to learn tricks and sharpshooting," Reba said stubbornly. "And I want to go to Wyoming and be in a show."

Henry Ray squeezed her shoulder reassuringly. "You know, if there were any girl who could do that, my money would be on you."

Secretly, Reba built an obstacle course in the woods. She taught Trixie to jump over a small log when she went riding. The thrill of learning new tricks with her horse excited the young woman, but the problem with riding was her dress. She had to sit sidesaddle until she got into the woods and "hairpinned" her legs on the horse. How could she ever be a trick rider if forced to wear a dress? She studied the picture of Prairie Rose. The one she'd hidden in her secretary when an idea came to her that the woman had altered her dress somehow, making it more movable, yet still presentable.

"Rebecca, teach me to sew," she asked the housekeeper. Since Reba's mother died when she was much younger, the woman acted as a mother figure and was happy to see her ward wanting to do feminine things like stitchery. The girl's father constantly battled her about why she didn't do "girly" things. Rebecca told Reba's father that his daughter would grow into a suitable marriage role, and today, she proved the housekeeper right.

Reba received a hoop with the alphabet imprinted on a piece of cloth and several bright-colored threads and needles.

"This embroidery will teach you how to sew," Rebecca told her as they sat in the parlor and stitched together, the housekeeper with her mending and Reba with her embroidery, learning square knots, cloverleaf knots, and straight stitches.

In between trick riding secretly in the woods, Reba learned different techniques of sewing to finish her sampler. It pleased her father when she proved to be a good seamstress. Unbeknown to Rebecca and Carl Boone, Reba's desire to learn how to sew was to make herself a costume out of one of her old dresses so that she would be able to ride Trixie in a typical fashion.

On her sixteenth birthday, she received the cowboy boots she desired, which had a taller shaft than the regular boots. The new boots would work perfectly with her new riding outfit. Her father couldn't deny his daughter anything. Reba was his "Little Princess," the name he called her by.

She received the best education Springfield could offer, and with the help of Henry Ray, who was sworn to secrecy, she learned a lot about shooting and riding. Only she and Henry Ray knew the extent of her talents.

"Now that you have finished your education, I think you should find a suitor," Carl Boone said to his daughter one evening while seated at the dinner table.

"Father, I do not want to be married this young. I want to go west and be a trick rider like Prairie Rose." Carl Boone laughed at his daughter lovingly.

"That is a child's dream. Now you are a woman."

"As a woman, I should be able to do as I wish before being married and having children." Her father's dark eyes brooded, and he chose his words carefully.

"Daughter, you must be reasonable. You have hardly been anywhere off this ranch, much less out west."

"Father, I love you, but I have dreams." She left the table upset while her father went out on the back porch to smoke his pipe.

Looking out the window, Reba saw the ranch hands putting their horses away for the night. Releasing his horse was a new hire, a young man who had caught her eye. Since Henry Ray had had a stroke, he was still being cared for by the Boone family but was no longer able to work in the barn. Her father hired a new man, and she was interested in knowing more about him, so she walked out to meet the cowboy.

"Hello, my name is Reba Boone. It's nice to meet you." The cowboy's mouth dropped at the outgoing rancher's daughter. He didn't know if he should shake her hand—it didn't seem proper—but there she was, up in his business with her hand extended toward him, so he took it.

"Dale Cope, pleased to make your acquaintance," he said back to her, suspicious of her boldness.

"Dale, what did you do before you came here?" He chuckled as he had already been through an extensive interview with her father before being offered the job.

"I did a little rodeo work out west."

This knowledge made Reba's eyes light up. "You are Dale Cope from Montana? That Dale Cope?"

"The very same."

"Why are you here on our ranch? You are famous."

"Got hurt the way most of us rodeo folks do. Came back to Springfield to heal. Can't do what I used to with my busted leg and shoulder."

"Oh, gracious. That is very sad."

"Reba, what are you doing down here? Get back to the house until the ranch hands have left for the day. You know better than to come out here," Carl Boone reprimanded her.

"Father, I wanted to meet Mister Cope and welcome him to the ranch." Reba, red-faced, hiked her skirts to walk back to the house. How dare her father disgrace her like that, as if she were a child. Reba was a grown woman and didn't warrant treatment like a child. She wouldn't disrespect her father in front of the hired help but would discuss it calmly when they were alone.

Reba was in her room working on the riding outfit when she heard Whitey pounding on the door and Rebecca calling her to come quickly.

"Whitey? What's wrong? Where's Father?"

"Miss Reba, that stallion reared up, and your pa came off him and hit the fence."

"Is he hurt badly?" Reba went to grab some first-aid supplies, thinking her father was bleeding.

"Miss Reba, he's dead. He didn't suffer none, broke his neck, died instantly."

"What?" The orphaned woman stood in the vestibule, unable to move. Her father was a strong man who'd been thrown from a horse many times and had always gotten right back up.

"I told him there was something wrong with that horse, but he insisted on trying to break him."

Reba grabbed the shotgun off the mantle and marched to the corral where men had covered her father. She pulled the coat away. Seeing her father like that froze her heart. Without a second thought, she walked up to the stallion and unloaded the shotgun. That horse would never kill again.

No one tried to stop her, nor did anyone say a word. They stood openmouthed and watched the slight woman march back to the house after leaving orders to bury the horse and to carry her father to the parlor, which the men obliged.

Reba cried for two days. What was she to do? Her father had left her a working ranch—it could support her, but Reba had other dreams. The day before they buried Carl Boone, she sent for Whitey.

"Miss Reba?" He took his hat off and bowed his head. "I'm so sorry for your loss."

She thanked him, asking Whitey if he'd made sure the pastor knew to come the following day.

"He knows to come. Reverend Pit assured me he would perform the funeral tomorrow. Do you need help preparing the body?"

"No, thank you. Miss Rebecca helped me do that already. Please, come in and talk with me." Whitey wiped his feet and stepped inside with his hat in his hand. They passed the parlor where Carl Boone was laid out in a pine box with silver coins on his eyes. Whitey followed her into the less formal sitting room where she had coffee set out.

"I would like to know if you are willing to stay on here and help me run the place. You were father's most trusted man. Do you feel confident you can run Eden Ranch and make decisions in my absence?"

"I am honored, Miss Boone. It's been a lifelong dream of mine to be able to run a place like this."

"Then you shall. I will have my attorney draw up the necessary papers. You will receive a sizable raise, and the men who stay on will continue at their present pay unless you find one who will step up to your old job."

"Yes, ma'am." Whitey stood and offered his hand to shake, looking uncomfortable at making a deal with a woman, but he knew she was in charge now. Reba shook his hand.

"Whitey, will you send Mister Cope in?"

"Yes, miss." Whitey left the room while Reba paced nervously. She had decided sometime in the night to fulfill her dream of being in a Western show. Dale Cope would hopefully accept the job she was offering.

She answered the knock at the door. Dale Cope removed his hat. "Miss Boone, you sent for me?"

"Yes, Mister Cope, please come in. Would you like some coffee?"

"No, ma'am, I'm in the middle of something, can't stay long. What is it you need from me?"

"I would like to hire you as a personal bodyguard."

"Come again?"

"Yes, Mister Cope. I am going to travel to Wyoming. I have been practicing for years and would like to become a performer in a Western show."

Cope's eyebrows went up with interest. "Wyoming?"

"Yes. I would like you to escort me. I will pay for your services and would pay extra for any lessons you could teach me about rodeo tricks along the way."

"Miss Boone, one doesn't learn 'tricks' overnight." The poor man looked uncomfortable.

"I know this. I have been practicing for years. I can outshoot, out rope, and outride any cowboy on this ranch. I am determined to get to Cheyenne, Wyoming, and find my hero, Miss Ann Robins, better known by her stage name, Prairie Rose."

"I know of her, Miss Boone. I don't know if she still performs. What would this guard duty entail?"

"A woman cannot safely travel alone in this country, unfortunately. It is simple. I want you to pose as my brother and take me to Wyoming. When I am there safely, you may return here to your present position, or if you'd like to continue in my employ, we can come to some mutual understanding. I have put Whitey in charge of running the ranch for me until I return."

You could have knocked Dale Cope over with a feather. After Carl Boone died, he waited for someone to tell him to leave, but now he'd been offered a job with more responsibility and pay.

"That's at least a month one way—Wyoming. I'll have to purchase supplies and make some protection for inclement weather. You could go faster by train."

"I want to see the West. How can I be part of a Wild West show if I've never experienced it? How soon can you be ready to go?"

"I would think a week or so to get everything together."

"Then start your preparations. As soon as my father is buried, I will be able to leave Eden Ranch."

"Yes, miss." Dale walked out of the house, stunned that he'd been given such responsibility. He didn't know much about the woman, but Reba Boone was self-assured and capable based on what he'd seen. She wasn't afraid. He knew this after she took out the horse that killed her father and didn't blink an eye.

The part that bothered him most was teaching rodeo tricks. Dale had watched the riders do their tricks but never learned in depth how one trained the horse or the rider.

Carl Boone's funeral was well attended by many friends and neighbors. The reverend did an exemplary service. Reba and Rebecca made plenty of food along with the other ladies who brought a dish to pass.

Soon, the heavy pall of the funeral ceremony gave way to good food and intoxicating beverages. When the people left, Whitey came to her.

"I think your pa would have loved his sending off."

"I believe you are right, Whitey. Another thing, I would also like you to take up a room in the house. It wouldn't do for the boss to live in the bunkhouse with the other men. Miss Rebecca needs to keep her employment, and I assured her that her job is still here, taking care of you. With me gone, there is no one to look after. The house will be a place to do business with other ranchers, and Miss Rebecca will run the household. You will tell her your needs. Please do any necessary repairs on the house. This ranch is my father's legacy, after all."

"Miss Boone, I will do whatever it takes to keep your family's legacy alive. I admired your father, and I do not take this assignment lightly. When you return, you will find Eden in shipshape. Speaking of that, when do you plan on returning?"

"There is no timeline for me, Whitey. I plan on trying out for a Western show. If I make it, it could be years. If I fail, it could be months. I will write to you when I am settled. Also, if Mister Cope comes back after settling me in Wyoming, give him a good job."

"I can do that. He's a good man and, Miss Reba, you'll make it in that Western show."

"How do you know that, Whitey?"

"Henry Ray always had me watching you. I saw your shooting and the tricks you put your horse through. You'll make it. I plan on being here for a long time."

"Thank you, Whitey." She was a bit embarrassed that she didn't know she was still under the watchful eye of someone when she left the house.

Before she left Springfield, Reba rode Trixie to the little house nestled closer to town on their property. There, Henry Ray lived with another man whose job was to care for him.

"Miss Boone, you've come to see Henry Ray. He will enjoy your company." Matthew took Trixie's reins, and Reba walked through the door, seeing Henry lying on his bed near a fire. One side of his face was pulled down, and his right arm no longer worked. She held back tears of love for this man who was more like the loving father she'd longed for.

"Reba," his voice was raspy, but his eyes shone brightly.

"Henry, I've come to say goodbye, I am going out west to fulfill my dream of being a Western show star."

Henry took her hand as she sat in the chair next to him. "Miss Reba, you will accomplish anything you set out to do, training all your life for this moment—my best student. I will enjoy reading about you in the newspapers. Go out and make your pa and me proud."

Reba left him with a heavy heart, for she knew the chances of Henry being here when she returned were slim.

SEVERAL DAYS LATER, Dale had the wagon set up for them to travel to Wyoming. He had fashioned a bed in the wagon with a rainproof tarp over the top. He would sleep beneath it in inclement weather. Feed and water barrels tied to the wagon gave them provisions for four horses and two passengers. He had all the basics to cook with, and they would depend on wild game for meat.

The morning came to leave. Dale tied the horses to the back of the wagon and waited for the woman to come out of the house, stunned when she came out in men's pants, tall leather boots, her father's oversized coat, and a beat-up cowboy hat on her head.

"Miss Boone, you can't dress like that," Dale said, red-faced. He knew she was going to be a handful, but this was unexpected.

"Mister Cope, we are going through the wilderness to places where we must walk. Do you expect me to do that in a cumbersome dress? I am wearing these dungarees. Don't worry. When we get to Cheyenne, I will appear as a proper woman. But during travel, I am putting my hair in a hat and will look like your younger brother. It makes things safer for all concerned."

She checked her horse and then hopped up on the bench seat. Dale Cope scratched his head. He was not married to the woman, and what she did was no reflection upon himself. So, he climbed up beside her, flicking the reins. The horses moved down the drive and out onto the road.

"What are you looking at?" She caught him staring at her.

"Never seen a woman wear britches before, is all."

"Well, times are coming when women will wear britches if they choose. Whoever thought it was right and proper to wear a dress every day should have their head examined."

They rode north out of Missouri, turning west. Every day when they stopped for the evening, Dale tried to teach Reba something new, like how to run and jump onto the back of a horse. But she wasn't tall enough to accomplish that task. She was good at roping and most definitely was a fine shot. He'd found that out after setting objects on a fallen log, and she used a mirror to shoot them aiming over her shoulder, shot backward, hitting every single one of them. Dale started to believe his student might be able to make the Western shows because she was phenomenal at what she did.

She never complained. Dale set up under the wagon at night while the horses were left to graze either by a creek or water was given from the barrels replenished at each watering hole they crossed.

AFTER TWO WEEKS on the road, they were seasoned travelers. Reba went to bathe in the river while Dale cooked a rabbit over the campfire.

"Hold it right there." Dale Cope froze, with hands in the air. "I'll take that rabbit, and I'll take whatever you got in your purse."

"I don't have money. I am a man for hire and won't get paid until I get my client's things to Cheyenne," Dale told the man. "But you can have the rabbit. I'll shoot another if you leave me my gun."

The man motioned with his gun for Dale to move away from the fire. He grabbed the rabbit, pulled some meat off the stick, and put it in his mouth. "I'll take those boots. What size are they?"

"Ten."

When Reba came out of the river, she heard voices and quickly got dressed. Grabbing her gun, she put it in the front of her pants, sneaking up on the would-be robber.

"Drop your gun. I'll take that too," the thief told Dale.

Reba aimed at the man's pistol and shot, knocking the gun out of the stranger's hand.

Dale grabbed his gun. The intruder yelped, and Reba shouted in a low voice.

"Come on, let's get him!"

The robber turned, running for his horse. When he was gone, she came out of the bushes.

"You saved me. Thank you," Dale said. He was still astonished at her shooting accuracy through bushes. He threw the gun down and said, "Leave it. He'll be back for it. We don't want him to follow us for keeping a cheap gun."

Reba did as he asked, then chuckled. "I have been practicing most of my life for this day. Glad he didn't get all the rabbit. Let's eat." She pulled a chunk of meat from the roasted carcass. Dale couldn't believe what he saw. This woman was as good as any right-hand man and better to keep company with. They sat by the fire and talked until they fell asleep.

>-···· ⇒⊱⇐ ····-<

"DON'T MOVE," DALE whispered. Reba woke to see a rattlesnake next to her. Instinct made her want to roll away, but the snake was coiled and ready to strike. Dale shot, beheading the snake in front of her. Reba fell back, nearly fainting from holding her breath for so long.

"You did good. Maybe you can be my assistant in the Western show. You can put an apple on your head, and I'll shoot it off." Reba chuckled.

"Not on your life, missy," Cope said sourly. "You could thank me for saving your life."

"Thank you, Mister Cope, for saving my life. I believe we are now even."

They broke camp. Dale didn't engage her for most of the day. She was a woman, though she looked like a young boy these days. Last night, they fell asleep around the campfire. Reba should have climbed into the wagon and turned in for the night, but that didn't happen. They needed to continue to keep their distance. Dale Cope didn't want anything to do with the woman. Once they reached Cheyenne, he would part ways and go back to the ranch where a job was waiting, according to Whitey.

After a month on their journey, Dale told Reba she had to dress appropriately. They would be in Cheyenne soon. Her days of being a young boy were over. He refused to take her into town dressed as she was. Reluctantly, Reba returned dressed as a woman.

"I shall miss my freedom," she lamented, putting the men's clothing in her trunk and climbing onto the wagon. Several hours later, they reached the outskirts of town.

Cheyenne, a large cattle town, made Reba's eyes grow wide as she saw the shops and ruffians in the streets. She would be sad to let Dale Cope go back to Missouri. Perhaps she could find another bodyguard here.

She paid for two hotel rooms and asked Dale Cope to take her to the grounds where the Western show was, bright and early the following day.

Reba came out of the hotel dressed in the outfit she made, the dress that tucked into the tall boots. When she met Dale on the street with their horses, she didn't ride sidesaddle. She hairpinned her legs over like a man. Dale nearly choked but didn't say a word. Reba Boone was his boss, and he would give her respect due to being a boss. They rode out to the grounds.

"Who is that?" Reba gasped when she saw her first Black man performing in a Western show.

"That's Bill Picket. Never heard of him before?"

Reba shook her head.

"He can wrestle a steer to the ground with his bare hands. He's an amazing cowboy."

Reba watched the man twist the steer's neck and bite its lip. Submitting to him, the animal lay on the ground and the crowd went wild.

"Do you have tickets?" a man asked them.

"I am here to talk to the person in charge. I am applying for a job," Reba said boldly.

The man chuckled and led them to a small building marked *Office*.

Dale followed her inside, where Reba sat and waited. They heard the man shout at the other man, who left the office quickly.

"Can I help you?" The boss looked at Dale, who threw his head toward Reba. "Miss?"

Reba got up from the chair and crossed the room, her hand extended. "My name is Reba Boone, and I've come for a job. I can out rope, outride, or outshoot any man you have in your show. Give me a chance."

The man looked at Reba's slight frame with a pinched face, then looked at Dale. "Now I know who you are. Dale? Dale Cope?"

Dale nodded and shook his hand. "Mister Nash, Miss Boone here is phenomenal. I've seen her shoot things from a mirror backward and get a perfect score. She's getting close to jumping on the back of her horse. It isn't her fault she's just short, that's all, but she's almost there. I think the crowd would get a kick out of watching her tricks."

Nash asked if she could do some tricks today.

"I can. I am prepared to go on now."

"Okay, get your horse and go out to Ferrit, the man out in the arena. Take this note." Mr. Nash scratched some words and folded the note over.

Reba didn't question. She mounted her horse and rode Trixie out to the arena, handing the note to Mr. Ferrit. Nash didn't care—he found his final act, and the audience was no longer shortchanged after a difference of opinion from his regular performer. The crowd would be amused at the slight woman's expense, if nothing else.

"Ladies and gentlemen, all the way from Springfield, Missouri, I present Reba Boone!" The crowd applauded, and a table with several bottles and cans was placed in the arena before the gate was opened.

"Just ride around and shoot at the table," Ferrit told her.

This was it, her chance. Reba took a deep breath, walked Trixie out to the middle, and made the horse bow. The crowd clapped politely. She started him in a slow canter around the arena, aimed at the first bottle on the table, and shot. She missed. The crowd groaned.

"We want our money back," shouted a man. Reba hung off the side of Trixie and took several shots, blasting bottles off the table. The crowd roared, and the trick rider's adrenaline soared. After that, she didn't miss. She shot behind her, taking the next bottle. The crowd no doubt had never seen an excellent sharpshooting woman before. Reba had them in her hand. When she finished, Nash stood outside the arena listening to the wild cheers.

"I want to offer you a job, young lady." He was all smiles, and so was she.

It took a week, but Dale was able to find another bodyguard for Reba, another cowboy on the circuit. She had a place to stay and a job. She was secure, and he was going back to Springfield.

"Thank you, Dale." Reba held her hand out as she had when they first met.

"You take care, Miss Boone. I wish you a successful career." Dale took his horse and tied him to the back of the wagon.

"I'll be back in Springfield before you know it," Reba told him. They had given her a six-month contract.

Dale tipped his hat and rode off.

Reba watched him until she could see him no longer, feeling a tinge of homesickness, pushing that longing behind her. There was a world to see, and she was going to do it. The show was moving tomorrow, and she with it.

Dale went back to work Eden Ranch under Whitey, a fair boss. He looked forward to reading the paper that came in the mail every week. Reba Boone had carved a name for herself. Being a local celebrity, she was featured almost every week, and Dale was able to see her smiling face, usually on the cover. Something tugged in his heart, a change that admired the spunky woman he had come to admire and respect. There was no keeping Reba Boone down.

Someday, she would return to Springfield full of stories to tell, and when she did, he would be waiting for her.

—*Dawn DeBraal lives in rural Wisconsin and has published over 700 short stories, drabbles, and poems. She was a 2019 Pushcart nominee and was awarded the International Literary Global Book Award for her first solo novel in 2024,* The Lord's Prayer, A Series of Horror. *Dawn also writes under the pen name of Garrison McKnight. You can find her on Facebook —https://www.facebook.com/All-The-Clever-Names-Were-Taken-114783950248991 and Amazon — https://www.amazon.com/stores/author/B07STL8DLX/allbooks?*

THE QUEST

CHRIS ENSS

NO ONE PAID much attention to Grace Harrington as she slowly limped into the Fort Worth Mercantile Company in the summer of 1887. She was barefoot and the dress she was wearing was little more than shredded material hanging on her emaciated frame. The thirty-nine-year-old woman's face was bony, weathered, and bruised. Across her neck was a dark red burn, a brand of some sort. She held a faded blue cavalry jacket against her left side, and a pocket watch on a long, tarnished chain dangled from her scarred and bloody wrist. Grace took two steps into the store and dropped to her knees. Her features were the color of wet sand, her eyes dark and bloodshot and mad. There was nothing in them that showed she saw anyone around her.

Samuel Minshall, the bespeckled, sour-faced proprietor of the business, glanced up from the crate of canned goods he was unpacking and stared befuddled at the scene. Grace tried to speak but a bubbling sound caught in her throat, and she choked on her words. She finally forced the name of "Henry" from her lips, put her right hand over the hand holding the jacket and watch, and fell. She didn't put her hands out. She fell as a tree falls and the bundle she was carrying dropped to the floor.

Only after Grace was lying face down on the ground did the customers nearest to her notice the two bullet holes in her back and the stains from the blood that gushed out of them. Minshall ordered his wife, who had been stocking shelves, to get help. She hurried out of the store and in a few quick moments returned with Doctor Augusta Baylor in tow.

The main thoroughfare of Fort Worth, Texas, was so crowded that the passing streams of people jostled each other, and strangers walked shoulder to shoulder. The air was charged with excitement. A carnival had come to town and citizens from far and wide had poured into the location to see the sights.

Doctor Baylor, a tall, no-nonsense woman with a shiny boyish face, arrived at the mercantile carrying a black medical bag. She knelt next to the unconscious woman and gently probed her wounds. She then opened her medical bag, donned a stethoscope, rolled Grace onto her right side, and applied the instrument to her chest. Satisfied the patient possessed a discernable heartbeat, the doctor motioned for a couple of ranch hands in the store to carry the woman to her office.

Several days passed before Grace awakened. Doctor Baylor had removed the bullets lodged in her upper torso and bandaged the deep and numerous cuts up and down her painfully thin frame. Apart from the military jacket and watch Grace had with her when she collapsed, there was nothing to show who she was or where she came from. She wasn't wearing a wedding ring and the rag masquerading as her dress had no laundry marks to study. The doctor examined the woman's battered hands. Fingers and wrists had been broken more than once and had either been set improperly or not at all, which accounted for the deformed knuckles and crooked digits.

Doctor Baylor returned to her desk to make a few notes in the patient's chart. She eyed the watch the woman had been carrying, now draped over a microscope, and picked it up. The doctor examined the timepiece thoroughly, looking for a name or initials. She pressed the stem on the top and the cover on the front of the watch swung open. A sweet tune emanated from a musical mechanism within the timepiece once the cover opened. The tender melody filled the room. When the refrain reached Grace's ears her eyes shot open. With effort, she lifted her head and searched the room until her eyes came to rest on the watch. The doctor noticed the woman stirring, closed the watch, and hurried to her bedside.

"Try not to move," she persuaded Grace. "You've been hurt. I'm a doctor and this is my office."

Grace said nothing. She was confused and wore the expression of one trying desperately to recall what had happened.

"Can you tell me your name?" Doctor Baylor softly inquired. "Do you have people somewhere?"

Grace didn't reply. A bead of sweat broke out on her forehead as she stared curiously at her bandaged arms.

"Do you have a husband?" the doctor continued. "Children?"

Grace struggled to pull herself up. She was hurting but physical pain was not what was troubling her. She stared around the room and at her body. The doctor placed a hand on Grace's shoulder and tried to get her to lie back. "It's all right," Doctor Baylor assured her. "You're safe."

Grace reluctantly laid her head on the bed. Tears of pain rolled down her face. "And Henry?" she asked weakly.

"Who is Henry?" the doctor responded, dipping a cloth in a nearby basin of water.

Grace furrowed her brow. She was confused, on the verge of re-membering, but stuck. She reluctantly laid her head down and tried desperately to fight from falling asleep. She quickly lost the battle and drifted off.

A SHROUD OF smoke settled on a battlefield littered with the bod-ies of cavalry soldiers. All is blurred like an old painting. The eyes of the slain are as immobile as their limbs. The smoke about them twirls heavenward as if it were taking souls home. Suddenly, a lieutenant atop a large sorrel horse rides fast out of the fumes. The thirty-two-year-old man is disheveled and sweating. His uniform is weathered and torn in places. With dumb, muted strain, the lieutenant's horse obeys his urging to move even more quickly. The horse's mouth is full of foam, his mane flies, and his hooves pound the greasy grass into dust.

Rider and horse are surrounded by Sioux braves and race headlong into hostile Cheyenne warriors. The lieutenant draws his weapon— lightning, smoke, and the blast of a .45-caliber shot scream from his pistol like a scythe, cutting down those in his path. Bullets are fired at the lieutenant but he's oblivious to the incoming rounds. A piece of his hat is blown away and epaulettes are shot off. His fellow soldiers who have ridden alongside him are killed and their blood splattered on his coat. More Sioux materialize from nowhere and charge after him. The sound of bullets cutting through the air can be heard from all directions.

KABOOM!

The report of a gun in the near distance jerked Grace awake. Her hair, matted against her face, drenched with perspiration. She's had the dream of the rider being pursued by the Sioux and Cheyenne many times before, and each time she awakens with a jolt. She wiped the sleep from her eyes and ventured a look around. Golden sunlight streamed in through a window adorned with white curtains directly across from her bed—one of two in the spacious, orderly room. Rolled bandages, a mortar and pestle, pitcher and washbasin, thick medical books, and the skull of a human head are arranged neatly on a tall dresser next to a half-opened door leading into an office. Apart from Grace the place is empty.

Somewhere outside and close by an oriole sings. The bright melody is in sharp contrast to the noise and chaos that haunted her sleep. As the daylight continued to tickle her eyes into full wakefulness, she glanced over at the small table next to the bed hoping to find some water. There's only a small vase with flowers, sheets of blank paper, and a pencil. Grace had a vague recollection of sharing her nightmare with someone who wrote it down and she shuddered at the thought. With rare exception had she ever talked about her nightmare, for to speak of it would give it substance and that was more than her heart could take. She tried to push the dream from her mind and concentrate on the bird's song. She listened for some time before she heard the crunch of bootheels and the growl of voices.

Two soldiers noisily entered the room. Both were members of the Second Frontier Regiment. The outpost in which they were stationed was located outside of Whitesboro, Texas, some eighty plus miles away in Gainesville. The job of the more than nine hundred mounted sentries assigned there was to patrol the area for outlaws, hostile Native Americans, and deserters. Having heard of Grace's dramatic entrance into town, an officer and enlisted man from the garrison hurried to the scene. Lieutenant Homer Corey was a slender, hawk-faced, silver-haired gentleman. Sergeant Jerome Neland was in his late thirties, stocky and powerful, with a great shock of vigorous hair and a pair of hard, blue eyes glinting out of a blocky, blunt-featured face. His voice rolled over her, sounding deep and harsh.

"I'm Sergeant Neland," he announced to a frightened Grace. "I want all your story on how and why you showed up here the way you did. And I want to know if anyone helped you get to Texas?"

Grace tried to pull herself up and move to the edge of the bed away from the pair. The forceful manner of the sergeant took her aback. She recoiled and tried to disappear into the blanket covering her.

"I need to know if someone helped you," the sergeant gruffly reiterated. His tone was jarring, and there was an implication there which tightened Grace's lips. His eyes bored into her intently. Just then Doctor Baylor charged in and positioned herself between her patient and the soldiers.

"I told you this wasn't the time, Sergeant Neland," the physician sternly reminded him. The doctor turned her attention to Grace, who was crying—her face a frozen mask. She was short of breath, and Doctor Baylor helped her lie back and straightened the bedding. "Nothing has changed since you pushed your way in here the morning after this woman was moved here," the doctor firmly informed the men. "She can't help you. At least not right now."

The lieutenant placed a hand on the sergeant's shoulder and the man relaxed a bit. "I recognize that brand," the sergeant noted, pointing to the mark on Grace's neck.

"She needs time," Doctor Baylor responded compassionately, determined to convince the soldier.

Sergeant Neland eyed both women gravely for a moment. "Two days," he offered. "That's all I can do." The sergeant turned on his heels and walked out the patient's room, frustrated but resigned. After apologizing profusely for the intrusion, Lieutenant Corey followed after Neland.

Doctor Baylor leaned over Grace and dabbed the perspiration off the traumatized woman's brow with a cloth she had tucked inside the pocket of her white cotton smock. Grace's face was a mixture of confusion and pain. "Were those men with the Seventh Cavalry?" she asked with tears in her eyes.

"No," the doctor replied. "They're with the Frontier Regiment. Do you know someone in the Seventh?"

"I do." Grace finally nodded. "I do."

Doctor Baylor gently took a seat on the bed next to Grace and wiped away the tears generously streaming down the patient's troubled face. In that moment Grace recalled everything.

>····· ⇒⫞⇐ ·····⤎

—Chris Enss is a New York Times *bestselling author of more than fifty books. Focusing on extraordinary women throughout history, her work has been honored with nine Will Rogers Medallion Awards, two Elmer Kelton Book Awards, an Oklahoma Center for the Book Award, three* Foreword Reviews *Magazine Book Awards, the DOWNING Journalism Award, and a WILLA Literary Award from Women Writing the West for scholarly nonfiction.*

Shadows in the Firelight

MICHELLE FERRER

THE TEXAS FRONTIER
OCTOBER 1857

"OLD WOMAN, COME on out here."

Clary Harper leaned out the kitchen door. "You callin' me, Old Man?"

"Sun's settin'. Come sit with me before it beds down over the ridge."

Clary watched her husband Asa set the logs alight in the stone-ringed circle between the barn and the cabin, just like he did every evening after supper. When the flames flickered steady, he relaxed into a willow rocking chair and puffed on his pipe. Tobacco smoke sweetened the cool autumn air. Tuckit, their yellow hunting dog, settled next to his chair and nosed Asa's hand for a scratch around the ears.

She dried and stored away the last supper dish in the cupboard, a recent purchase from a neighboring family who called it quits and abandoned their farm to the wild prairie. She patted the log walls of the newly added kitchen and breathed in the damp musky aroma of fresh chinking made from the Brazos River clay nearby. Her lips tilted up in a satisfied smile. Seven hard years in the coming, the original eighteen-by-eighteen foot log cabin had grown with the addition of two private sleeping rooms, and now a proper kitchen to cook in. At last, the family home was complete.

She strolled to the fire circle and settled in a chair next to her husband. "That's a good fire you got going tonight."

The couple rocked side by side watching the autumn sun splinter the sky into dazzling rays of color. Reflected in the river, the sky and land appeared to merge as the sun sank below the horizon leaving behind a darkening sky sprinkled with shining stars.

"Ain't no denying it. You can't beat a Texas sunset. It's almost like God's sayin' good night to the whole world."

"You almost missed it tonight, Old Woman. I can't seem to blast you out of that kitchen these days."

Her warm laugh tinkled in the twilight. "It's been a long time comin', Old Man. Now, I've got a proper place to cook a meal and put up preserves. I'll be spending some days fattening you up from here on out. You can count on that!"

Asa's lips curled into a smile around his pipe as he patted his stomach. "You started tonight. That was a fine meal, a fine meal indeed."

A clipped, raspy caw and flapping wings interrupted their conversation. Reflected in the firelight, the shadow of a large crow swooped across the barn wall. The bird circled the couple and landed on the back of Clary's chair.

"Hey, Midnight. Comin' for your bedtime snack?"

Clary pulled an unshelled pecan from her apron pocket and offered the nut from her hand. In one motion, a glossy head stretched forward grasping the treat before taking flight for his roost in the tall oak tree beside the barn.

"You've witched that bird, Old Woman. He ain't never gonna leave if you keep spoiling him."

"I don't want him to leave. He warns me when you're away and I'm here alone. Three caws says trouble's afoot. Sometimes, it's a cougar prowling. Or maybe some stranger lost or passin' through. When I hear Midnight's alarm, I get ready for whatever comes. It's sure a comfort."

Asa puffed small clouds from his pipe as he rocked. "You don't need a bird's warnin'. You can talk the Devil out of his brimstone."

Clary nodded and shifted a sly look at her husband. "Have a time or two."

"Too bad ole Lucifer wasn't listening when he drowned our boy in the Brazos last spring."

Clary swallowed back sudden tears remembering their son's body jammed in the river-swept brush piled up at the curve of Miller's Bend. Her voice trembled slightly. "Can't give the Devil credit for that. Henry was always reckless. He didn't respect the Texas wilderness, thinking he could ford that river in flood surge. That mistake cost us all."

"For a spell there, I thought I was gonna have to bury you right alongside him."

She rocked in her chair guarding her grief. "Took me a while, but I finally figured as long as I say his name, he ain't dead. Just sleeping."

Asa reached over and patted her hand. "Well, we've carved out one hundred sixty acres in this rough country that I'm going to tame. Come this spring, I'll prove who's boss around here."

"You can't tame the wild land, Old Man. You just make your peace with it. That's what the Indians do, most of 'em, anyway. They don't pull against it. They're part of it, like the grass and the sky."

"And, speaking of the sky," Asa pointed. "Moon's rising. Real full tonight and spreadin' silver light bright enough to read by. A Comanche moon."

Clary rose. "Time to head in. Mornin' comes early. C'mon, Tuckit." She glanced back at Asa still gazing at the moon. "You comin'?"

"First time I saw you was at that dance social back in Tennessee. I stepped out for a smoke and there you was with the moonlight gleaming all over your mane of auburn hair. We danced a waltz right there in the garden. How come you didn't dance with nobody but me?"

Clary grinned. "'Cause you were the only one tall enough to dance with me. Those men didn't like me being a head taller than them."

Asa sidled over and wrapped her waist in his arm. "Nah, they figured that fiery hair of yours would make you hard to handle. How about we waltz our way home. You remember how to dance?"

"Think you can manage not to stumble over your feet this time?"

"You just keep up with me, Old Woman!" Asa led her through a lively jig. Tuckit joined in barking and prancing side to side while the firelight cast their dancing shadows against the barn wall.

CLARY BLEW OUT the lantern as early morning light crept through the kitchen door. She poured Asa a second cup of coffee along with another helping of bacon, eggs, and fresh biscuits.

"Want some soppin' gravy with those biscuits?"

"You're makin' good on your promise to fatten me up. Pack me some vittles to take along, and a bone for Tuckit. It might be a long hunt."

She laid out biscuits, along with beef jerky and dried plums. "I'll make you a venison stew when you get back. Be a nice change from wild turkey. Try to get a buck. I'd sure hate for a fawn to be left alone to starve."

Asa smiled at his softhearted wife. "Don't know if a buck will volunteer, but I'll give it my best. I'm gonna check out the cornfield on my way out. Saw signs of wild pigs rootin' through it the other day. Cliff can help me finish clearing that field when he gets back from selling the horses in Fort Worth."

Clary handed him a wrapped food bundle. "When do you expect him back?"

Asa sucked his teeth, calculating the journey. "Herd's small, and they're all trail broken. Even with rest and grazing, shouldn't take more than a week to get there. Less time to get back if he don't lollygag. Should see him by Sunday supper."

"What if he doesn't come back. You two had a ripsnorter of a row. He was still steamin' when he left."

Asa spread his hands on the table and studied his calloused fingers. "The boy vexed me. I was harsh, I know that. I'll make it up to him."

"He ain't a boy no more. Maybe he won't forgive you. Not this time."

Chair legs scraped the floor. Asa stood and shot her a sharp look. "He'll be back. I know my son."

Clary watched him strap on the Walker Colt revolver and stuff three loaded cylinders into his saddlebags. "You expectin' trouble?"

"Maybe. Seen Indian signs. Comanche probably. Don't know if they're friendly." Asa took his rifle down from the wall. "Might not get back before morning. Shotgun's loaded if you need it. Take the Paterson Colt when you leave the cabin but keep close to home."

He paused, seeing her face go pale. The crease between her brows silently noted her concern. He grinned and gave her a frisky wink to lighten the mood. "Don't worry. Midnight will give you a three-caw warning."

Clary sputter-laughed and threw her dish towel at him as he went out the door. Chuckling to herself, she took a sip of her hot coffee. The sudden harsh clang of metal crashing against the cabin startled her. She dropped the cup. A loud curse followed the sharp crack of the Colt revolver. She grabbed the Paterson and peered out the door. Her eyes scanned for the shooter. Asa lay face down on the ground barely moving. Tuckit whined over him nosing his neck.

Clary flew out the door and threw herself over him. Alarmed at the blood pooling around his hips, her hands searched him for the wound. "Where are you hit?"

"Tripped over the milk pail. Gun went off when I fell on it. Damn fool thing. I thought I set that cylinder to the half cock."

Clary wrapped her arm around his shoulder and pulled. "Trust you to trip over those big feet. Push on the ground… help me turn you over. Let's check the damage."

Already pale and clammy, Asa's face twisted in pain as he rolled onto his back. Clary's eyes widened at the blood pulsing from the severed artery in his thigh. Using his kerchief to make a tourniquet, she wrapped the cotton around the dinner bell's striker iron and wound it tight. She pressed her apron against his leg, but nothing staunched the bright red flow. His lips began to turn blue.

"Gotta get you in the house."

"Too late. I'm bleedin' out."

"No, you ain't. I can fix it." Unable to hoist him off the ground, she grabbed handfuls of dirt to pack the wound. Her hands began to shake as the blood kept bubbling through. She looked for anything that would stop the bleeding.

"Tell Cliff I'm sorry."

"Tell him yourself. You're gonna be all right." She swallowed hard to mask her panic as his face turned ashen. His eyes began to dilate.

Asa reached blindly for her. She grabbed his hand tightly in hers. "I'm right here."

He struggled to speak as he panted in shallow breaths. "Ain't never loved... no one... but you, Clary."

"N-no, Asa. Stay with me." Her voice began to crack. "I'm not lettin' you go. Oh, God, please... this ain't happening. Hold on, Asa."

His glazed eyes stared at nothing, his grip loosened, and he lay still. She looked down on him as her tears streamed.

"Asa?" She shook him, screaming. "Asa...! *Asa!*"

Her wail echoed through the trees.

LOW GRAY CLOUDS and chilled gusts blew over the hill behind the cabin warning of autumn storms to come. An ancient bur oak tree sat on the crest of the hill. Its twisted and corded bark served as testament to strength and age. Standing strong against the wind, the tree sheltered the two mounds of earth where Henry, and now Asa, rested. Clary sat hollow-eyed on the ground between her son and her husband. She didn't feel the chill or notice the clouds.

Every day for the last three days, the chickens somehow got fed and the cows were milked although Clary had no recall of those chores. She only remembered hauling rocks from the river's edge to the top of the hill. She had felt nothing as she muscled the stones into tidy borders around each grave. But every step with those heavy stones pulled the tears and her grief into the earth where her heart wanted to lie.

She brushed away wind-tossed leaves from the twin mounds. "Well, Asa, Henry. Here we are. The three of us sittin' up here on this hill and I'm doing all the talkin.' Since you got each other for company, how about the two of you get together and tell me how I go on without you."

She tried to hum a favorite hymn, but no song made it past her parched throat. All of her felt as dried out as those bur oak leaves dropping down in the gusts. The clouds turned darker gray as the sun behind them began to set. Tuckit nestled closer and poked her with his nose. Clary buried her fingers into his fur and gazed down into his soft brown eyes.

"You're right, Tuckit. Time to light the logs."

The fire crackled in the circle spreading light and warmth as night fell. The flames reflected Tuckit's image as he stood in front of Asa's empty chair wagging his tail. Flapping wings and a dark shadow announced Midnight who landed on Tuckit's back. Startled, Tuckit yipped and leaped sideways shaking the crow loose to tumble on the ground. In a huff, the bird fluffed his feathers. He bellowed two caws to regain his dignity and hopped on the back of Clary's chair.

She chuckled at the comic antics and rewarded Midnight with a pecan snack. "Leave it to critters to make a body laugh. Old Man, see what you're missin' tonight? Asa... You ain't dead if I call your name. You'll never be dead to me."

>····· ⇒⁄⇐ ·····≺

CLARY WOKE BEFORE dawn. She reached for Asa, caressing the empty space beside her. But the demands of the farm had no patience for mourning.

She had lost track of the passing days, but the daily routine starting with farm chores and ending at the fire circle made waiting for Cliff's return bearable. Asa had said he would return by Sunday supper. Sunday had come and gone. This morning, like every morning, her eyes scanned the eastern horizon for the telltale dust of an incoming rider. Tuckit brushed his shoulder against her leg.

"Not today, boy. Looks like we'll have to wait a little longer." She gave him an absent-minded scratch behind his ears. "How about if I make us a corn pudding for breakfast? And fresh honey bread and cream. It's Cliff's favorite. Asa's too. And I'll fry up some bacon for you. What do you think?"

A wagging tail gave approval.

Sweet aromas of fresh-baked bread and pudding soon filled the kitchen and drifted into the yard. Clary set the bread and pudding on the table to cool. Tuckit managed to stay out from underfoot. With no warning, he sprang to his feet and stood stiff-legged at the kitchen door. His fur bristled and he growled a warning. Three caws echoed from the oak tree in the yard.

Alerted by the animals, Clary slipped Asa's Walker Colt into the holster under her apron and cautiously looked out to the yard where two Comanche waited, both on foot with a single horse in tow. One she recognized. Kwihnai, who stood a head taller than her and whose calm, penetrating golden brown eyes matched those of his namesake, Eagle. The other was a stranger. His hooded dark eyes set in a face like chiseled stone gave her a chill.

From the porch she smiled. "Kwihnai. We welcome the Eagle's visit."

Kwihnai lip-pointed toward the house and signed for Asa. Clary shook her head and signed "away." She offered the hospitality of hot coffee, warm honey bread, and crisp bacon. Kwihnai tucked in and motioned the dark one to eat. Tseena, the Wolf, stood silent.

With the greeting ritual observed, Kwihnai fetched the horse to the porch. "We bring you gift."

The young horse stood about thirteen hands high. Too short for Clary to ride comfortably but looked strong enough to pull a plow. Her practiced eye also noticed that the mare favored her left foot caused by a mild swelling on the hind leg. The rough riding required of a Comanche horse meant she would likely go lame and end up in a Comanche stew. Clary nodded in understanding. The horse was meant for trade.

She offered two sacks each of coffee and flour. To sweeten the deal, she also tossed in a pouch of Asa's tobacco. With a nod, Kwihnai handed Clary the bridle.

The Wolf's wooden façade came alive. She didn't understand the words, but his harsh tone and angry gestures toward her and the milk cow made his intentions clear.

Clary spoke to Kwihnai. "Your friend is greedy. He shames you."

Tseena reached for the pony's bridle. Clary slapped his hand away. He grabbed her hair braid and jerked her toward him. Even though she was taller, his grip was powerful. The more she struggled, the harder he tugged.

Clary kicked and clawed, fighting to keep her footing. "Turn me loose, you thievin' piece of dry goods!"

Midnight's raucous caws set off a chorus of nearby crows filling the air with their cries. Flapping wings churned in the sky and swooped over the tussling pair. Tuckit attacked and sank his teeth into the arm holding Clary. In the scuffle, she ripped Tseena's sacred medicine bag from his chest.

Instantly, he let her go and backed away. Blood dripped from his fang-bitten arm. He paid no attention to the wounds. His eyes were riveted on the medicine bag she had defiled with her hands.

Clary's pent-up tears turned to rage. Her outstretched arm trembled as she held the bag of sacred amulet tokens in a stranglehold grip. "You call yourself Wolf, but you have no honor. You're just a flea-bitten coyote. Here's what I think of you!" She threw the bag down and ground it with her heel.

Tseena stood frozen. He paid no attention to her words but stared at the crushed bag holding the destroyed remnants of his protection and magic. His face turned hard as stone. His eyes became slits as he focused all his hate on her. He drew his knife and moved toward her.

Clary pulled the revolver and aimed for his chest. Kwihnai leaped between them and shoved Tseena back with a warning. Tseena charged and the two warriors grappled, neither willing to give ground. Kwihnai slipped and Tseena plunged the knife into his side.

Clary heard Kwihnai gasp as he slowly sank to the ground. Tseena stood over him, his hand holding the knife covered in the blood of his friend. His eyes focused on her as his face twisted in rage. He bellowed a war cry and ran for her. She raised the revolver and fired. The knife flew out of his hand as he staggered back from the bullet's impact. Blood spurted from his shattered shoulder. She cocked the gun again, but Tseena hobbled into the trees where his horse was tethered. He labored to mount and ride away.

Kwihnai lay nearby. He struggled to rise but fell back. She managed to get him on his feet. He leaned heavily on her as she half walked, half dragged him into the cabin where he collapsed unconscious on the floor.

Clary knelt down and turned him on his side to examine the wound. The cut looked deep but appeared to angle away from any vital organs. The gash was too big to cauterize. She would have to stitch it shut.

She clicked her tongue and checked to see that he was still unconscious. "Good thing you're out cold. You ain't gonna like this next part."

THE FARM REMAINED quiet after the ruckus with Tseena. Clary stayed close to the cabin for the rest of the day but kept a watchful eye in case he returned. Kwihnai had awakened briefly after she stitched him up. He tried to get up, but she fed him some laudanum-laced hot tea to make him sleep. He hadn't moved since. Toward late afternoon, she checked his bandage and found no leakage. His skin was cool and dry. No evidence of fever. He snored softly in even breaths.

Farm chores called and with no evidence of trouble waiting outside, she headed for the barn. The young mare she traded for quietly grazed in the grass nearby. Her bridle trailed the ground. Clary gently stroked the animal.

"I'm sure sorry, girl. I forgot all about you. C'mon. I've got a lead horse who'll make you feel right at home."

By sunset, she'd laid out hay for the horses, milked the cows, and bedded down the chickens. Tuckit waited by Asa's chair in the fire circle. He circled her legs, wagged his tail, and whined for an ear scratch.

"Time to light the fire, huh, boy? It's gettin' so I can set the clock by you these days."

She relaxed in her chair. Tuckit lay down between her and Asa's chair. Clary stared into the fire forgetting to watch the sunset.

"Asa. I need you tonight. So, tell me, what am I gonna do with that Comanche boy in the house? I owe him for saving my life. Ain't forgettin' that. Doin' my best, but if he dies, I'll have his whole tribe down on me, I guess. As for that other, I hope I blasted his sorry ass to Hell. And don't lecture me on swearing. I've earned the right!" She rocked in the chair listening to the nearby creek splash and gurgle its way downstream. "You seen Midnight, yet? He's never late for his snack. That's a worry."

A rustling in the house turned her attention to Kwihnai. He was asleep but restless. She wiped him down with a cool damp cloth and adjusted the blanket. "What you need is sleep, boy. Good thing you ain't used to laudanum. It'll keep you still long enough so those stitches can set."

Two caws echoed across the yard. With a relieved smile, she made for the kitchen door with two pecan treats to feed the tardy bird. Three sharp caws stopped her cold. Through the firelight, Tseena's shadow hobbled across the barn wall. She slammed the door shut—dropping the latch—and flew through the house forting up the windows, then blew out the lamp. The dark and the loaded shotgun served as allies. For extra measure, she took Asa's rifle down from the wall and kept it close by.

Too late, she realized Tuckit was locked outside. She peered through the peepholes in the doors and shutters, but there was no sign of him. The only shadows reflected on the barn wall were those of the crackling fire logs dancing in the night.

The door rattled but the latch held. Clary softly pulled back the hammer on the shotgun. Outside, she heard Tuckit snarl and the sound of his jaws tearing into flesh. Something slammed hard against the door followed by a loud yelp. Then, silence. She raised the gun to the peephole and scanned the empty yard. A harsh war cry split the air. Tseena's carved gargoyle face popped up as he charged the door. Clary pulled the trigger, and the shot exploded through the opening.

All went suddenly still. Even the fire hushed its crackle. The quiet was louder than the pounding of her heart. An hour dragged by in the silent dark. Kwihnai moaned slightly but didn't wake. A horse whinnied near the barn. Through the peephole Clary glimpsed a shadow reflected in the firelight. A figure, bent over, crept toward the house and quickly crossed out of her line of vision. Footsteps shuffled softly along the porch. The door latch rattled. Clary raised the shotgun and aimed at the door.

"Mama, it's Cliff. Open up."

CLIFF'S HOMECOMING WAS bittersweet. Clary held her son tight, relieved he had come back. The loss of Asa lay heavy on Cliff who blamed himself for the hard words left between them that couldn't be undone.

Cliff took over the farm chores leaving Clary free to tend to Kwihnai and Tuckit. After three days, Kwihnai awoke anxious to get back to his people. His side stayed stitched shut, but she worried he'd be able to ride the distance even though the camp was just across the river. Cliff agreed to ride along to see him safely home. When Kwihnai asked about Tseena, Clary shrugged and signed that he was gone.

Come Sunday afternoon, mother and son climbed the hill to pay their respects despite the promise of early November frosts. They stood side by side at the stone-lined graves of Henry and Asa.

"I can't believe you moved all these rocks by yourself, Mama."

Clary could only nod. Her lips pressed tightly together to hold back tears.

Cliff shook his head side to side. "I should have been here. I was wrong to say what I did. I feel bad about how we left things, Pa and me. Should have been man enough to make it right."

"Don't blame yourself, son. He felt bad about it too. Said he'd make it up to you. Told me to tell you he was sorry."

Clary felt a chill as the breeze shifted to the north. "Sunset's comin'. Time to light the logs."

Cliff supported her by the elbow as they made their way down the hill to the fire circle. Tuckit limped along beside them. He had taken a beating and left a tooth in Tseena but was mostly recovered now. Clary was still angry with herself for not keeping Tuckit out of harm's way.

"Cliff, I was sure I shot that bad one, but he must have got away. He better not come back. I'll make sure not to miss next time."

Cliff nodded. "He won't bother us no more. Something I didn't tell you. I found his horse grazing in the cornfield. And his body not too far away. I couldn't leave him out there for the pigs. Ain't Christian. So, I buried him deep over by the woods. I know the Comanche don't bury their folks, but I didn't want them knowin' you killed him either. Could go hard on you. Oh, and I took his horse across the river and let him loose to chase a wild herd passin' through. Let's keep all that between us, though.

"Mama, how about you let me get the fire going tonight, while you warm us up some supper. We can eat out here by the fire and watch the sunset. Might help me feel a little closer to Pa, if you don't mind."

Clary smiled and turned toward the kitchen. "Cliff... look!"

From the porch rafter hung two fresh-killed rabbits along with a beaded lodge token. It was Cliff's turn to smile. "Well, I'll be. That'll be from Kwihnai. I never did tell you, Mama, I was a might worried when I carried him home to his people. They were none too friendly at first, until Kwihnai gave me the good eye. I guess we can count him a friend after all."

Clary hurried to put a meal together so that they could share the sunset while they ate. Tuckit sat between the two of them, waiting for crumbs to fall. Clint had built a good fire like Asa used to. Mother and son sat quietly rocking, content in the warm heat and each other's company.

"So. You plannin' to stay?"

Clint nodded. "Yep, soon as I get back from Fort Worth. Met a gal there, Mama. I'm gonna marry her."

Clary arched both eyebrows. "Well, why didn't you bring her with you?"

"Had to square things with Pa, first. Make sure we'd be welcome. Sure wish I'd taken the chance so he could have met her."

"You gonna tell me about her?"

Cliff smiled as he rocked. "Her name's Laura-Mae. Met her at the sale barn. Her Pa's the one who bought our horses. Hair like midnight. Wears it in a braid over her left shoulder, like you do. She's got… sea-green eyes that you get lost in. Nothing seems to matter when she looks at you. Ain't tall, like us, but holds her own.

"And fearless. She rides like an Indian and wrangles cattle like she's witched 'em. Soft on the inside, but don't make her mad. She lit into a guy at the barn who was whipping a horse. They had to pull her off him. Then, she made her pa buy that horse. Yeah, softhearted on the inside and tough as iron on the outside. You'll like her, Mama."

"Well, then, best you get an early start in the morning. Get that ring on her finger and bring her home. Go on, now. I'll be in directly."

Alone in the night, Clary stared into the fire. "Well, Asa, you were right all along. Our boy's home, like you said he'd be. And he'll make you proud. Right soon, now, we'll be a family again. This wild land has tested us hard, but we're making our peace with it. Day by day. We're gonna be all right, Asa."

She stood and stretched her back. High overhead, the full moon glowed silver in the night sky. A month ago, she had stood on this spot gazing at a Comanche moon just like tonight. She could almost feel Asa's arm around her holding her close as he did that last night.

Clary stared into the fire remembering all the nights she and Asa had shared their thoughts and dreams. She would always feel him rustling around in her heart, especially on quiet nights under a full moon.

Tuckit rubbed against her leg and whined toward Asa's chair, wagging his tail like he expected an ear scratch. They stood together in the firelight that reflected their shadows on the barn wall.

A woman, her dog, and a tall man with his arm around her shoulders.

—*With a business career behind her, Michelle Ferrer has returned to her passion for writing stories—mostly historical fiction and other stories that can't be ignored. In addition to writing short stories, she is also working on her first novel. She lives in Texas with an understanding and supportive husband. Her writing efforts are assisted by a creative chihuahua who perches between lap and keyboard.*

BANNER

SHARON FRAME GAY

WYOMING
1898

"NO, ANNIE, AND quit askin'. You can't have that colt." Papa's voice was firm, the kind of firm that sounds brittle as winter rain that can't decide if it wants to ice up or not. I felt it clear down to my bones, and my heart sang a sad song.

I've had my eye on the foal since he was born, slipping out of Papa's prize mare, Bonnie, and drifting to the ground like a snowflake. He was ebony and white, with little tufts of mane and tail the color of the hills on Christmas morning. His eyes were dark as raisins, and I swear he lifted his head, looked straight at me, and winked.

That's the first time I begged my father for him. Papa said I could name him, but that's as far as it goes. I couldn't think of a name fittin' for the colt right then. I was too upset, so decided to wait and have him tell me himself what he wanted to be called. Then I cried all the way back to the house. I fell into my mother's arms, thinkin' nothing could be as sorrowful as that day.

I was wrong.

>····· ≈⁄≈ ·····≪

IT HAD BEEN two years since the colt was born. That September, our mares and foals journeyed down from the hills where they had spent the entire summer feasting on sweet grass in the upper meadows and growin' fat and shiny. The pinto colt didn't lag behind the rest of the herd but swaggered up front, budding into his role as a stallion, his neck arched and tail high. His meager mane had grown into a billowing cloud that swirled and danced along his neck, and his tail rustled in the wind like a flag. I knew right then and there I'd name him Banner.

"I like it," Papa said as he slapped a lariat against his thigh and helped the cowboys settle the horses into a large holding pen. "Suits him. A great name for a stud." Then he turned to his foreman, Hank, and told him to cut Banner out of the herd and put him in a large corral behind the barn.

It was separation day. My father was looking for horses to sell, colts to geld, and mares to turn back to pasture or keep in the paddock for breeding. His practiced eye moved along the herd. Before long, all forty horses were sorted, and the wranglers tasked with the job of separating them.

Five colts were to be gelded. They were not good enough, in my father's opinion, to be used as studs. But Banner would remain intact. As if he knew, he raised his muzzle and blasted through the autumn air with a whinny so loud his shoulders shook. Far off in another pasture, a mare answered. Papa smiled. Banner wouldn't disappoint.

I walked to the corral and whistled. Banner tossed his magnificent mane and trotted over as I hopped the fence and hugged his neck. Even after a summer in the highlands, he remembered me, rubbing his head against my chest.

I sighed. I'd been with Banner since the day he was born, crawling into the birthing pen with Bonnie and stroking the foal for hours. From the moment he walked, he followed me like one of those disciples in the Bible, his head close to my shoulder like we were tied together.

He was my horse. There was no question. Everyone on the ranch knew it. Everyone except my father, who only looked at his ledgers and papers, staring long into his coffee cup. Papa spoke of the price of this, the value of that, and never about the heart. Or about a young girl who needed that colt and him not even hearing her beg, only hearing what's sensible and not what's right.

Two years ago, I thought my heart would break because I couldn't get Banner from my Papa. But since then, I've learned that some things can hurt even worse, especially when you aren't bracing for it. It comes about anyway, the way a storm hovers over the mountains and then marches down the hills to the homestead and covers it all with snow.

That's how my sorrow felt. Like it covered everything and couldn't warm up or cool down. It sat in my heart like a rock that's hard and dark, even though I watered it every day with my tears.

My mother fell ill, right about the time Banner was learning to gallop in the fields with his mama. Bonnie was healthy and swept through the grass in an elegant lope that looked like she was ready to jump for the moon.

But my own mama grew weaker by the day. The doctor said he thought there was something eating her up inside and spreading like seeds. When he said that, I ran to my room and stripped off my clothes. I stared in the mirror, looking to see if that thing was trying to eat at me too. I checked for a ripple in my skin or a lump on my back, but all I saw was the hide of a young girl, clean and innocent as spring. It scared me. What if the sickness came to eat me too? Or my father?

For a few days, I stayed away from Mama. I was afraid her breath might leak seeds, and I'd catch it. But I yearned to hold her and feel her warmth, as it seemed like Papa was getting colder and more distant. I needed to feel like the earth wasn't tilting upside down, trying to shake me loose. So, I'd go down to the corral and hold on to Banner. Sometimes I'd grip his neck so hard, he'd snort and back away. But he'd always step right back into my embrace as though he knew I was aching. He nudged me with his muzzle as I wept.

Mama was in bed all the time. Her body was as thin as a husk, as though she'd already moved on and left just her skin behind. I'd sit by her side and read from her favorite books. I barely heard the words as they passed my lips, and I doubt she heard much, either, but we wove love back and forth between us like a loom. I knew without her telling me she was keeping my voice in her memory, so she'd have something to hold on to when she was called to heaven.

Every night I prayed for a miracle, and every morning I went to visit Banner. I'd tell him my troubles and lean on him as he stood in the shade of an old cottonwood tree.

It was hot for September, and even Banner seemed listless as the sun beat down on the land and took the shine off of everything. Papa was so busy running the ranch and looking after Mama that he hardly noticed me in the corral with the young stallion. I'd put a bridle on Banner and laugh when he'd show his teeth like he aimed to spit it out but then took it into his mouth like he wanted to please me. I rubbed an old Indian blanket all over him in gentle swipes until he stood quiet as can be and let me spread it over his withers.

The day I pulled myself up on top of him, my heart pounded so hard I thought it would spring clear out of my chest. But Banner stood there like a statue, letting me throw my leg over his back and sit on him. I ran my fingers through his milky mane and pressed my cheek into his neck, feeling the warmth of his hide and hopin' he'd feel me, too, so he'd know me forever. We'd walk round and round the corral every day. I swear my thighs grew into him, as both of us grew into ourselves, and together.

"What the hell are you doing, Annie?" Papa's voice cut into my dreamy thoughts one morning, and I slid off Banner and stared at my boots. "For God's sake, that horse is too young to be ridden! You could ruin his back."

"Papa, I'm thirteen, and small for my age. I ain't hurting Banner. Why, he likes it! He told me so."

"Told you so? Stop playacting, Annie, and get along now to the house. Your mama needs some supper, and I have to clean the barn."

The house smelled like pain—the walls caked with a thousand sad thoughts. My mother was dying, and it was as plain as day. She'd never get up out of that bed, and now she barely talked to me. I'd press a spoonful of soup to her chapped and bloodied lips and she'd swallow like a little sparrow, then drop back into the depths of her pillow again. These days I was lucky to get just a few drops down her. Then her cloudy eyes closed, and I'd take her rigid hand in mine and cry.

It hurt me so. I didn't want to be here anymore, and I shamed myself for the thought. But I was scared and lonely and I just wanted it to end, but I didn't know how or where it should end. I only knew sorrow clawed at me like a wild animal. The only time I felt whole was when I was with Banner.

By the time the leaves were falling, my mother slipped away. I held her wrist and felt her pulse weaken, then slow, and finally leave her altogether. Papa pressed his forehead against hers and cried in great sobs. I curled up by her side on the bed and held on, hoping I could fetch her spirit back and make her wake again.

We buried her in a pasture where the sun sets in a meadow that looks like a notch between Wyoming and heaven. All the cowhands sang a song as Papa shoveled dirt onto her coffin. It was the same sad song they'd sing to our cattle to keep 'em from getting jumpy during a thunderstorm. I sank to the ground and covered Mama's grave with my body and felt the whole world spin in circles until Papa pulled me off, tucked me under his arm, and carried me back to the house.

From that moment on, things changed. I didn't talk much, except to ask for the butter, or to say good night. I didn't even talk to Banner, even though his ears pricked forward when I walked up to him and he nuzzled my neck. Papa had changed too. He went into town more often and came back smelling like whiskey, his boots soundin' so heavy on the floor I swear there were nails in the soles trying to tether him to the wood so he couldn't move. Sometimes he didn't, so full of drink he'd just sink into a chair and cover his eyes with his hands. I wondered if he'd forgotten about me. If everyone had forgotten about me. And there was nothing I could do but float along like a log downstream, with nowhere particular to go, but goin' in one direction and never returning.

"It's gonna be an early winter," Papa said one morning. "Annie, I want you to make sure there's enough firewood. Get Hank to help you count up the logs and start placing them around the house outside. He'll get more if you tell him."

I nodded. This was my mother's job, but now she was gone. I'd watch her out there in the yard every autumn, squinting at the firewood, then sending the cowboys out to the woods to come back with felled trees they pulled along with their horses.

Hank and two other cowhands brought in the wood, and I helped layer them against the house and the bunkhouse. A chill came off the mountains and crept down my collar, giving me the shivers. Off in the distance, Banner saw me and nickered. I smiled and waved as he pawed the ground, then broke into a proud trot.

"Damn, that's a good-looking little stallion," one of the hands said.

Hank nodded. "Sure is. I think John will get a good price for him. He should become a nice stud in a couple of years."

My breath stilled. "What? What do you mean? My Papa ain't selling Banner."

Hank rubbed at his jaw, his eyes shifty. "Well, I guess not, Annie. I don't know why I said such a silly thing."

I knew he was lying, the way grown-ups say things to make a kid feel better. Right then and there, I knew Papa planned to sell Banner. Heat rushed up from my boots, covered my body, and flicked away any sort of chill as my face burned like the righteous and I turned on my heel and stalked to the barn.

I found my father pitching hay from the loft. His arms moved in mighty passes, stabbing the pitchfork into the hay, then tossing it down into a pile on the ground below. When he saw my face, he slowed, then stopped.

"You aren't selling Banner!" I hollered up at him, then threw myself into the hay and screamed. I rolled around like a crazy thing, tearing at my coat and kicking my feet, letting my anger burst through the silence of the barn and drench it with fury.

My father climbed down from the loft and stood in front of me. I saw his boots at eye level and at that moment, I hated him. Hated him as much as I loved Banner. Hated him for my mama dying. I hated him for siring me, and raising me, and now leaving me adrift on an ocean of pain so restless, it hardly knew where to put itself.

His voice was gentle. "I wasn't gonna sell him at first, Annie. But he's so special, I figure he'd get a good price in Jackson. Enough to keep the rest of the animals in feed this winter. More valuable to sell him than keep as a stud, and, well, we need the money." He knelt and put his hand on my quaking shoulder.

"I'll tell you what, honey. Bonnie's in foal again. This spring, I promise you, the foal will be yours. Colt or filly, beauty or not, if you want it, I won't argue. Maybe it'll be another pinto like Banner."

I heard through the words. Words meant to calm me but only served to light a match inside. I couldn't even talk. I was so full of embers, if I opened my mouth, they'd fly around the barn and set the whole ranch on fire.

"When?" I choked out, fists clenched so tight my nails bit into my tender palms and I welcomed the pain, wanted the pain, and for a moment, I loved the pain.

"Soon. Winter's on its way and I need to get him to Jackson before the snow falls." He looked up at the sky with a practiced eye. "Soon," he echoed.

I didn't eat supper that night. I stayed in my room and soaked the bed with tears. Banner was my horse. He was from the moment he dropped from Bonnie and nestled in my arms and heart. He would never belong to anybody but me. Why, we were stitched together at the soul. It couldn't unravel. If it did, I'd lose my grip on this earth and leave it altogether like Mama. That's when I knew I had to take Banner and leave. Leave before one more thing got wrenched from me. Leave before the first icy flakes hit the ground and kept me prisoner in this valley until spring.

THE NEXT MORNING brought leaden clouds, so close to earth it looked like I could climb inside them and hide. Snow was coming. I smelled it in the wind that came down off the cliffs and wound its way around the cross where my mother lay in silence.

Papa was already out of the house. I saw him leave with the cowhands, their horses nose to tail, as they traveled over a knoll to check the fence posts and barbed wire so the cattle would be safe in the lower pastures.

I hurried. Packed a rucksack with food and layered myself in as many pieces of clothing I could muster, until I looked like one of those clouds—thick and heavy.

Down at the barn, I took my mother's saddle and bridle. She was small, like me, and the saddle was light. A cowboy glanced over with a puzzled eye. I glared at him until he looked away and went back to work in a stall.

Banner took the bit, but he'd never worn a saddle before. He flinched when I pulled the cinch under his belly. I tightened it slowly until it felt snug between my fingers. Then I pulled the stirrup down and let it flap along his side. I jabbed my foot into the stirrup and swung my leg over his back. He crow-hopped a little and snorted, then settled in. I'd ridden him bareback plenty of times, but we'd never left the safety of the corral. I patted his neck and whispered in his ear.

"Banner, take us away. We'll go somewhere safe where Papa won't ever find us. You can't be sold. But you have to do your part. Don't buck me off. Don't bolt when I open this gate, and we'll be together forever."

His ears pricked forward as I eased the latch off the gate and swung it wide. We stood there for a moment. Banner raised his head and nickered across the valley. Then I touched him with my heel, and we bounded into the icy morning.

Papa went east, so I turned Banner west toward the mountains. I loosened the reins, and he broke into a gentle lope. Feeling his muscles beneath me, I realized he'd turned into a full-grown horse. Powerful. It scared me a little because all this time he'd been my closest friend, but now I realized he was separate from me. He was a mighty stallion, and I'd just set him free. His lope turned into a gallop, and I held on to his mane as he reveled in newfound freedom.

I gave Banner his head, and he ate up the ground, hungry hooves carrying us farther and farther from home. By late afternoon, we were beyond the foothills, and Banner struggled as his hooves rang out on the granite of the mighty Tetons. He gathered himself and hopped along deer paths, so narrow my legs scraped against tree limbs and brush until my pant legs seeped with blood, but we kept moving.

I tasted a snowflake on my lips. More landed on my hands, turning my fingers red and cold. The flakes fell harder, swirling around us like a mad thing. The wind blew in great gusts, painting the hills so white that the sky and the ground merged as one, and my head reeled in confusion.

I turned Banner into a small canyon and dismounted, then pulled his saddle off and wrapped the blanket around me. We huddled together near a rocky overhang, away from the blizzard. There was no wood for a fire here above timberline, and I figured we'd have to climb back down as soon as the snow let up. Banner stood with his head lowered and eyes shut, his tail to the storm. I crawled close to him and looked for warmth, but there was none.

Somewhere in the canyon, a series of howls broke through the swirling silence. Wolves. Banner raised his head in alarm, snorting and backing away. I tightened my hold on his reins.

"Whoa, now, whoa. It's okay. We're fine. They're far away." I patted and soothed him, but he knew it was a lie, just like the grown-ups lied to me sometimes. That's when I realized they lied to bring me comfort, not hurt. I missed my papa, missed the ranch. Tears rolled down my face and froze on my cheeks.

The yaps and howls grew closer. The sun fell to the other side of the mountains and darkness flickered in the final arc of dusk. I could see the white spots on Banner's flanks, and little else.

Out of the last slivers of light came the wolves. There were five of them, approaching us with their heads lowered, circling and growling.

Banner snorted and yanked the reins from my fingers. His eyes rolled as he backed away, then bolted. Two wolves lunged and snapped as he galloped by. Then they turned to me. I pressed myself against a rock and reached for the saddle. I held it against my chest like a shield and hollered at them.

"Get away! Go away from here! Go home!" The largest wolf stared at me and lowered his head, then snarled and took a step closer. Another raised its muzzle into the wind and howled. Others in the distance answered. I swear, every hair on my body stood up in fright. I wished I'd packed a rifle with me, or a knife, but I had nothing, not even a fire. And Banner had abandoned me too.

"Mama!" I cried out for my mother, praying for help. Or maybe to let her know that I'd be joining her soon. Night was shutting down, the wolves were closing in, and there was nothing between me and them but an old saddle and terror.

The wolves hesitated and cocked their heads, listening. I heard nothing but the angry wind in my ears and the pelting of snow on my face.

Then, a fierce whinny and the sound of hooves ringing on rocks echoed through the canyon. Banner broke through the darkness and lunged at the wolves, biting and kicking. They turned on him in a dark wave, snapping at his neck and haunches. The biggest wolf grasped his back leg and ripped at it, taking pieces of hide and flesh in his massive jaws. Banner fell to one knee, and the wolves closed in.

"No!" I screamed so loud I swear the mountains shook, but the nightmare in front of me showed no sign of stopping. My heart ached as I watched Banner fight bravely but lose the battle as the pack grabbed at his throat and withers, and he fell to the ground.

The wolves stopped abruptly and stepped back. They snarled and snapped at something in the distance that I couldn't see.

A wolf yelped when a bullet hit him, then another. Two more cried in pain as they fell. The others backed away and melted into the darkness.

Banner struggled to his knees, then stood, head down, bleeding into the snow and blowing through his mouth in great gasps.

Papa stepped out of the mist and stared at the scene before him. I dropped the saddle and ran into his arms. Papa held me so tight I could hardly breathe.

"You're safe now, honey. But you're so cold. We have to climb down this mountain. Are you hurt?"

"No." I looked around at the men and shivered. "How... how did you find me?"

"Joe said he saw you saddle Banner and leave. He rode out to us, and we turned around right away and followed your trail. We lost your tracks at times in the snow. Another few minutes, and I can't even think about what might have happened."

He tightened his grip on my shoulders. Two cowboys took blankets out of their bedrolls and wrapped me in them.

"We have to go now," Papa said. "It's gonna take us a long time to get off this mountain in the dark. But we have to keep movin' before we all freeze."

He straightened and looked over at Banner, who still stood with his head down, blood flowing from his battered leg. Papa raised his rifle and aimed.

"*No!*" I yanked on the barrel and the shot went wild. The sound rolled through the canyon.

"Annie, I have to! He'll slow us down, and his wounds are so bad I doubt he'll survive. I don't want to just leave him here to die in agony from the wolves. It's the right thing to do to put him out of his misery."

"It's not the right thing, Papa! I have to help Banner. He tried to save me. I'll walk along with him all the way home. Please!"

My father stared at me for a long time. He walked over to Banner and ran his hands over the injured leg and torn shoulder. Banner trembled and blew out through bleeding nostrils. He sighed.

"No, Annie. You can't walk him down the mountain. We need to get you home before you get sick, and he'd only slow us down. You can't help him walk. You're just a young girl." He reached for my hand and squeezed it. "But I will."

"Hank," he said, pulling his collar up around his ears and loading his rifle. "Take Annie home on my horse. You all go on ahead. I'm bringing Banner home."

Then he turned to me, and I saw a deep sadness in his eyes. "Honey, Banner might not make it, but I promise I'll try. But I also promise you I won't let him suffer if he can't make it. Let me do this, Annie."

I hesitated. Then it was like I heard my mama's voice sayin' that I had to let down my guard. I had to trust my father, and I had to let it go, even if it ended up in heartache. Even if I lost Banner too.

"Okay, Papa." I touched his cheek and nodded. Then Hank picked me up, put me on a horse, and swept me into the swirling darkness.

⊶••••••━ ⇒⟋⟍ ━••••⊷

HANK RODE BACK out to the mountains as soon as he brought me home, carrying blankets and food on a packhorse, heading west to find Papa.

It took two days for my father to return to the ranch. Two helpless days while I peered up toward the Tetons and prayed.

At sunset on the second day, I saw figures in the distance and counted the horses. Two. Just two. Papa on his gelding, leading the packhorse. As they drew closer, I knew Banner wasn't with them. My heart turned heavy with grief.

I walked to the empty corral where I grew up with Banner and sifted dirt between my fingers. What had I done? If I hadn't run off with him, he'd still be alive today. It was all my fault, and I had nobody to blame but myself. If I could do it all over again, I'd never open that gate and let us out. Banner fought off those wolves for me. He gave up his life and showed me how much he loved me. I could only hope he knew I loved him just as much, only I didn't show it very well.

My father drew near and reined in at the barn. He dismounted with a weary sigh and nodded as a cowboy came out to lead the horses away. Hank wasn't with him. Did he get hurt too? I walked toward Papa with leaden feet. Then I placed my head on his chest and heard his heartbeat, steady as ever, and tried to match mine to his.

"I'm so sorry," I said, feeling the need to comfort him, despite my grief. He smelled like snow and sweat and fatigue, and I wanted things to be how they used to be.

"Banner's not here," he said, his voice raspy and tired.

I nodded. "I know. He didn't make it. I know you tried your best, Papa." I took a mournful breath and peered around. "Did Hank get hurt too?"

My father cupped my head and rocked me back and forth like I was a little baby. "No, no, Annie! Hank is with Banner. The horse tuckered out a few miles from here, so Hank's resting with him. I'm sending Joe back up with food and water. They'll make camp, then Hank will bring him in tomorrow."

Papa tilted my chin up. "Look at me, honey. Banner's gonna be okay. It will take a long time healing, but he's got spirit." He gathered me in his arms, his breath warm on my face. "He was always your horse and always will be. I ain't taking him from you. Not now, not ever. The two of you need each other. I'm sorry I didn't understand sooner just what he meant to you." Then he held me while I sobbed.

IT TOOK A YEAR, but Banner healed up, just like Papa said. I could ride him again, but we had to be careful and not go far from home. Banner knows the way to Mama's grave, and we go there often. I sit by the cross and tell her all about my life, how I'm growing up, and how much I love her.

My father quit drinking, and we get along better. I hear him whistling in the barn sometimes, his footsteps lighter as he goes about his day.

As for me, I learned that love can hurt, but it's still worth it, anyway.

I hope I show those I love the best part of myself and never hold back. The way Banner did for me.

Now it's late spring, and the world is full of promise. I kneel in the meadow at dusk and place flowers on my mother's grave. Mounting Banner, I pat his sleek neck and bury my face in his billowing mane. Then I whisper goodbye to Mama as we head home.

—*Sharon Frame Gay is an award-winning author whose work has appeared in many anthologies and magazines, including* Chicken Soup for the Soul, Typehouse, Fiction on the Web, Literally Stories, Lowestoft Chronicle, Thrice Fiction, Saddlebag Dispatches, Crannóg, *and others. She is a Pushcart Prize nominee, award winner in several genres of writing, and the recipient of the Will Rogers Medallion for excellence in Western writing. Collections of her short stories,* Song of the Highway *and* The Nomad Diner, *are available on Amazon.*

A
KNOT OF
TOADS

K.S. JONES

QUINCY, ILLINOIS
1878

AT DAYBREAK, MARIETTA Truett and her eight-year-old son, Rand, climbed up onto their wagon loaded with a traveling trunk, two carpetbags, a scarred Winchester rifle with a shortened stock, a tapestry bag with their necessaries, papers, and money, and her husband's Colt Peacemaker.

With a last look at the homestead, she snapped the reins.

Spring bore a burdensome chill, but Rand had a jacket, and they both wore two sets of clothing after being unable to fit more into their trunk.

Although it was still early when they arrived in Quincy, the town was alive with activity. Turning onto Vermont Street, sunlight squinted their eyes. If she had her wish, they would never travel east again.

West was the dream.

The courthouse took up the entire north side of Jefferson Square. Newspapers claimed the new two-story building had a jail in its basement, but Marietta didn't talk about that to Rand. The boy was fascinated by outlaws and thought they were brave, diligent, and adventurous men.

She hadn't had the heart to tell him differently because it was the only true thing he knew about his father.

Josiah was brave. He was adventurous. And his diligence had made them landowners. But she'd been naïve to believe they could afford seed, farm tools, and the armament Josiah regularly brought home and often resold.

Rand jumped down from the wagon at the courthouse, pointing to the white stone towers and turrets. "Is this a castle?"

"It's a courthouse. Only kings live in castles, and we have no king, only a president." Marietta secured their wagon and horses and retrieved her bag from the seat, calling to Rand.

The boy looked so much like his father with his cinnamon-brown hair and brown eyes. She was grateful he had not inherited the moles that marred her own face.

When Rand reached her, she bent to straighten his jacket with a tug, easing the bulk under his armpits. Without any intent of a reprimand, she said, "You might be a plain farm boy ignorant of the city, but you'll soon be an important young businessman. Hold yourself out as one today."

With no disrespect in his voice, he said, "Papa wasn't a business man."

Maybe it was nerves, but she took hold of his shoulders and squeezed. "And that's why he's dead. Now do as I say."

Marietta stood and brushed the road dust from her black mourning dress before picking up her bag. She led her son to the courthouse. Together, they walked the polished wood floor, finding offices on the main level and signs pointing upstairs to the law courts and downstairs to the jail.

Through an open door, Marietta spotted a clerk. "Excuse me. Can you tell me where the land office is?"

"Yes." The woman came and pointed down the hall. "It's four doors down on your right, just before the bench where those men are seated."

Marietta nodded, and then she and Rand walked toward the land office. The two men she was slated to meet dutifully stood as she neared the door, hats in hand.

"Mister Ellis," she greeted. He was their neighboring farmer and a friend to Josiah. Then, to acknowledge the man's grown son, she said, "Thomas."

"Mornin', ma'am," the elder Ellis greeted. "We've taken the liberty of talkin' to George Brophy 'bout you. He's head of the land office and has some standard questions." He reached out and took a gentle hold of Rand's shoulder. "Would you like your boy to sit with us while you're conductin' today's business?"

"No." Instinctively, Marietta nudged Rand behind her. She hadn't meant to appear mistrusting, so more softly, she said, "Thank you, but no."

She opened the land office door, only releasing her son's hand after it closed. Inside, behind a counter, stood a man.

"Missus Truett?" His tone was firm but not intimidating.

"Yes," Marietta said. She looked at her son, motioning with a side glance that he should seat himself, which he did without question.

"I'm George Brophy." He reached for a handshake.

Marietta shook his offered hand. He was known to many local homesteaders as a man of unblemished morals, but a woman often had a different sense of things. She was prepared to make her own determination.

"I understand you plan to sell your husband's homesteaded property."

"It is my property, Mister Brophy. I am his widow and entitled." Josiah had died before the five-year homesteading requirement had been met, but still, she was his wife. It belonged to her, and she had every right to sell it, if she could acquire the deed.

"You're aware there are conditions?"

The 160-acre homestead was some of the best farmland in Adams County. It was Josiah's way of starting life over as the respectable family man he'd promised her he could be. Within three years, he had become a productive wheat farmer, and after his first good crop, he had sent for her and Rand. But it hadn't mattered. Redemption was always one step behind retribution. Marietta had buried him almost nine months ago.

"I've met the conditions. I have proof!" She'd expected opposition, but now that it was afoot, her heart pounded. "You'll prepare the deed, or...."

"Or *what*, Missus Truett?"

Marietta stopped. "My apologies." She said the words so softly she barely heard them herself. "It's already been a long day."

"Of course." Brophy reached beneath the counter and pulled out a printed paper with a smattering of blanks and then took a steel pen from his drawer. After donning his spectacles, he asked, "Do you claim yourself to be head of household?"

"I do," Marietta said.

He dipped his pen into the ink. "Husband's name and date of death?"

"Josiah Samuel Truett. He died last year. On the fifteenth of August."

No reverent moment followed. Not even a nod of sympathy.

"And your full name?"

"Marietta Helen Truett."

Without lifting his gaze, Brophy asked, "Do you have the homestead affidavit?"

"Yes." Marietta opened the bag at her feet. Finding the document, she stood with it.

"Did you also bring a death certificate and marriage certificate?"

"Yes, I have those." She handed him the affidavit and then retrieved the other two certificates.

Brophy spent the next several minutes transferring information onto the document.

In wait, sweat sprouted on her brow, but she dared not wipe it away, fearing he might become suspicious of her unease.

"Missus Truett." He held up a paper. "It appears that your husband was the original filer. The *only* filer. Your name is not on this homestead affidavit."

"Y-yes...." She knew the stuttered word was punishment for the sin of lying. "Josiah was told his name was all that was required. No one said both names were needed." Summoning grit, she pressed him. "Was that the fault of someone under your tutelage?"

"No. Well, perhaps. Mistakes happen, Missus Truett."

She sighed. An act well practiced. "I understand. As long as you can correct any errors today and provide me with my deed, I'll not file a grievance."

His stance stiffened. "Missus Truett, the issue is, you and two credible witnesses must attest that you, yourself, have lived on the property the full five years and have made the improvements alongside your husband." He pointed to the paper's date. "Per the Homestead Act, I'll need proof these conditions have been met. Otherwise, I cannot issue you a deed today."

Marietta was grateful for the two dresses she was forced to wear, for if she'd only worn one, her heart surely would have pounded right through the first garment.

"Mister Brophy," she said tersely. "I was told my two witnesses had already spoken to you."

If the Ellis men wanted her homestead badly enough, they'd be willing to swear under oath that she had occupied the property since the beginning of May 1873, even though she'd only returned to the land two years ago after Josiah made amends to her. What choice did she have but to lie? Other than the homestead, Josiah had left her nothing but broken promises.

Marietta glanced at her son. Her obligation was solely to him now, and their future in the Dakota Territory awaited. Thank the Lord for her brother and his prosperity. She would have her boardinghouse next to his restaurant, which was booming, just like the town of Deadwood.

Brophy narrowed his eyes in thought. "The same two men who intend to purchase your homestead are also your witnesses?"

"Yes," she said, more timidly than intended. Perjury, she'd been told, was a punishable offense.

Brophy put down his pen and removed his spectacles, though he still held them in one hand. "It's none of my business, Missus Truett, but before your witnesses are called…." He paused. "Are you certain you want to sell? Quincy is destined to be the most important city in this state. I'd hate to see you taken advantage of. Your land will be worth much more next year."

"I've made my decision." Marietta fisted her hands to keep them from shaking.

"And when you sell, where will you go?"

"The Dakota Territory. It's been opened up, as I'm sure you've heard."

"A widow, going alone?"

"I'm not alone. I have my son."

Brophy's glance landed on the boy. "He's what? Nine? Ten?"

"About," Marietta answered. Rand was an advanced eight-year-old of considerable merit, and she thought him a laudable companion in lieu of a worthy man.

Brophy sighed, slid the paper to her, and handed her his pen. "Sign at the bottom and then call your witnesses."

After she, Thaddeus, and Thomas swore an oath to her full five-year residency, Brophy handed Marietta her deed. In turn, she relinquished it for a new deed, naming the Ellis men the new owners—after she collected their two thousand six hundred dollars.

Outside, Thaddeus fitted his hat. "Bein' a friend to your late husband and all," he told Marietta, "I'm obliged to say again that I think you're makin' a mistake about the Dakotas."

"I have a brother in Deadwood."

"It's still no place for a woman or a boy," he said. "But if you're hell-bent on goin', you shouldn't go alone." Thaddeus pointed across the street but then swirled his hand at the whole town. "There's eight breweries in Quincy and probably a dozen men in each." He eyed her. "Don't get the wrong idea. They're not all lazy, beer-guzzlin' men. Important business deals happen in a saloon, so if you're fixed on Deadwood, go find a man willin' to go along." After a glance at the boy, he lowered his voice. "Plenty of men are lookin' for a wife too."

It wasn't as if she hadn't thought of that herself. Distractedly, she touched the moles on her face.

"Naw," Thaddeus said, shaking his head. "Don't worry 'bout those."

Marietta glanced at Rand, who she knew was looking and listening even though he pretended not to. Quietly, she answered Thaddeus. "I tried that a month ago. There's nothing but a knot of toads in those places, and I won't have them hanging onto my skirts or expecting me to pull it off for them." She hardened her stance. "We're going to Deadwood. I'll run a respectable establishment, and my son will become a businessman. Our lives will be different there."

"All right then, good luck to you." Thaddeus tipped his hat before walking away.

There was no reason to linger, but Marietta waited on the bottom step of the courthouse anyway, watching the Ellis men leave with the deed to the only home she had ever owned, even if it was for only a few minutes.

"Missus Truett!"

Marietta glanced back to see George Brophy hurrying down the steps toward her. Had her lie been realized?

Her instinct was to run, but instead she gave Rand a heart-thumping be-brave look, released his hand, and turned. "Yes? What is it, Mister Brophy?"

When he reached her, he proffered a folded paper. "I've just learned that a local man is on his way to deliver an order of flour to Camp Sturgis under an Army contract. He'll sail on the new packet ship that just arrived in St. Louis."

"How does that concern me?" Marietta asked.

"Camp Sturgis is in the Dakota Territory. Perhaps you can travel alongside Mister Morgan so that you're not entirely unescorted." He unfolded the paper and pointed to the name he had written there. "Virgil Morgan. You'll find him at Eagle Mills on Second and Broadway." He took her hand and placed the paper into it. *"Please,* Missus Truett."

Marietta took the paper.

Was it a plan to steal their money?

She studied his eyes in search of deceit, but when she found none, she simply said, "Thank you, Mister Brophy."

EAGLE MILLS WAS painted in bold black letters across the width of the building. At the back, men were busily loading barrels onto a mule train.

Marietta stopped the wagon and set the brake bar. She handed the reins to Rand. "Stay here. I shouldn't be long."

"Ma, you don't even know him," Rand warned.

"I know." She had promised him honesty. "But Mister Ellis and Mister Brophy are right. It would be safer if we traveled with a man." Marietta looked around and, seeing no one, said, "We have a lot of money in our bag. We must safeguard it. Sometimes that means doing things we don't want to do." She forced a smile.

"Are you plannin' to marry him?"

Her smile straightened. "Only if I have to."

"What if he's a toad? You said you wasn't marryin' no toad."

"English, Rand...." Marietta squeezed his hands tight around the reins. "Speak properly." Then she scooted the bag beneath the seat. "Papa's Colt is there if you need it."

When Rand nodded, Marietta climbed down off the wagon and headed for the mill's front door.

"Hello?" Marietta said to two men behind the counter, discussing a ledger entry.

One man looked up. "Can I help you?"

"I'm looking for this man." Marietta unfolded the paper and presented it to him.

He glanced at the name written there. "She's looking for you, Virgil." He handed off the note. "Come get me when you're done."

"You're Virgil Morgan?" she asked.

"I am. And who are you?"

"Marietta Truett." She looked him over, trying to decide whether to continue. He was tall and carried the girth of a healthy man, but his nose was too wide, his ears too big, and his bushy, reddish-brown eyebrows, arched too high, were oddly lighter than his short, much-too-curly hair. His green eyes, though, were kind, and his close-mouthed smile was friendly. "George Brophy from the land office said I should speak to you."

"What about?" Virgil asked.

"About accompanying you to the Dakota Territory."

"Accompanying me?" He shook his head. "No."

"Why not?"

"Have you been there?" he asked her.

"No, but it's where my son and I are headed, with or without an escort."

"Look," Virgil said. "The only thing traveling with me is flour." He turned and took a few steps but then stopped and looked back. "How old is your son?"

"Rand is eight." More quietly, she said, "I've heard there's a new treaty."

Virgil lowered his head, shaking it as if she had no sense at all. He walked back to her—the movement of his eyes counting her moles before shifting. "An agreement exists with the Sioux, but I can't say it's peaceful." He lifted his focus, but this time, his eyes met hers without a blink. "Missus Truett, if you think the Dakota Territory is an El Dorado, you're wrong." He drew his hands to his hips. "Where's your husband anyway? Why do you need me?"

"My husband is dead," Marietta stated. "My son and I are headed to Deadwood, where my brother is. He has a restaurant and a boardinghouse."

Virgil sighed and shook his head again. Then, after a moment, he said, "Fine. You can travel the route with me, but I can't assure your safety."

Stunned he had accepted, Marietta nodded. "Yes, of course. Thank you, Mister Morgan."

"What was your name again?"

"Marietta."

"All right, Mari," Virgil said. "Why don't you meet me at the docks tomorrow morning."

MARIETTA SOLD THEIR wagon and stock, and then she and Rand boarded the steamboat to St. Louis.

Rand attached himself to Virgil. Perhaps the man's friendly smile had captured him too. Wherever the flour man went, Rand followed.

"Does this boat go all the way to Deadwood?" Rand asked Virgil from the rail, watching the Mississippi River churn below.

"No, tomorrow we'll switch to a Missouri River steamboat. It'll take us to Fort Pierre. From there, I'm traveling by bull train. It's the only way to transport one hundred twenty barrels of flour."

Rand called to his mother. "How are we getting to Deadwood?"

Marietta walked to him. "Uncle Dandy's last letter said his friend has an ox-train. He'll find space for us."

Rand's face fell. "I wanted to ride the bull train."

Virgil laughed. "Bull train and ox-train mean the same." Then, to Marietta, he said, "Dandy is your brother's name?"

"Yes, well, his name is Danny, but he was such a friendly child that people called him Dandy. The name stuck."

The next day, at the St. Louis steamship office, Marietta secured passage on the *F. Y. Batchelor*. Their belongings were delivered to a cabin on the passenger deck.

After settling in, Marietta told Rand, "I need to see the captain." She handed him loose pages from a book. "Study your words."

"Ah, Ma," he complained. "Can't I go find Mister Morgan? I could count barrels!"

"No," she scolded. "I'll be back soon."

On deck, Captain Marsh was supervising the onloading of supplies when Marietta approached him with her bag.

"Captain, may I speak to you?"

The captain turned to see her. "Missus Truett, isn't it?" He was tall, broad-shouldered, and clear-eyed. His blond hair and mustache gave him the appearance of a Boston businessman, rather than a riverboat captain.

"Yes, that's right," Marietta said, and then she made arrangements to store their money in the ship's safe before returning to find Rand enthralled with the riverboat readying itself for a voyage.

Each day, Marietta waited for Virgil to search them out. In his absence, she kept busy by using pages from the book for spelling lessons.

"Spell sympathetic," Marietta challenged, but Rand jumped up from his chair, pointing to the stairs.

"There's Mister Morgan!"

Virgil approached, pulling a nearby chair with him. He ruffled Rand's hair as he passed, but then to Marietta, he said, "May I sit a while, Mari?"

"Yes." Marietta knew she was smiling but couldn't stop the grin. No one had ever called her Mari, but here on the riverboat, headed for a new life, she didn't mind it at all.

Virgil settled into his chair. "I'm curious to know about those pages."

"I found them in our wheat field," Rand told him.

Marietta sat straighter. Why was she so attracted to this unattractive man? "A twister, we think," she explained. "Rand was helping plow the field when he found these pages scattered about one day. We don't own a single book, and school isn't an option, so we use the pages for spelling words, but he is curious to know the story."

"Ma's real smart," Rand told him. "But we don't know what a farthing is. Do you?"

Virgil reached for the page. "Can I see?"

Rand handed it to him. "It's at the top."

A Flat Iron for a Farthing." Virgil read the printed title of the book. "A farthing is a coin. Money and flour, I know."

Marietta kept her eyes on Virgil. "I'll bet you know lots of things."

When Virgil fixed his gaze upon her, Marietta felt the insecurity of her ugliness. She lowered her head, turning her face away.

"Mari," he said. "You don't need to do that."

"Ma doesn't like her moles," Rand explained, even though he appeared to be reading his pages. "And she won't tolerate toads." He looked up. "Ma, Mister Morgan isn't a toad, is he?"

"No," Marietta said, a flush heating her cheeks. "Mister Morgan's face has character."

"I don't know about that," Virgil said with a bashful smile. "My character has never turned a woman's head."

"Yes, it has." Then, bolstering her courage, she asked, "I suppose you'd mention a wife if you had one."

Virgil glanced at her. "I would, Mari." Then he rose. "I should check the flour again to be sure moisture from the river hasn't dampened it."

Clearly, he wasn't married, but he also hadn't expressed an interest in her. And why would he? Between the two of them, she was the toad and needed no reminders. She wouldn't broach the subject again. If she paid no attention to his eyes or his smile, she would be fine.

The remaining days on the river ran their course. Nary a snag slowed the steamboat. Virgil visited them on the upper deck many times daily, often staying and talking for hours.

Ahead of schedule, the *F. Y. Batchelor* arrived in Fort Pierre amid a rousing celebration of whoops, hollers, and gunshots in the air.

The place had a strange mix of people, many speaking different languages, but they all seemed to share the white-hot excitement of gold in the Black Hills.

Scores of miners, military men, and travelers went about their duties while Marietta and Rand awaited the unloading of their belongings.

"Mari, I need to supervise the transfer of flour from the boat to the ox-train." He smiled. "It'll be a while, but I'll be back."

"No, don't leave," Marietta said, cradling her bag. In a whisper, she confided, "We have almost three thousand dollars in here."

Virgil gripped her arm. "Why didn't you tell me?"

"Fear, I suppose. Anyone could steal from us." As ashamed as she was, she admitted, "Even you." Then, apologetic, she offered, "I didn't know you at all."

Virgil escorted them to the livery near the ox-train, isolating them in the scant shade of its roof, and then hurried to help load the barrels onto the last freight wagon.

At the head of the bull train, a fiftyish man wearing a brown felt hat checked the canvas tie-downs. He looked like the man her brother described. She approached him with her bag and Dandy's letter. "Excuse me. Are you Wade Hager?"

The man turned. "That's me."

"My brother said you would take us to Deadwood."

"Sorry, we're full up."

"But Dandy said—"

"Dandy?" The man gave her a good look. "You his sister?"

"Yes," Marietta said, then waited when she saw Virgil hurrying toward her.

"Everything all right?" Virgil asked.

"Yes. Mister Hager is the friend Dandy wrote to me about."

Virgil offered him his hand. "Mari and the boy will ride with me."

"Well, that's just it," Wade said. "I've already told the lady, we're full up."

"When can you take them?" Virgil asked.

"Well, I'll be back in thirty days, but then it's another fifteen back to Deadwood."

"Forty-five days!" Marietta protested.

"Yep, but you can ask at the store about other transportation," Wade said.

"But we need to go today. Surely, you can find room. I'll pay!"

Wade shook his head. "I promised Dandy if you ever showed up, I'd get you to him, and I will, but not this trip. You three will have to wait or find another way."

"Whoa," Virgil said. "I go where the flour goes or the flour doesn't go. That's half your transport."

"You the Eagle Mills man?" When Virgil nodded, Wade went to the wagon box, pulled out a leather satchel, and began looking through his papers. "Your name again?"

"Virgil Morgan."

"Yeah, you're on here," Wade said. "But we're full up after you."

"You'll take all three of us," Virgil ordered.

"And where do you expect me to put them? On the back of an ox?"

"Give 'em my seat. I'm a big man. They can both fit in whatever space you reserved for me. I'll give up my passage and work my way across as a bullwhacker."

Wade sized up Virgil. "All right."

When Wade walked away, Marietta said, "We can take shifts."

Virgil shook his head. "It's gonna work out just fine."

Two teams of twenty oxen pulled three wagons each for the 200-mile trip to Deadwood. They traveled from four in the morning until noon, rested and grazed until four, and traveled again until dark.

Reaching the pine-covered mountains was bumpy, grueling, and hot, so any wisp of a breeze or shade from a cloud found praise.

On the fifteenth day, they came across hundreds of bison. Beyond the immense herd was Deadwood.

Before sunset, the ox-train rolled down Main Street, passing saloons, gambling halls, a theater with bawdy ladies out front lifting their skirts, and several shabbily built businesses. The road itself was filled with drunken sots. From the Gem Saloon, a patron stumbled out its doors, falling dead in the street. A man with a pistol followed him out, shooting him three more times.

Marietta gasped, shouting, "This godforsaken place!"

In answer, a woman on the Bella Union balcony called back, "This place ain't just forsaken by God. It's forsaken by the devil too!"

They were on the far side of town before Marietta saw the restaurant and darkened boardinghouse. "There it is—Dandy's Place!" But the ox-train continued to move down the deep-rutted street thick with the muck of manure and mud, finally settling on the outskirts of town near Whitewood Creek.

Virgil helped Marietta and Rand off the wagon and paid a boy for the delivery of their belongings.

Inside the restaurant, Marietta's gaze landed on the face and physique of each man. "I don't see Dandy."

Virgil waved his hand, signaling a waiter.

A man in an apron hurried to them. "You need a menu?"

"No," Marietta said. "We're looking for Dandy."

"I'll get him."

Virgil and Rand sat at a table, but Marietta stood waiting.

Dandy appeared, calling, "Marietta!" He had her in a hug before she could say hello.

"Oh, Dandy! I thought I might never see you again." Marietta kissed his cheek, but then pulled back, looking at him. "This place is not like you described. We saw a man shot and no one came to his aid or apprehended the assailant."

Dandy shrugged. "Law is just a matter of opinion in Deadwood."

"Shouldn't we report it to the sheriff?"

"Rumor will get to him soon enough." Then his glance landed on Rand. "Can this be my nephew?"

Rand stood, grinning, and stuck out his hand. "It's good to see you, sir."

"Well, look at you." Dandy shook the boy's hand. "You've grown into a fine young man."

"Dandy," Marietta said, motioning to Virgil. "This is Mister Morgan. He escorted us from Quincy."

"Much obliged." Dandy shook his hand. "Take a seat, all of you. Supper is on the house. Tonight's special is beef and dumplings, which took the last of my flour. The whole town is out now."

When Dandy left for the kitchen, Rand whispered, "You could sell your flour here instead of to the army."

Virgil leaned in. "I didn't want word getting out, but twenty of those barrels are mine. Only a hundred go to the army." Then, he whispered, "I plan to open a mill."

"Here?" Marietta asked. "You're staying?" When Virgil nodded, she sat back and grinned. "Deadwood has more promise already."

After supper, Dandy led them to the boardinghouse. He unlocked the door, lit two oil lamps, and handed Marietta the key. "It's all yours. Well, fifty-fifty."

"I expected it to be full of patrons."

"It will be," Dandy told her. "Both places were too much for me alone. I decided to wait for you." He led them through the house, past the second-floor stairs, and into the kitchen. He lit another lamp. "Follow me."

At the rear of the house were private quarters—a receiving room with a boy's bed in the corner, plus a separate bedroom for Marietta.

"You've got eight rooms to rent. Two downstairs and six upstairs. I only ask that you serve coffee, tea, milk, and maybe something sweet, but then send them to the restaurant for meals."

"Yes, of course," Marietta said. "Thank you."

The next afternoon, Marietta and Rand opened for business. Their first customer was Virgil Morgan.

"And how long will you stay?" Being near him weakened her knees.

"How long will you allow me?"

"I would never presume to limit your time with us."

"I was hoping you'd say that, Mari." Virgil reached for her hands and held them. "Because I've come to believe we belong together."

Her throat tightened, and in a whisper, she asked, "What does that mean?"

"It means I want to marry you."

"Virgil, I…." Marietta looked down at her dress, but tears blurred her vision. "It's not yet a year. I'm still wearing black."

Virgil released her hands but then lifted her chin. "No one knows us here. There's no one to judge."

She had so many imperfections. "I'm almost thirty-four."

"Tell me why that matters."

"Children."

"You're young enough to have more children."

Marietta covered the left side of her face with her hand. "But what if—"

For a moment, his eyes questioned her unease. "I know I'm not a handsome man, so be honest, are you afraid we'll have a knot of toads?"

She hesitated. "Rand is a perfect boy. How will you feel about me if the next one isn't?"

"I'll love you just as much." Virgil gave her chin an affectionate pinch. "And if we have a knot of toads, we'll just dress 'em up nice, teach 'em some manners, and nobody'll know the difference. The whole world is full of toads, anyway."

—*Karen (K.S.) Jones is a multi-award-winning Texas author who lives an hour northwest of San Antonio in the Texas Hill Country. She writes American historical fiction and contemporary Western romance. In 2014,* Southern Writers *magazine awarded Karen their grand prize for Best Short Fiction of the year, and soon after her first two novels were published. Her work has since garnered numerous literary awards, including the WILLA Literary Award, the Chaucer Award, an* InD'tale Magazine *RONE Award, the Laramie Award, two Literary Classics International Book Awards, and two prestigious Will Rogers Medallions. In 2021, Women Writing the West awarded high honors to her Western short story, "The Pretender." Her current books include the Depression-era novel,* Two Sides of Truth, *her contemporary Western romance novels set in the Texas Hill Country titled* Tastefully Texas, Once in a Bluebonnet Moon, *and* Lone Hearts of Topaz, *and her California gold rush novel,* Change of Fortune, *which rose to #30 on Amazon's list of "Top 100" in American historical romances.*

SUIT YOURSELF, COWGIRL

JOYCE B. LOHSE

A BAY HORSE burst into the rodeo arena at a flat-out gallop. His black mane flapped in the face of the woman who leaned low over his neck. They streaked ahead of a gang of noisy, mounted cowhands in hot pursuit as they performed a stunt known as, "Chase for a Bride."

After a furtive glance over her shoulder, with her red neckerchief and white blouse sleeves fluttering in the breeze, the cowgirl swung a leather quirt overhead with her fringed gloved hand. The horse increased his speed a notch when he heard the rawhide braid whiz through the air above his ears.

As she continued her escape, she heard cheers from ranch hands who watched as they leaned against the arena's fenced perimeter. Some men and a few women on horseback angled toward the railing for better views. Brass band parade music blared from a crackly Victrola gramophone on the announcer's stand. The aging Rocky Gulch Rodeo grandstand, with splintered benches and peeling paint, was half full of wranglers and ranch families, gathered to enjoy summer entertainment on Colorado's eastern plains.

The chase posse was intent on narrowing the gap between them and the runaway "bride," who distanced herself from her pursuers. She looked for the cowboy riding a golden palomino, who pulled away from the posse to follow her. She slowed her horse enough to allow him to catch up. When the rider was next to her, he nodded with an encouraging smile and reached his arm toward her. "Jump!" he yelled. "Jump now!"

The woman kicked her boots out of the stirrups and pulled her knees in a split riding skirt up into a crouch. With reins looped over the saddle horn, she prepared to push away and cross the gap between the two running horses.

When she looked down at the chasm between the two mounts, she froze. The blur of flashing hooves and rock-hard arena soil whizzing past made her dizzy. She squeezed her eyes shut to avoid feeling sick as her hat blew off of her head.

Her eyes flew open when she again heard the cowboy yell, "Jump!" She grimaced and launched her body across the open space between horses. With an awkward grab, she clutched his arm and back as he pulled his new passenger closer. When she steadied herself, his horse snorted in protest from the added weight. She swung her leg across his hindquarters while he continued to run. With her arms clamped around the rider's neck and shoulders, she balanced herself behind his saddle.

With a strong hold on the cowboy, she adjusted to riding double while the palomino continued to gallop with white mane and tail flying. When the pursuit group gave up the chase and slowed to a walk, one rider followed her loose horse as he trotted away from the commotion.

The woman listened as the announcer's deep voice bellowed through a megaphone from the grandstand. "There you have it, folks, 'Chase for a Bride.' Once again, the young lady escapes danger into the arms of a brave hero. Let's give a big round of applause to Bronc Rider Duke Nelson and his partner, Miss Florence Gaines." A wave of clapping hands and cheers erupted from the spectators.

Florence Gaines, who grew up on a farm in the Midwest, fit in well with Western cowgirls. At nearly thirty years old, she relished time spent riding a horse on open range among rock formations, fragrant sage, flowering cactus, spiky yucca plants, and thirsty cottonwood trees signaling the presence of precious water.

In 1910, performances such as "Chase for a Bride" developed from Wild West shows, which were popular live entertainment during the late 1800s. When cattle drives ended, cowboys and rodeo riders portrayed scenes to keep Old West spirit alive.

At the end of the chase, Florence loosened her grip on the cowboy's back as they rode an extra lap around the arena. She knew Duke was smiling under his sandy brown mustache while he waved his hat toward the crowd. She held on to his shoulders as his horse, damp with sweat, slowed to a bouncing trot.

When they rode through the exit, she dropped her hands from Duke's shoulders. "For goodness sake, you almost dropped me out there… and after you said, 'this is for fun… it won't be dangerous.'"

"Relax, darlin', I didn't drop you." He nodded to some friends who waved at them. "You did fine. The crowd loved it."

"It was pointless."

"It was great! They thought you were in danger."

"Imagine that," she said with a tight smile.

They rode on slowly in silence behind the arena to allow the horse to cool down. They passed loading chutes, pens, and corrals. Horses and mules, saddled or harnessed to buggies, spring wagons, and pony carts, were tethered to hitching posts and fence rails.

Florence was relieved that motorized vehicles did not yet share the rural road. Few automobiles had been seen in Rocky Gulch, a remote prairie town east of Pikes Peak and the Rocky Mountains. Passenger cars were hard to ignore when they appeared out of nowhere and frightened skittish horses unaccustomed to noisy vehicles.

As they rode past a group of cowhands, a voice shouted, "Nice catch, Duke!" Florence frowned as the cowboy on the saddle in front of her laughed and tipped his hat toward his pals. Among the compliments, she heard a female voice say, "Well done, Ben." Who was Ben? Florence wondered if the woman confused Duke with somebody else.

They continued to meander through the maze of barns and sheds. Random calls of, "Good ride, cowgirl," and, "Well done, Duke," floated their way. His horse's breathing was normal when they found a stock tank half full of water. They let him drink until he had his fill and started splashing water with his lip.

Their next stop was a bank of empty stalls shaded by a roof over-hang with a pleasant breeze. Florence was more than ready to stand on solid ground. Duke held her arm while she slid down from the back of the saddle. Her legs were shaky, but she quickly regained her balance. She smoothed out the folds of the skirt she designed and sewed for riding astride.

Florence watched as Duke dismounted with effortless motion, patted his horse's neck, and said, "Good job, Sunny." He removed his saddle and exchanged the bridle for a halter and lead rope. With the tired animal standing between them, she located an empty burlap feed bag, so she could help wipe him down.

"You're a pretty good rider," the cowboy said from across Sunny's back. "With a little practice, we could perform more stunts together."

She concentrated on rubbing the horse. "Oh, I don't think so."

He looked over at her. "I thought you did a great job. You weren't frightened, were you?"

"Not really, well, maybe a little. It was... exciting, but dangerous." She hesitated, then said, "To be honest, I dislike pretending to be a helpless female in peril."

"Oh, come on, now. It's just for fun."

"A woman on a horse chased by a bunch of ruffians... I don't see the humor."

"It's an exciting story with a hero and a happy ending. There's nothing wrong with entertaining folks with some Wild West excitement."

"It's fake," she grumbled.

"It's history!" He found a brush and started grooming his side of the horse. "Rodeo stunts remind folks about days past. With your riding skills, you could perform in other events too."

Florence collected her thoughts as Sunny leaned into the wipe-down from her gentle hands. "I'm not sure about that. As soon as I find my horse and hat, I'm going to ride back to the ranch." She walked around the horse and tossed the burlap bag in the cowboy's direction.

Duke caught the sack. "You know… we really should plan another ride together."

Frowning, she started to walk away, then turned to face him. "I might consider riding with you again, but under one condition."

"Oh… what is it?"

"I will choose and plan the stunt."

His expression was quizzical. "What do you mean?"

"Well… we need to change the story."

"In what way?" He wiped his sleeve across his forehead.

She smiled. "Next time, you will be chased into the arena. When I ride up next to Sunny, you can jump over to my horse and ride behind my saddle." She was beginning to enjoy this. "Don't worry… I'll catch you."

Duke shook his head. "No. Huh-uh. That won't work. It's too dangerous. You need more strength for that."

She gave him a hard stare. "Too dangerous? Well, suit yourself, cowboy."

Duke shook his head. "We could try something else…."

"We'll discuss the new ride later."

Florence straightened up to her full height, a couple of inches short of six feet tall, and walked away with a confident stride toward the arena. A stray wisp of chestnut hair drifted over her collar from the neat roll pinned up behind her head. Braided horsehair from her riding quirt, which was firmly wedged under a woven waist sash, swayed gently as she walked.

Florence did not stop when she heard Duke call after her. "You'd be a helluva good saddle bronc rider. Stirrups are hobbled in place now to make ladies' events safer."

From a distance, she hesitated, then continued walking. She would have been amused to hear him say to his horse, "Don't worry, Sunny. She'll come around."

Florence located her bay cow pony. He stood peacefully resting a hoof, with his bridle reins looped over a corral fence post. The cowboy who retrieved him brought her hat over to her. She thanked him, mounted up, and eased away from the arena to ride back to the ranch alone.

Although the excitement of the rodeo was a distraction from her problems, the chaos of the event did not provide much comfort. She welcomed riding in solitude.

>-..... ⇒⊱⊰⊱ .....⊰

SEVERAL WEEKS EARLIER, Florence arrived in the "Queen City" of Denver by railroad, ready to start a new life. She hoped to acquire a job using bookkeeping skills she learned in school and to save enough money to buy or homestead a piece of land.

Florence arrived by train in Denver's bustling Union Station. She was delighted when she walked outside through a huge *Welcome* arch made of ornate ironwork. However, she was soon jostled by a cluster of people as they left the station and hurried toward the city. Although she had visited Chicago, she was a country girl unaccustomed to busy streets where automobiles and streetcars outnumbered horse-drawn transport. Noise and stink from automobiles, streetcars, wagons, and animal filth were overwhelming.

Florence clutched her carpetbag and a small, beaded purse in her gloved hands. Her initial excitement turned to distress when a ragged, wild-eyed woman tried to grab her handbag, which she quickly stashed under her jacket. When she continued walking, a man stepped in front of her. He tipped his skimmer hat and said, "Hey, there, going my way? I'll carry your bag." As a streetcar rushed close by, she turned and walked away as fast as she could in the other direction.

Florence was lost. She stopped to catch her breath and reached into her purse to retrieve the address of a ladies' rooming house on a wrinkled piece of paper. With relief, she located a policeman and showed him the crumpled note, written in her mother's handwriting. He walked with her a short distance and told her she could ride the streetcar or walk to the address. He added a stern warning for her to be wary of her surroundings. She thanked him and chose to walk so she could gather her bearings.

Based on the policeman's instructions, she found the boardinghouse. The place looked sparse but appeared to be clean and tidy. The landlady was kind and welcoming, so Florence moved in.

Her initial confidence soon faltered. She had no luck with newspaper ads or inquiries about clerk and bookkeeping positions, most often filled by men. Ladies were sought for sewing, cleaning, cooking, teaching, and nursemaids. Florence was aware that some women ended up working in brothels. With that distressing thought in mind, she was determined to find a fitting job for her skills.

After a few more weeks with no success, Florence decided to leave Denver before she spent all of her money. She was discouraged, but not sorry to leave Denver City behind when she purchased a train ticket for the return trip to the Midwest. She left the next day.

When her train followed its eastbound route along Colorado's Arkansas River Valley, Florence noticed a cowboy who boarded her passenger car in Pueblo. He was of medium height with light brown hair, a mustache, sturdy build, a well-worn cowboy hat and boots, and a weathered leather saddlebag slung across his shoulder.

Florence was startled when he stopped next to her bench. The man appeared to be friendly, amiable, and tough as nails. She also noticed that his clothes were rumpled, and his hazel eyes were a bit bloodshot.

He touched his hat brim and said, "Howdy, ma'am. I'm Duke Nelson. Do you mind if I sit on the bench across the aisle from you?" She smiled and nodded. She was surprised when he reclined and propped himself against his satchel, bent his legs up, pulled his hat over his face, and fell asleep. She returned to watching the landscape outside her window.

When the cowboy woke up about an hour later, he sat up, yawned, unfolded his legs, and looked around. When he saw Florence looking at him, he grinned and said, "Are we there yet?"

Their conversation flowed easily. Duke listened with interest to Florence's tales about her travels alone, then failed attempts to find work and settle in Denver. She asked questions about his life and job as a foreman at a historic ranch near Rocky Gulch in eastern Colorado.

The miles flew by. When the conductor announced they were approaching Rocky Gulch, Florence was surprised when Duke suggested that she leave the train and come stay at the ranch. He explained that for extra income, the owners hosted guests who sought lodging for an affordable price without luxuries included at popular dude ranches.

Florence, who was not anxious to leave Colorado, accepted Duke's suggestion. If the price fit her budget, she could stay for a few weeks while she figured out what to do next. If the ranch did not work out, she would catch the next eastbound train.

Her unexpected appearance at the ranch was met with cordial handshakes and hospitable smiles from the owners, Sam and Irma Jensen. Without batting an eye, they offered her an available room for a modest price, which she gratefully accepted.

Irma showed Florence to her room in the guest lodge. She had lost weight and had not felt well in Denver. Irma was not joking when she told Florence to bring a good appetite to the evening meal, served to a dozen or so guests and wranglers. Hearty food and friendly company was just what she needed.

Guests were encouraged to participate in ranch routine, and Florence blended right in. She was experienced with horses and was encouraged to enter a special event at the local rodeo. When her ride with Duke in "Chase for a Bride" was a success, she was amazed and a little perplexed that she was regarded as a rodeo rider.

When Duke asked if Florence would ride with him again, she agreed, but only if they changed the story. They discussed her idea, which she called "Chase for a Cowboy." He was skeptical, but he kept his promise to perform the stunt her way.

Florence was assigned to a different horse from the ranch herd, a sensible roan cow pony named River. He had plenty of speed and was sturdy enough to carry two people. She and Duke tried a few practice rides when he could fit time into his work schedule.

A new posse was organized to help Florence catch the cowboy. She invited riders from the ranch, along with a couple of teenagers from the nearby Cheyenne tribe, whom she met earlier at the rodeo grounds. The chase group would follow Duke on his horse, Sunny, into the arena. Florence would peel away to catch up next to him. With her help, he would jump onto the back of her horse and ride behind her saddle. Florence said there would be no problem, but Duke was worried.

On rodeo day, the sun was bright on the western plains. The temperature was milder than it had been at the rodeo a few weeks earlier. Local residents, ranchers, and a few members of the native Cheyenne tribe gathered to watch the new event. The same scratchy parade tunes crackled from the announcer's Victrola while onlookers chose the best places to sit in the sagging grandstand.

The posse on horseback was ready to go when Duke on Sunny galloped into the arena. Florence and her riders launched after him, and the chase was on.

While the announcer described the action, Florence broke away from the chase gang. She pushed River hard to catch up and keep a steady pace next to Duke on Sunny. He looked down as the space between them wavered. When he kicked his boots from his stirrups, she nudged River with her heels to keep up and stay close.

Florence waved her arm and yelled, "Okay, jump! Jump now!" Duke pulled his knees up on the saddle, then looked again at the gap. She reached toward him as he reached toward her. Then he hesitated. He slipped but stayed in the saddle to keep from falling. Dust swirled as Duke grabbed Florence's arm and swung across the opening. One leg landed across River's hindquarters, while his other leg slid under the horse's belly. His hat slipped off into the dust.

Florence's eyes widened as Duke's lower leg jostled and dragged in the dirt. When he pulled up his foot, his boot slid off in a tangle of galloping hooves. The pack of horses and riders was close behind as Florence grabbed for Duke's leather belt and held him steady. Sunny veered away without his rider to leave River and the chaos behind.

With Florence clutching his belt in one hand, and River's bridle reins in the other hand, Duke held on to her waist and saddle. She did not detect fear from him to match the panic she felt as he clung to the side of her galloping horse. She pulled Duke up with a mighty hoist as he pulled himself up farther until he was balanced behind the saddle. River snorted when the load shifted, and Florence slowed him to an easy lope.

The pursuit group eased back and circled out of the way. With the two riders out of danger, they cheered with relief. The two Cheyenne kids left the pack to catch Duke's horse and retrieve the remains of his boot and hat. Florence waved at the youngsters, a sign for them to ride an extra lap before they left the arena. With big smiles, they led the flashy palomino at a lively trot past the grandstand.

The announcer said, "Ladies and gentlemen, you don't see a new event like this every day. That was a fine ride and a valiant rescue… or was it a capture? The cowgirl and her gang caught the cowboy and reclaimed his horse. No wonder they call it 'Chase for a Cowboy.' Let's give these riders a round of applause."

Florence loped River slowly around the arena with Duke firmly in place behind her saddle. With her hat still in place, she gave a brief wave toward the audience. The cheering spectators were delighted to witness a new and different stunt at their hometown rodeo.

When she looked over her shoulder at Duke, his hair was tousled and a grin showed under his mustache. After he waved at the crowd, he leaned forward to plant a kiss firmly on Florence's cheek. She played along with a surprised look on her face, which caused some laughter. She then slowed her tired horse to a trot, then a calming walk through the exit.

Florence and Duke did not talk as they rode double behind the arena. A few cowboys nodded and cowgirls waved as the two riders and horse rode past.

Duke broke the silence. "Florence?"

Florence was exhausted. "What is it?"

"I lost my boot… and my hat too."

Florence looked at him over her shoulder. "That's not all…."

"What else?"

"You have a big hole in your sock."

After their horses cooled down, Florence and Duke rode back to the ranch with the other riders. When they arrived, she unsaddled and wiped down River, then turned him out in a corral with other horses. He promptly rolled in the dirt. While Duke took care of Sunny, she went back to her guest quarters to clean up before the evening meal, an outdoor cookout.

By the time she arrived at the campfire, the sun was setting, and she was hungry. Most of the guests and cowhands had eaten, but a few lingered by the fire. When she saw Duke, he nodded at a space next to him on a bench built from a tree trunk.

Fortunately, the cook saved food for them. As sunset turned to dusk, they filled their plates with barbecue brisket, beans, biscuits, and fruit cobbler.

After they ate, Florence and Duke lingered awhile to drink coffee. They sat by the campfire and laughed as wranglers congratulated them for surviving their exciting ride. When a whiskey flask was passed around, Duke poured some in his coffee. Florence declined and said, "Some other time."

Duke was smiling. "Well, darlin', looks like you're a rodeo star. What do you think?"

Florence picked up a long stick and poked it into the coals. "Actually… I was frightened this time. I was afraid you would fall off and be trampled."

"Well, I was a little concerned about that too. You did just fine when you pulled me up. That was quick thinking."

"I couldn't think at all. I was looking for a handle. I'm glad that leather belt didn't break. I hope my shoulder still works, though." She grimaced as she rubbed her upper arm. "Did you find your hat and boot?"

"I did. They suffered some damage, but they were past their prime anyway. Guess I need to buy some new duds... maybe next payday."

Florence held her hands around the warm cup. "Sorry about your sock."

His eyes lit up. "Can you fix it for me?"

She straightened up her posture. "No, but... I can show you how to darn a sock."

Duke shook his head. "Well now, I'm not good at that sort of thing. We have different skills, but we're a pretty good team. That's why I think we can perform more rodeo events, and maybe even make some money at it."

Florence sat back. "I don't think so. I don't see the benefit of it, except to promote the ranch. We're lucky nobody was hurt, including the horses."

He stared into the fire. "Think about it. We could visit a few rodeos when work is slow." He picked up a stick to prod the fire and nudged a few embers back into flames.

Florence collected her thoughts and responded carefully. "The ride was exciting, but I don't expect to repeat it." When Duke looked quizzical, she continued.

"Women performing in rodeos and Western shows are popular attractions, but it can be hard on them. Traveling, injuries, working through pain, worries about livestock, money, family... and heartache.... Bones heal faster than broken hearts."

She looked at Duke to see if he understood. "It takes a long time and a lot of hard work to become a skilled rider. You said lady bronc riders are safe with their stirrups tied down. Hobbling doesn't work when a foot gets stuck, and a bronc flips over. I'll keep riding slick with loose stirrups and leave the rough stock broncs and bulls to professionals." With a faint smile, she reached for the coffeepot to reheat Duke's cup as well as her own.

Duke watched her over his raised coffee cup, then forged ahead. "I hoped you would agree to ride with me again, so you would stay longer."

Florence was pensive and looked down at her hands. "If rodeo riding is what you want, then you should do it. I plan to find a job using my skills so I can be independent and find a place for myself in the West. I love it here, and I enjoy riding with you, but I am not a rodeo rider."

Duke rubbed his chin. "Well, suit yourself, cowgirl. The thing is, I've been a cowboy my whole life, and so was my pa. I don't have much of a grubstake yet, but I plan to buy my own ranch and build a herd. At least I have a decent saddle and an ornery palomino horse. That's enough for me on most days, except when I start thinking about the future."

Florence smiled and shook her head. "I don't have a saddle and a horse yet. I've worked and saved money, but I don't have a place of my own, except where my parents live."

"It's still your home."

"Not really. I came out West to build my own life." She broke a stick apart but did not toss the pieces into the fire. It was time to let embers die down.

"I enjoy our time together, Duke, and I'm glad you suggested I visit. I've been helping Irma with meals, guests, and horses. Sam asked for my help with bookkeeping and office work, and I enjoy learning about ranch management."

Duke sat up straighter. "I didn't realize that. I've been busy moving cattle and fixing fences and irrigation. I really looked forward to our rodeo practices."

"I did too." Florence watched the fire's dim glow, which would soon turn to gray ash.

"Oh, I almost forgot." She reached into her skirt pocket and brought out an envelope. "Irma told me this came in today's mail, and she asked me to give it to you."

She handed the letter to Duke. It was addressed in flowery hand-writing to Benjamin F. Nelson. Duke studied the envelope briefly and slipped it into his shirt pocket.

Florence changed the subject. "So, Sam and Irma offered me a job which includes free room and board if I want to stay at the ranch. They need an assistant with bookkeeping, managing guests, and leading trail rides. The job is mine if I want it."

Duke straightened up and looked at her, to make sure she was not joking. "Are you going to take it?"

"I'm thinking about it. I can give it a try and see if it works out."

"Well, then." He smiled and adjusted his hat. "I guess you won't have much time for rodeo riding."

She smiled. "I doubt it. I'll probably try the job through summer and fall, then decide if I should stay on."

"That sounds fine. You know, if you need anything, I'll be around."

"Actually, there is something… I would like to learn how to handle a rope. Can you teach me how to throw a lasso?"

Duke laughed. "Well, now. If you fix my sock, I'll teach you how to handle a rope, lasso livestock, whatever you want. I can show you a few tricks and spins that will dazzle the guests."

Florence laughed. "I can't refuse a deal like that."

As they stood up together, Duke said, "I'd better check on the horses. River had a rough day, and so did Sunny and the others. I hope none of them pulled up lame."

With a tentative smile, Florence placed her hand on Duke's arm. It felt warm and natural. They walked slowly together toward the corral, enjoying the cool night air as crickets and locusts tuned up for their nightly chorus.

At the corral, Florence and Duke leaned on the fence rail together while they watched the small herd moving around in the dark. A few horses made snuffling sounds while eating stray wisps of leftover hay.

"Florence?" Duke's voice was uneasy.

"What is it?"

"About my name…. It's Ben, but my rodeo name is Duke."

She smiled. "Well… both names suit you."

As clouds parted, dark shadows yielded to light from a bright, waxing moon. River walked toward them, looking for a handout. Florence let out a sigh of relief. The sturdy roan with a big heart was walking steady and appeared to be alert and sound.

—*Joyce B. Lohse is a Colorado journalist and author who combines research and Western history to write articles and award-winning books for all ages. Her seven Filter Press books include four titles in the* Now You Know Bio *series. Awards include three Women Writing the West finalists, five Colorado Independent Publishers Association awards, and a Colorado Authors League Top Hand award. Her articles are included in Pikes Peak Library District compilations. Joyce is a member of Western Writers of America, Women Writing the West, and the Denver Women's Press Club. She is currently writing and researching among the canyons of Western Colorado.*

ᗷUTTERNUT SKY

RHONDA LOMELI

TERRITORY OF NEBRASKA
1859

NOTICING AN INKLING of discomfort, Adeline lowered her ever-increasing bulk into the rocker with an *oomph*. "This late in the game it's normal for new aches and pains according to Doc McCoy," she said to Lee, whose six-foot-two-inch frame leaned against a support on the cabin porch.

Her husband of one year said, "I hope he's born soon, you know, to relieve you of your misery."

The sultry night carried no breeze. Grabbing her fan, Adeline opened it outward with a snap. "He?"

The proud father-to-be, smiling coyly said, "Yes, I can tell." Then, shaping his hands in an oval on the sides of her stomach, said, "You see, your belly has a manly shape to it. Wait, that didn't come out right! What I mean is...."

She shook her head slightly. A grin emerged from the corners of her mouth then blossomed into laughter.

Reprieved from his blunder, Lee said, "Seriously, Adeline, we need to talk about tomorrow. I'll light out before dawn. If all goes well, we'll be done in a few hours. I'll head back straight away and return after suppertime." Then as an afterthought, he added, "Hopefully before dark."

"You think you'll be gone that long? I didn't think it would take that much time," said Adeline.

"Why sure, darlin'. Putting up a barn is no quick task. We were lucky several joined to help us finish our barn. Roy put in extra time too. I know he comes off as a ne'er-do-well, but believe me, he's there when the chips are down. He arrived before the others and was the last to head out. It's only right we return the favor, and I know you feel the same way."

"Of course. I'm so grateful for our neighbors. Securing a place for their animals and hay is important, baby coming or not." Thinking out loud, she continued, "Besides, last time we saw Doc McCoy, he mentioned it could be about three more weeks. He also said the first baby can take a long while comin'. I suppose you'll have plenty of time to come home," Adeline said, a hint of nervousness in her voice.

Lee, proud of his wife, smiled. "I imagine you're uneasy. When the time comes, Doc McCoy will be here, and I'll be right outside the door pacing around like an ol' fool not knowing what to do. The doctor will be calling orders to his wife, but no need to. I heard she assists him at all the births. Did you know he's delivered most people in this county under twenty years of age?"

"No, I wasn't aware of that," said Adeline.

"Yes, it's a fact. That's a lot of people. I heard about it just last Sunday at church from Missus Turner. You were talking to your friends, and she came over, put her gloved hand on my sleeve, and said not to worry. She was looking at you. She said Doc McCoy was an expert." He ran his fingers through his sandy blond hair.

"That's good to hear. I like Doc McCoy and his wife. I've felt better in the last week and a half, and I've accomplished a few chores without effort. Remember the items I didn't have the energy to complete like the quilt for the crib? I finished it and the baby clothes are now folded in a drawer. The wooden baby spoons I started carving a while back are smooth and splinter-free," said Adeline. "I'll be fine tomorrow. If the birth was near, I likely would be too tired to do all that."

Rebel, the collie, bounded in from the field. Not far behind was Petie, the black-and-white fox terrier.

"Suppertime already. I tell you, those two can tell time without a watch! I'll see if I can get up and get us something to eat," said Adeline, rocking harder to gain forward and upward momentum. Heaving once more, Lee darted from his place at the post to help her out of the rocker. Grabbing her hands in his, he pulled her gently to her feet. Moving a lock of her auburn hair, he said, "You've got the most beautiful cornflower blue eyes I've ever seen. It's easy to see why I fell for you."

Adeline could see sincere love in his eyes, and with embracing arms, welcomed his kiss. *I feel so lucky to be loved.*

Supper was a meager affair. On their small Blue Willow platter Adeline had arranged a roasted chicken on a head of shredded lettuce from the garden. Two glasses of milk were positioned by each placemat, and the conversation was light. Bedtime came early and sleep arrived without delay.

IT SEEMED ADELINE had just closed her eyes when she heard Lee moving about the cabin gathering his clothes and boots. He packed up a muffin from the day before and crept to the bedside. "Adeline, you awake?" he said.

"Kind of," said Adeline, rolling over. "The morning has a chill to it," she added, pulling the Wedding Ring quilt about her body.

"You rest tight, sweetheart. I'm heading to the barn to saddle up Rumble and gather my gear." His voice changed and he said tenderly, "Addy, you take care of yourself while I'm gone. I'll be back as soon as I can. I mean it."

As she settled in for a deep sleep, Adeline heard the horse nicker then the powerful hoofbeats of Lee's blue roan head out in the dawn.

An hour later, Adeline awoke for good this time and wiggled her way to the side of the bed. She stood up slowly and made her way to the outhouse. *I wish it wasn't so far.*

Heading back to the cabin, she noticed the day was different. *It's the sky. It's the color of butternut squash. I'll call it a butternut sky.*

Dressing for the day, Adeline put on a skirt that she tied loosely to the side. It had been her aunt's. The aunt, rotund in her day, had given it to her as a new bride, preparing to leave for Nebraska. She had said, "Now, Adeline, you take these three cotton skirts. Right now, two of you could fit in them, but there may come a day when you're 'in the family way' and there are not too many general stores on the prairie. When you're done with them you can always turn them into a tablecloth or curtains. Please send me a letter when you view that Chimney Rock and let me know what it looks like." Adeline smiled at the memory, remembering how she had blushed. *Thank you, Auntie.*

As she finished up a quick bite of breakfast, Adeline felt a new ache. *What is it and where's it coming from?* She moved her head from side to side stretching the muscles in her neck. Rolling her shoulders, she looked up and shaded her eyes from the rising sun.

Adeline heard a *cluck, cluck, cluck,* and grabbed the wire basket. She started down the hill, calling to Rebel, "It's 'bout time we opened the coop, isn't it?"

Straightening from his first nap of the day, Rebel reluctantly left his place in the sun and trotted behind her billowing skirt. Petie yawned, returned his head to its resting place, and exhaled deeply. His sigh said it all.

The barnyard rooster, crowing since before dawn, was indignant at having been kept waiting. He strutted out first. Amid a cluster of squawks and a blizzard of feathers, the flock paraded down the board ramp and fluttered out to the yard.

Adeline grabbed the rake from outside the chicken coop and began fluffing up the straw to look for eggs. "Rebel, if I could just teach those hens to lay their eggs in the boxes we made, I wouldn't have to dig around for them. Ah, there's one."

After collecting the remaining eggs, she found herself looking at the sky on the horizon. There was something unusual about it. The color seemed to capture her interest, mesmerizing her. *I'll be sure to tell Lee when he gets home. Perhaps he sees it too.*

It had only been a couple of hours since he left, but it seemed like a long time. Deciding it was best to get herself busy, she headed for the cabin to deposit the egg basket on the table. "Okay, Rebel, we'll get some firewood by the fireplace and some extra on the porch. I can feel a cold wind kicking up."

Firewood gathering seems to be a struggle these days. Her added size coupled with the inability to bend at the waist made the chore slower than usual. "Petie, at least I won't have to do this in the dark," she said to the dog wagging its tail by the hearth. "I gathered enough wood to be comfortable if the weather turns chilly come nightfall."

Out of nowhere, she felt the unusual pain once more. "What if it's labor starting, Petie?" The dog, hearing its name again glanced in her direction. "No. I've heard it's much worse. This is likely the uncomfortableness the doc was talking about."

Adeline sat at the kitchen table and smoothed her hair. Drinking the cool glass of water in front of her, she wiped tiny perspiration droplets from her upper lip. "That's probably what was wrong with me, Petie. I just needed water after all that wood collecting." The dog stared at her, wagged his tail, then put his head down.

Before long she busied herself getting the flour and other items ready to make bread for the day. Deciding to make a double batch, she got the additional supplies and began the process. Pain distracted her, but she quickly returned to her task. Taking a sprig of rosemary from her windowsill garden, she pulled off the leaves. Cutting them into smaller bits, she kneaded them into the dough. When satisfied with the consistency, she formed two balls and covered each with butter, then sheltered them in a tea towel in the sun. *It'll make things easier should Lee come home extra hungry after a hard day's work. If he isn't, at least tomorrow's bread will be made, and I'll have one fewer chore.*

Time passed. *I feel vulnerable like a turtle on its back. I wish Lee was here. Until today I've been able to keep the actual birth process in the back of my mind. It seemed far away. It's crept into my thoughts more often now that my "condition" is blatantly apparent with every pain.*

Having grown up on a farm, Adeline was familiar with the birthing of animals from horses to cows, several dogs, and even cats with their kittens. The animals, for the most part, seemed to address the situation with a naturalness and ease. *I should be just fine. I just wish someone was here. My mother would love to be here....*

A chill blew through the open window with a gust. She had slipped her shoes off to keep her swollen feet comfortable and now had to use each foot to help the other foot slip them back on. Adeline closed the window and the door, but not before enjoying a glance at the butternut sky.

Afternoon arrived. Grabbing her shawl, she ventured out to pick some crops from the garden and several ears of sweet corn from the cornfield. The basket she carried was large. After filling it, she decided to take out a few ears. "Rebel, I'll have to make a couple of trips back to the cabin. This thing is getting heavier each minute."

On her second trip the odd pain returned, prompting her to set the basket down for a spell. *Perhaps I need to make a trip to the outhouse.*

It seemed that today the outhouse would be her best friend. The visits became more frequent. *I feel a strange pressure.*

Something came to the forefront. Adeline began thinking of all the stories women had whispered about giving birth. *It seems each story was more frightening than the last.* She began to miss Lee. Adeline hoped to hear hoofbeats announcing his return. "Rebel, it's silly of me because Lee won't be returning for hours."

Rebel, attuned to Adeline's mood, seemed to walk closer to her as they headed for the cabin. *Perhaps one of our neighbors will stop by. I'd love to talk to a woman right now who's given birth. She'd know if this pain was normal.*

ALTHOUGH IT WAS customary to have a light lunch at the table, Adeline chose a different arrangement today. Sitting on the bed offered soft comfort. Nibbling at an apple, Adeline found herself resting on one elbow. A short time later, she stretched out because it seemed a better idea. Her heavy eyelids closed, and she felt herself drifting off to sleep.

It was a deep sleep, but short. Startled awake with an unpleasant twinge, Adeline began to think it wasn't normal aches after all. She eased herself onto her elbows then moving her legs to the edge of the bed, struggled to sit up. Grabbing the bedpost, she pulled herself to her feet. After a time, the pain eased, then subsided altogether.

Walking over to the window, Adeline moved the flour-sack curtains and pushed them far to the sides. She let in the full view of the sky. The butternut sky was beautiful, and she could now enjoy it from anywhere in the cabin. *The sun is still high. It's going to be a few hours before Lee returns.*

Stirring the coals in the woodstove, Adeline threw in a log and then prepared the pans to bake the bread. Once the pans were in the oven, she felt the pain return. *I believe I need to walk around. Maybe that'll help.*

A GENTLE WIND swirled the dust as she headed back to the cabin. The temperature had dropped since she had last come outside, and the butternut sky was changing. "Rebel, I think before we go in the cabin, we better coop the flock. I'm not used to this Nebraska weather yet." Something about it felt strange, ominous.

There was no need to gather the flock. The rooster was halfway up the board to the entrance and hens were in line behind him. They would be fine cooped up until tomorrow. There was food and water, and the weather seemed to be changing fast. They would be much better off inside.

It seems to be getting dark, but why? It's nowhere near suppertime. Adeline shut the cabin door as the pain returned. It was coming at regular intervals now and was intensifying. *I believe this is labor. I still have a way to go before giving birth. Lee has time to come home.*

Looking out the window in the far distance, Adeline noticed that the cloud base had a slow-rotating look starting to develop. She noticed a part of one cloud that seemed to be forming into a pipe-shaped pattern. It was coming down from the large dark cloud but then disappeared back into it.

That looks like a "dust devil." At least that's what we called them as kids. They were tiny in comparison.

She said, "Rebel, where's my butternut sky? The clouds must be covering it." A gripping pain in her stomach came and shrouded the thought. When the hurt subsided, she had lucidity, and a realization developed. Adeline gritted her teeth from fear of the unknown. *It's not just the imminent birth, but the weather.*

The weather was getting stranger by the minute. There was an added chill that concerned her, and a kind of spark was in the air. She noticed the cows were circled up and were mooing. The ache returned.

Entering the cabin to take the bread out of the oven, Adeline noticed the gingham blue tablecloth fluttering. *The gaps in the cabin walls are certainly pronounced, but I didn't think this much! It's going to fill the cradle with dust.*

After securing the bread, she pulled on her shawl and grabbed a basket of onions and potatoes to put in the root cellar. The dogs followed close on her heels.

Struggling with the double doors, she tried three times before finally getting one door open. It was a set of doors that were angled from the ground up and about two feet off the soil at the top of the doors. *What an odd design. I wonder why Lee positioned them this way. It's like going into a dungeon.*

Once inside the cellar, Adeline smelled the earthy scent that reminded her of the home she had left behind, and her family. She was melancholy of the past until the discomfort returned her to the present. It took her concentration now. She leaned against the dirt wall for the time being trying to distract herself by feeling the coolness the wall offered to her outstretched hands. The smarting inside her body concluded slowly.

Taking a deep breath, she put the potatoes and onions on a shelf and realized it was quiet in the root cellar. There wasn't the high-pitched whistling sound of the wind. *It's peaceful here.* A sense of security came over her. *I'll wait in here until Lee returns. I just need a couple things.*

The sky darkened and Adeline made her way back to the cabin. It wasn't as easy as she had hoped. She noticed Petie peering from the cellar, refusing to leave.

Walking into the cabin, the ache returned. Adeline held on to the back of a chair until it subsided.

<hr />

SHE LOOKED AROUND the cabin with clarity. Grabbing a couple of quilts and a pillow, she happened upon a wooden bucket of water with a ladle. Water sloshed a little with each step, but at least most of it made it to the cellar.

The sky sprinkled drops in a steady flow. On the next trip, Adeline packed some soft, clean baby blankets and two little outfits. She wrapped everything in the tablecloth to keep them clean. The ever-increasing wind picked up swirling, relentless dust. It stung her eyes like piercing needles.

Walking against the wind took effort. She was soaked by the time she made it to the heavy doors. Adeline used all her strength to open one door. Tossing the items in one at a time worked best. Miraculously, she was able to close the door.

Outside the double cellar doors, Adeline heard a loud sound almost like being at the bottom of a waterfall. There was the combined sound of a loud whine but also a low roar. The sound lasted through a couple of contractions and her "rest" between them. *Either this is a long storm, or my contractions are getting closer.*

Adeline was thankful Lee had made the cellar so large. There were still items packed from the journey west to Nebraska. When their wagon had rolled to a stop, Lee was more concerned with making a shelter and getting the crops planted than unpacking. *Thank goodness, there may be something in here I can use. I haven't looked at these items in months.*

Glancing around the cellar, she found a place in the very back and decided this would be where she would set up the birth bed. It was far from the doors that it would likely stay dry even with this heavy rain. Rummaging through a box, she found another quilt. It was dusty anyway, so it was put on the ground with the cleaner ones on top.

Rebel had circled three times and was curled up in a large ball in one corner of the room closest to the doors. Petie had found a spot farthest from the doors and closest to Adeline's makeshift bed.

Heavy rain came, then hail that pounded the doors. The sound was deafening.

Rebel, on alert, got up often and did a patrol around the root cellar. He sniffed and looked through the crack in the doors in an apparent effort to check the perimeter.

The hurt was coming at regular intervals. It began at her sides and would wrap slowly toward the center of her stomach until it reached her belly button area. The intensity lasted seconds or hours, then slowly subsided as it crept back toward her sides.

Catching her breath, Adeline continued setting up the area. There wasn't much to do, but it was a distraction. She looked around and found a box within a box. For the most part, it was clean. She put the baby items in it and placed the box near the shelf by her bed. A loud thundering wind could be heard. Adeline gripped the dogs, then gathering her wits, released them.

Observing a small piece of wood from the larger box, she pulled it off then removed the splinters. Adeline recalled that she had seen her mother put a piece of a branch between her brother's teeth once while she wrapped his broken arm. Adeline placed the piece of wood on the blankets she had placed on the ground. *I hope I don't need that.*

Inside a box she found jerky meat. "Together with the bucket of water, this will have to be our nourishment if we're stuck here awhile," she told the dogs.

She was certain Lee would not be returning anytime soon and she'd have the baby in the cellar... alone. Momentarily, she wanted to panic, really panic. The kind that makes one want to run screaming into the prairie.

Time passed. Adeline wasn't sure how long but finally took a deep breath. *All the people walking around the earth, and they all got here because some woman gave birth to them. Many even have a brother or a sister. If it was that bad, women would never have more than one child.*

IT WAS AS if something turned off the sound. The heavy rain and hail stopped. Had it not been for Rebel's tail hitting a shelf, Adeline would have thought she had gone completely deaf. The dead-calm silence was frightening, eerie.

As another contraction gripped her, she forgot about the strange goings-on outside the cellar. When it was over, she felt relief. From her quilt on the floor, she looked out the crack between the double doors. She noticed twigs and leaves were blowing in the yard. That's strange. They're blowing from the other direction. Adeline saw that the once beautiful butternut sky had now turned a blackish-green color.

After several contractions, each growing in intensity, Adeline began slowly pacing around the small room. It seemed to help her body, but she knew it was temporary. She would need to save her energy for the birth.

Longing for Lee's return, Adeline wondered what he was doing. Looking at the dog, she said, "Rebel, I hope he's safe from this storm. Thank you for protecting me."

A loud pounding began, and large "balls" of ice hit the doors with fury. The sound continued for what seemed like time without end. *Will it ever stop?*

The painful compression like a large, wide belt tightening began at her sides and met in the middle of her abdomen. It was overwhelming and involved all her concentration to breathe through its powerful grip. When it was over, Adeline took a few gulps of air to collect herself and get ready for the next one.

Petie made his way onto the quilt and snuggled as close to Adeline as he could. During one contraction she could hear him whine, then he gave her a lick on the hand and snuggled closer to her. He did that during the next contraction and the next. *He's always been so intuitive. He knows I'm hurting.* The next time she was between contractions, she petted him. "It's all right, Petie. I'll be all right."

Adeline was on the quilt for the last few contractions, walking around was too much now. She heard a scream. *Was that me or the wind playing tricks?*

It now took everything she had to get through them. *I don't want to be here. I don't want to do this anymore! Can I finish tomorrow? I'll come back and finish tomorrow!*

Determined to find a way through this, Adeline remembered that once while playing with her friends, she had jumped in the river and one of her feet got stuck between two rocks. She had looked up and seen a butternut sky then too. She saw the waterfall and her friends playing on the riverbank. They were unaware of her dire situation. From her spot under the cool, clear stream, the seconds seemed to tick by like lightning or maybe eternity. It was hard to tell since she was frightened out of her mind. She had to have a stern talk with herself and come to a decision. *I had to think about how to free my foot rather than panic, or worse, succumb to the situation.*

Adeline remembered that moment when at last she had freed her foot and swam breathlessly to the surface. Gulping for air, she looked at the butternut sky with both river water and tears streaming down her cheeks.

She glanced down at the scar she now carried, a jagged reminder of how she had overcome fear and kept her wits about her when it was imperative.

It's like that for me now. I must gird myself. When this baby is born, I'll feel the same relief. But for now, it's time to get down to business. She took a deep breath and said aloud to herself, "I can do this. I can do this. I *can* do this!"

She could hear a scream and moaning and realized it was her, but it was uncontrollable. Feeling an urge to push, she did. The next contraction she pushed with all her might and Adeline could feel progress. *The baby's coming!*

On the next contraction, Adeline pushed hard again. She felt the baby emerging, and then the agony stopped. She felt her whole body relax and heard a quiet cry. *I did it!*

Reaching down, she lifted the baby to her heart, wrapping it in the quilt while kissing and snuggling it. She wiped the tiny face clean. Adeline held the baby in this position for a long time, looking into the most beautiful face she'd ever seen.

The baby fell asleep, and turning on her side, Adeline held it close. Tucking the baby safely in the quilt with her, she could feel herself slipping into a light sleep. At the slightest gurgling, her eyes would fly open to check on the baby.

Once when this happened, she noticed it was dark through the split between the double doors.

<hr />

ADELINE AWOKE TO Rebel and Petie barking, and voices. *Am I dreaming? Is that Lee I hear? Is it the wind or some other strange thing the crazy storm has come up with?*

"Addy! Addy!" yelled Lee's familiar voice. "Doc, I can't find her. She's not in the house or the barn. What if the tornado took off with her?"

Adeline, too stunned and weak to call out, managed to whisper, "It's your papa. He's home."

Adeline saw the light of a lantern and the root cellar door opened. She held the baby tight as Lee picked her up. On the way out the cellar door, Adeline inhaled the fresh cool air smelling of wet earth and damp cornhusks. The lamplight showed the whistling wind had had its way with the cabin, but at least it was still standing.

Doc McCoy said to Lee, "Please put her on the bed. I've got to examine her and the baby. Could you get a fire going? And water, please boil up some water." Lee bolted into action.

"You did good, young lady," he said while appraising her. "I'm going to do a few things here to help you."

Once Adeline settled in, Lee smiled with admiration. "Thank you, Addy. Wish I could have made it back to you sooner."

"I'll take the baby now, mama. I need to check your little one." Doc McCoy turned to Lee. "Could you please get me warm water and some small clean cloths?"

Lee accomplished the mission in record time. Adeline then saw Lee move anxiously behind the doctor, staring over his shoulder.

Adeline watched as the doctor ever so gently placed the baby atop the table on a clean tablecloth. She watched Lee's eyes surveying the blanket. As Doc McCoy removed the swaddling, Lee's eyes beamed like twin sunrises and a barn-door grin covered his face.

A sense of accomplishment and pride filled Addy's heart. *I got through it. I did it!*

—*Rhonda Lomeli is the author of* Semper Fi, Marine: Two Brothers in the Pacific Theater, WWII, *a children's book on bullying titled* There's a Tussle in the Coop!, *and her latest book,* Make a Splash with Your Dash!, *is a top seller in inspirational books. She has also published short stories and magazine articles. Her writing journey began early, when a winning poem submitted to a school contest revealed a gift—and a passion—that would follow her into adulthood. That moment marked the beginning of a lifelong commitment to storytelling. An enormous fan of the Western genre, her deep appreciation for vast expanses is sprinkled throughout her writing.*

Her current endeavor is a trilogy set in the 1800s. It follows the saga of female protagonist Sage Weston over many adventures and miles across the continent. While possessing an admiration for horses, she does not have room for one but instead has a miniature Manchester terrier.

CHARLATANS

DEVON MCKAY

SAN FRANCISCO, CALIFORNIA
1851

"MADAM BORDEAUX, HUH? Sounds foreign. French?"

"*Oui,*" Delilah Westbury answered curtly. She bobbed her head, the blonde curls framing her face bouncing from the movement. She was as French as the man who stood before her, but he didn't need to know that. Nor did he need to know she'd borrowed the title from a bottle of wine. *Which had also been stolen.*

But lies, deceit, and trickery come easy when you are hungry.

The name was nothing more than an illusion, one of many in her bag of tricks. Crystal gazing, palmistry, and a casting of the cards would follow. At her prompt, the showstopper would be added, signaling the entrance of a loved one. This included the shaking of the table as well as the strung apples used to mimic the sound of footsteps her sister Lydia had perfected. They were standing knee-deep in the art of deception, duping those who wanted to believe by *"communicating with spirits"* and fake séances. Yet now, they had little choice in the matter. What had started as a fun performance had now become their only chance at survival.

It was a foolish notion—thinking they could make a living from a parlor game they'd witnessed in St. Louis. Criminal, in fact. Naïve to think their actions wouldn't cause harm. Preying on those who wanted one last interaction with a passed loved one hadn't been their intention. But that's exactly what she and Lydia had done. Or were attempting to do. Providing those in mourning some relief from the grief made the fraud bearable, almost… *forgivable.*

A thirst for adventure had led them west. More specifically, San Francisco. A booming seaport in California that was wild and untamed, both in nature and occupants. And though it had been a struggle, they had started to build a following. One that paid. Which for now, was all that mattered.

Truth be told, it was the one position they were qualified for. They'd been so pampered in St. Louis that they weren't prepared for life outside of a wealthy household. Their skill sets consisted of a knowledge of fine wines, playing croquet, practicing archery, and the making of potpourri. None of which were in high demand here.

They knew nothing about providing services such as laundering, cooking, and cleaning. And despite their willingness to learn, no one wanted to take a chance on two silly, spoiled girls who had never worked a day in their lives. The choice to start the frivolous business had been their only option.

Delilah was determined to make it work. There was no other recourse. They couldn't return to St. Louis if they wanted to. Their father would never welcome them home. Not after the rebellious exit. Pride had closed that door.

The ploy began with a crystal ball, quickly followed by the tracing of lines on an eager palm, and lastly another form of divination, tarot reading. Usually, she saw nothing in the clear glass. Nor did she have a clue what the lines on a palm meant, but the casting of the cards was where she truly shined. It was the only part of their act that proved true. Tarot told a story—one she was able to tell. Delilah simply let the images speak.

Yet, this often came at a cost, both to her and the person wishing for their fortune to be shown. Physically she'd be spent, both shaken and tired. Emotionally, the readings left her slightly drained. Which is why she always closed with the cards.

First, a quick study of the man was in order. He was tall and lanky with a shifty, untrusting stare. Not unusual in the rough mining town. Nor was his rugged clothing or the shiny six-shooter housed in the gun belt slung low over his slim hips. Most of her clients were armed in some way or another, even the soiled doves. She preferred to focus on the way he carried himself. A lot could be told by a person's demeanor.

Unfortunately, this client couldn't be trusted. Unease balled in her stomach. He made her uncomfortable. There was an edge to him. Something she couldn't quite place, nor did she want to. Mentally, she took note of this yet chose to ignore her gut and continued anyway. This would prove to be a mistake.

Despite the brief introduction, and inquisition about her heritage, the man said little else other than asking gruffly the cost of her services. The funds were exchanged, then Delilah invited him to sit so she could begin.

She started with crystal gazing. She stared into the glass sphere, narrowing her gaze until the surroundings went fuzzy, and her vision blurred, purposely distorting and magnifying the shadowed outline of the man. "I see a woman from your past." This was always a starting point. A woman for the male clients and a man for the ladies.

Delilah saw neither. To be honest, she wasn't focused. Her thoughts were on her next meal and paying rent. The only clarity the crystal ball brought was the fact that she was the one who couldn't be trusted.

"Someone you cared for, loved deeply. They are here with us." This was Lydia's cue. As anticipated, the rapping began, with three sharp knocks to draw their attention. Delilah braced her knees on the table's edge in preparation. "This person... someone you lost."

Lydia continued behind the scenes, bouncing the apples off the stairs to feign the sound of approaching footsteps. Abruptly, the descent was stilled, replaced with a shrill scream and the thumping of apples racing to freedom. The severity of the situation hadn't quite filtered in and for a second, Delilah was reminded of their early attempts before her sister had perfected the act. But that didn't explain the scream.

Her stomach churned as the small hairs lifted on the nape of her neck. Images of what could have happened flashed in her head, flawing all reason. She lifted her head, meeting his dark gaze and noting the hint of a grin pulling at the corners of his mouth. Whatever game he played, he felt as if he'd already won. Maybe he had.

"Appears I'm not the only one who has lost someone," he agreed shrewdly. He was toying with her, enjoying the control he had over the situation. This was the edge she'd ignored. The warning her gut had spoken.

"What do you want?" Delilah asked, hating the shakiness of her voice.

He leaned forward, close enough that she could see the black of his pupils, smell the soured tang of rotgut whiskey on his breath. "The truth?" His smile widened, showcasing a row of rotted teeth. "Give me what I came for. And your cohort will remain untouched. However, if you cross me again, my boys have permission to do what they may."

He hiked his thumb over her shoulder toward the velvet burgundy draperies separating the rooms. A grimy hand pulled back the curtain, exposing her worst fear—the men were holding her sister hostage. A moment later the heavy material fell back into place, forcing her to return all attention to the ringleader. "And you can drop the accent. We both know you're not French."

The man stood, towering over her for a moment before walking over to the window and flipping the *open* sign to *closed*. He paused, taking a moment to trace a dirty finger over the fortune teller logo and image of the crystal ball they'd etched into the glass. He then proceeded to shut them off from the world by drawing the curtains, a perfect match to the door's drapery.

The room was instantly cloaked in darkness. She fumbled to find a candle and matches to light the room. Somehow, she managed, flooding the space with an ominous glow and highlighting the man seated at the table again. Though his face was partially hidden by the dancing shadows of the candle's flickering flame, his expression was not. Irritation. Impatience. Expectance. None of which promised a favorable ending.

"I've told you. You caught me. It's not real. I'm a charlatan. An imposter. A fake. Why would you believe anything else I'd say?"

"I believe Rosie. From the saloon. Liquored up she's real chatty. Says everything you told her came true. Her friend… the one you told her was with child. She ran off. Like you warned her would happen. The barkeep waters down the whiskey. The madam takes a larger cut than what she says she's giving the girls. And lastly, who won the game of bluff. All of it true. Granted, some I could've figured out on my own. But not the poker game. Or how it ended. With the dead man's hand. Two pairs of black aces and two black eights. So, either you're one hell of a guesser or you might have some kind of natural ability. How about we get down to business and you just tell me when the stagecoach will get here?"

"The stagecoach?" At first she was confused, but then it dawned on her. He wasn't a normal client. He wasn't a miner asking when he'd strike it rich. Or a working girl wanting a glimmer of hope. Nor did he come to seek comfort from grief. The information he sought was for personal advancement, one of selfishness and greed. And possibly, the intent to harm others.

"Yeah. The one with all the gold. Tell me or I'll let my boys do what they may." Delilah returned her gaze to the curtained room. A muffled cry sent shivers up her spine. Furthering her fear, he withdrew his gun and held it for a long moment before placing it on the table, the muzzle pointed in her direction.

It didn't take experience to note the blackness of the man's heart. He was here for whatever insight she could share and then he'd conveniently dispose of her and Lydia. One didn't need a crystal ball to see that. Her only hope was to outwit him.

"Very well." Reaching for the tarot deck, she forced herself to remain calm. Oddly, the cards helped. They always did. The worn deck, weathered from frequent use, grounded Delilah in the way of only knowing the possibility of one's fate could.

She held them close to her chest for a moment, to breathe in their scent. They smelled of the sprig of lavender she used to cleanse the deck. The floral fragrance washed over her, further calming her nerves. Closing her eyes, she whispered her intentions, then placed the stack in front of him.

He chose his gun over the cards. Palming the six-shooter, his index finger slid over the trigger. Doubt had settled in. That much was clear. "Maybe, this is a waste of my time."

"You came to me," Delilah countered sharply. Perhaps she should've held her tongue. There was no reason to poke the bear. But his callous words irked her. He was the one wasting time.

"Do you wish for me to continue?" A dry lump was lodged in her throat, making it hard to swallow. "I could explain the process."

He held her gaze for a long moment, then nodded. His hand never left the gun.

"It's like a book and each card is a chapter. When put all together it tells a story. You simply think about what you'd like to know and then pick a card. Like this." She picked up the deck again and shuffled, then spread them out into a fan, and plucked one out. The Wheel of Fortune. A flitter of hope spiked through her. As far as the cards went, this was a sign in her favor. One of the best. A turning point. "Luck. Fate. Destiny. Perhaps we were meant to meet."

"Destiny?" He scoffed. The shiftiness in his stare became more pronounced. "In other words, this is just a game. Another trick."

"Is it? Rosie didn't think so." Delilah shrugged, attempting her best to appear nonchalant. She returned the card to the pile. "At this point, what do you have to lose? You may as well play the game. Shuffle, then ask your question."

To her surprise, he did as she instructed. "Tell me when the stagecoach will be here," he asked again, repeating the same question from before. "How many men will be guarding it? And..." he hesitated, inhaling a ragged breath before continuing. "Ask if me and my men live."

This was the first time he'd shown any sign of weakness. The thought was rooted by his exhale, a deeply weighted sigh. The outlaw wasn't as sure of his abilities as he let on. A part of her relished this and another part feared it. A man fueled by desperation was a dangerous man.

"Good. Now, cut the deck three times and spread them out. Pull ten cards." Again, he conceded.

Slowly, she flipped them over, one by one. Taking her time, she studied the images allowing the story to unfold. Fool. Devil. Eight of Wands. The Lovers. Tower. Judgment. Three of Swords. Death. Four of Pentacles. She left the last one unturned.

"The fool is you." She tapped the card with a long fingertip, noting his ruffled response. As expected, he took the definition at will thinking it was meant as an insult and not a counsel. The reversed image told a tale of taking too many risks and acting recklessly but she didn't explain this further. Let the man think what he will. She continued.

"The Devil, temptation. Eight of Wands is swift movement. Answering one of your questions. The coach is on the way. The time frame is within an eight, could be minutes, hours, or days. The Lovers is an interesting twist. It speaks of a partnership—a choice to be made." The card also indicated a need to use your head but not ignore your heart and intuition. More of a warning meant for her than him. An interesting twist, indeed.

"And the Tower, chaos. The destruction of a shaky foundation. See how the building is collapsing?" Delilah tapped the image. After a brief pause, she continued, "Judgment is self-explanatory. The reverse position seconds your actions are not the right path. Three of Swords is about heartache and betrayal. Death shows an ending. And the Four of Pentacles portrays a person of greed."

He picked up the card and studied the picture of a man surrounded by gold, a treasure chest hoarded in his arms. "That's me on a pile of gold. I'll take it." He tossed it back onto the table, then picked up the Death card, displaying the image of the Grim Reaper. "But this? Death? That's how this will end?"

"Could be. Or a new beginning," she offered, in hopes a different perspective might sway him in the right direction. It didn't.

"Death will do." He grabbed the gun and pointed it at her, cocking the trigger. The sound was incredibly loud and foreboding in the small space. "The only loose end is you."

"I'm not done." She pointed at the last card. How she was able to maintain her composure was a mystery. "There's one left. Let my sister go and tell your men to leave. Then, I'll finish the reading and tell you what it means. It may be something you want to hear in private."

He stared at her, a lack of trust highlighting his stare. He glanced at the cards, as did she. Delilah could have gone another route. She could've easily made up the meanings, but there'd been no need to. The reading was clear and concise, pointing out exactly what needed to be said. And done. The privacy suggestion was merely a final grasp of preservation and hope. It simply made mathematical sense. The odds of surviving one man with a gun were better than facing many.

Curiosity prevailed.

Demanding she stay put, he shoved the weapon into its holster and excused himself. Outside the curtain a muffled conversation was held, followed by the shuffle of feet. The bells on the door rang, confirming his men's exit.

A moment later, he emerged from behind the covering with Lydia in tow. Though rattled, her sister was unharmed. Trembling with gratitude, Delilah whispered a thankful prayer. He released the girl, allowing a brief hug to be shared before motioning them both to sit. Once settled, he returned to his seat.

"Let's finish this. What's the last card?"

She held his gaze, as she grazed her fingertip over the back, circling the colorful paisley design. "That's up to you. It's your fortune, turn it over and see."

He scooped it up, stared at the image for a moment, and then slammed the card face down on the table. "Is this your idea of a joke?" he demanded, spittle spewing from his twisted mouth. Face red, he was past the point of reasoning. He withdrew his gun, waving the six-shooter menacingly in the air, before aiming it in her direction.

Cautiously, she retrieved the card. A woman holding an upright sword in her right hand and two scales in her the other came into focus. Justice. No wonder he was upset.

"What does it mean?" The gun appeared inches from her face. Seconds later, the cold steel was pressed against her forehead, promising an ugly demise. With the card still in hand, she slowly rose to her feet, then took a few steps back to gain a small amount of distance. It was hard to think straight while staring at the wrong end of the barrel.

"Fairness, truth, and the law. Being called to account for your actions and judged accordingly." Meaning this could go either way. Her heartbeat accelerated, thundering loudly in her ears and racing to an erratic beat as her limbs shook, barely holding her weight.

She spared a glance at her sister, before returning her focus on the man. A choice must be made, and she knew exactly what needed to be done. They had to try to escape. Or the man would kill them both. The fear in Lydia's stare had solidified the decision. If the wheel rang true, then luck would be on their side.

With a flick of her wrist she flung the card, the sharp edge slicing his neck in a clean line as it whirled by. He never saw it coming. The blood wasn't immediate. Nor was the realization that he had taken his last breath as the air gurgled in his throat. Yet, both quickly set in as he crumpled to the floor.

A turning point for certain.

She stood over him until the life had completely drained out of his body. His face, contorted in a stunned expression, was now set in stone. The outcome shocked her as much as it did him. Evidently, Delilah had more tricks in her bag than even she was aware of. Her attempt was simply to catch him off guard so they could get away. Not slit his throat. But, if one seeks justice, then justice will be served.

The man was a fool after all. One should never challenge their fate. The tarot told a story. The only part of their act that proved true.

—*Devon McKay writes historical, paranormal, and contemporary romance with a Western flair. If she's not writing, she's busy with chores on her mini farm, working on a stained-glass project, or walking one of her three dogs through the woods. Her greatest joy is putting a smile on a reader's face and hearing from fans.*

She's a Hand

DANI NICHOLS

THE SNOW WAS slick with blood and membrane, dotted with bits of hay and pine needles. The world shrank to the size of our headlight beams, and right in the center, the mother cow sprawled in pain. She bawled at us angrily and tossed her head—we could see there was something inside her, but it was not life.

"Get the winch," Cox said. I fumbled, fingers slipping on frosty metal. Together, we—well, really Cox—got one end on the bumper and the other around a tiny cloven hoof, protruding from just below his mother's tail. I tried to help but my small stature and general lack of knowledge was a hindrance. Exhausted, her big brown eyes rolled in pain and fear as I tried to soothe her.

"It's okay, mama," I cooed, patting her heaving sides.

"Let's go, girl, we better pull this calf or we're gonna lose the mama too," Cox grumbled, working the winch.

Centimeters, inches, then feet—four feet to be exact—and a tiny, lifeless calf came out backwards as his mother heaved painful sighs. The afterbirth followed with a gurgle and blop, spreading even more blood on the frozen ground. My eyes filled with tears—I still wasn't used to the commonplace experience of death.

Cox moved quickly. "We gotta get her to the barn. Winnie and I'll walk her up, bring the truck."

With practiced movements, he twisted the mother's tail and got her standing, and then with firm motions and a whistle to Winnie the cow dog, the unlikely trio started walking. He positioned himself right behind her hip, too close to kick but not so far she might forget to keep moving. I climbed back inside the rumbling diesel pickup, where the AM radio softly burbled an ad for an auto parts store, and headlights illuminated the snowy, rutted road to the barn. The truck cab smelled like manure and blood and iodine and mud and hay, all brought into nose-melting confluence by the blasting defroster. My thin fingers tingled with the heat, and I noticed hay stuck in the bottom of my braid, which hung down from under my wool hat not unlike the mother cow's muddy tail. Cox clomped with his broad shoulders bent against the wind, while our faithful dog nudged the mother's heels forward like an uncompromising doula.

Once back in the barn, the fluorescent lights wheezed and wavered, but it was a relief to be out of the single-digit wind. The mother obediently staggered into a stall and Cox, with a whistle to Winnie, had her pinned between the metal pipe gate and the wooden wall in the time it took me to realize what was happening. "Get me antibiotics," he snapped as I watched the mother stamp and snort, while Winnie, a far more accomplished hand than I, stood guard at her hind feet. All I could feel was cold and dread. While most of my classmates were working in heated coffee shops and fast-food joints, I'd wanted to be a hand. I believed that even a skinny, weak girl like me could work with the men. I wanted to prove it to everyone, even myself.

By the time we'd administered drugs and supplied hay and water, it was two a.m. I could hear the wind whipping across the broad valley and making the tall pines throb and sway to their own gloomy winter song. I sat on a pile of empty grain sacks, absently rubbing Winnie's ears and listening to the mother chew. Cox was washing his hands of blood and grime, and I assumed we'd soon head back to the ranch house, job done. Instead, he commanded, "Gerrup, girls," and Winnie sprang to attention. I wobbled up less eagerly.

"We gotta calf to skin," he said. I didn't ask. We got in the truck, the radio was now crackling with a talk show about extraterrestrial activity, something we actually heard a lot about during calving season. Sometimes we even shared a laugh at a sincere caller's expense, although not tonight.

When we got to the dead calf, laying in the short pasture grass, it was cold but not completely stiff. I had to force myself to see it as shapes and tasks and not a being who should have been shaking his ears in wonder at the cold air and hunting for milk on the warm underbelly of his mother.

Cox needed no such mental preparation. He pulled out his folding knife and went straight to work, leaving the fore of the calf untouched and cutting the skin in half behind the shoulders. He was careful to leave the tail bed completely intact. He grunted quietly at his work, with a careful, sure, even gentle hand which belied the grisly job. We left the carcass—we'd go out with a tractor in the morning to bury it.

Quiet, we headed back to the barn with half a calfskin in the truck bed. Just the crackle of radio callers' Martian sightings and Winnie's comforting dog breath, snoozing at my elbow.

When we got there, Cox punched two holes in the skin with his pocketknife, stringing it through with hay twine like a grisly, medieval superhero cape. We went one stall over to catch an orphaned calf who'd been living in the barn since her mother died last week.

"Hold her," Cox grunted. I strained to keep the calf's and my combined distrust and panic from destroying Cox's hard work. I gritted my teeth so as not to wimp out or cry. I could cowboy with the best of them.

We tied the skin on, and the calf looked at us like we'd lost our minds. Honestly, I wasn't sure we hadn't. The bereaved mother moaned in the stall, her milk had come in and she instinctively looked for her calf, calling in a primal voice. Cox held the orphan and pushed her toward the mother's bulging udder. "Steady," he said. "If mama smells her head, it's over. She has to smell her calf's tail to think it's hers."

The calf gave a perfectly timed, gleeful headbutt to the udder and began to suck as the mother turned toward the calf's tail. She sniffed, bawled, and sniffed again. Cox and I held our breath. The calf's actual tail, partially hidden under the skin of her predecessor, began the furiously joyful wiggle of satisfied youth, and the mother grunted in contentment.

"We did it, girls," Cox said, and we closed the barn door and walked to the ranch house, where woodsmoke drifted out of the chimney and there was always hot coffee in a dented pot, at least this time of year.

—Dani Nichols is a cowgirl and writer from Central Oregon. Her independently published children's book about her quarter horse, Buzz the Not-So-Brave, *has won five book awards, including a silver Will Rogers Medallion Award and placement in the Western Writers of America Spur Awards. Dani's essays are popular on Substack and have been published in* The Other Journal, Oregon Humanities, Reckon Review, Barren Magazine *and more. When she's not writing, she is probably riding her horse, chasing her kids all over kingdom come, or cooking for family and friends.*

SHERIFF HARPER

BETSY RANDOLPH

DESPITE JUST WINNING the election, Suzannah Armstrong Harper—first female sheriff of Logan County, Oklahoma—groaned, *"What have I done?"* She didn't want the job. But the former sheriff's mantra, "Women have no business in law enforcement," flew in her face again—a stye in the eye. His sexist comment—the mentality of very few—was often spoken aloud when she was a state trooper assigned to Logan County.

Retirement could wait. That's when she threw her hat in the ring. And now, she'd won. She was the new sheriff in town. Her smile, tight across her teeth, stayed in place as she raised a closed fist in the air. Supporters shouted her name as she looked across the room at them. She wished she were home—in her red silk pajamas—sipping a glass of chardonnay, not standing on a stage in a crowded, Egyptian-themed auditorium sweating profusely. Her black blazer, too snug under the armpits, showed sweat stains. She imagined huge salt rings crystalizing around each drying ring of sweat—a lake shoreline, receding.

She raised her arms and waved regardless. "Thank you, all, for your support."

Politicians—I'm one of "them" now.

Her right-hand man, Dwight "Goldfinger" Rawlins, stepped behind the microphone on the glossy oak stage as the crowd continued shouting. Smooth black skin on his forearm covered chiseled muscle. His uniform shirtsleeve—always too snug—screamed for relief. He pointed toward the double brass doors behind the crowd, his deep voice booming.

"Sheriff Harper invites you all to a reception in the atrium just behind you there. Please join us for some light refreshments."

Amid shouts of her name, whistles, and something like catcalls from the back of the packed room, Suzannah exited the stage. She, Goldfinger, and her twenty-two-year-old son, Levi, waded through the crowd to the large, rectangular-shaped room through the auditorium's doors. The Guthrie Scottish Rite Masonic Temple acted as a part-time wedding venue and event center, likely due to its marvelous architecture. Each room in the 400,000 square foot temple was unique. The atrium, with its white Italian marble floors and walls, ornamental plaster, and gothic-like pillars was especially popular for receptions. One of her wealthy supporters paid the $2,500 rental fee for the watch party. She wasn't sure if he thought the Egyptian Room, with its deep green carpet and partial Pharaoh busts protruding from each wall, was somehow apropos. Her, ancient of days, starting a new career. She considered walking like an Egyptian—wrists and elbows bent and stiff, as she exited stage right.

She took up her place behind one of the many tables covered with refreshments. Her best friend, Phillis, "Phil" for short, organized the food and drink. The sheriff's table held a large chocolate-covered vanilla sheet cake—already cut into pieces. The other tables held fruit platters and heated stainless-steel servers of little smokies swimming in Head Country barbecue sauce. She slid her fingers inside a pair of latex gloves, then slapped her hands together.

"Who wants cake?"

Her whitened-toothed smile, genuine. Though tired and somewhat unsure about being sheriff, she was grateful to the people who'd helped her get elected. She handed cake to an elderly woman with long silver hair. "Thank you so much for…." Her sentence was cut short by a loud pop.

Was that gunfire?

The round entered the back of her wool blazer—knocking Suzannah into the table in front of her, then down to a kneeling position on the marble floor.

Screams pierced the air as she yanked her Smith & Wesson .357 from its pancake holster concealed on her hip. People flattened themselves to the floor, a few ran from the building while some continued to scream. Suzannah had not screamed. And although hit, she felt no pain. Her Kevlar vest had done its job, she guessed.

About fifteen feet away, Goldfinger and two other uniformed deputies made quick work of the shooter. They'd tackled him and wrestled his arms behind his back, clicking handcuffs on his wrists. His pistol lay nearby—a black, compact Taurus.

Suzannah stood, twisting her upper torso, scanning the room for any additional threats.

None.

She holstered her weapon. Levi, who'd been somewhere in the crowd, rushed to his mom's side. He ran his hands over her arms.

"Where are you hit? Are you bleeding? Mom, Mom… look at me… answer me?"

Suzannah stopped and looked at her only child. "I'm fine." She glanced down at her body. Nothing was amiss. She felt her back to look for blood but there was none.

Levi stepped back, searching his mother's eyes. She did appear to be fine. They looked over at the shooter about the same time. The deputies stood him up and patted him down. He didn't look familiar to Suzannah. His straight, jet-black hair and dark eyes said Indian or maybe Mexican, could be Middle Eastern, mid-twenties, five seven, 140 pounds. Tattoos covered his neck and hands. He glared at Suzannah with black eyes, mere slits. His lips pressed together forming one ugly line until he opened his mouth to scream.

"I'm gonna be famous! Kill'n the first girl sheriff!"

His rotten teeth said meth when he smiled at Suzannah. She threw her thumb over her shoulder, nodding her head the same direction.

"Get this dumbass out of here."

Two uniformed deputies hustled him out of the room by lifting his cuffed wrists, making him bend forward at the waist to walk on his tiptoes. They moved at a quick pace toward the large revolving glass doors in the foyer.

Suzannah raised her arms in the air. "We got him, folks. Everything's okay. That's why we wear our body armor." Her closed fist pounded her chest—one of the Spartan 300.

Some people cheered and clapped. Others took their time getting up off the floor—fear or age likely playing a role in their slow movements.

Goldfinger whistled loud and the room fell silent.

"Let me have your attention. We'll need to get witness statements from everyone. Especially those of you closest to the shooter and the sheriff."

He moved his arms around in a large arc. "No one leaves until we've gotten your information. Thanks for your patience."

Goldfinger hadn't finished speaking when white searing pain flashed over Suzannah, stabbing into her back. "Ohhhh!" She staggered, pressing a hand against the sudden fire. She took a knee, unwillingly, as a drill bit dug into her spine—mercilessly twisting this way, then that. She tried standing up—to move away from the pain, but the drilling continued, digging deeper and deeper into her flesh—her athletic legs suddenly wouldn't cooperate. She reached for her boy.

"Levi...."

"Mom! Mom, are you all right?" Levi grabbed her arm. "You're hit! Help! Someone, help!" He eased Suzannah down onto the marble floor.

"No, not on my back. The pain...."

She couldn't catch her breath. Everything hurt. She wanted to scream. To cuss.

So, *this* was the delayed pain response she'd been hearing about her whole career.

"I'm fine." She pressed a palm toward Levi to calm him. He was showing signs of shock—pale, clammy skin, shallow, rapid breathing, pupils dilated. She patted his cheek.

"Son, I'm all right. Take a deep breath."

A warm sensation tickled the back of her knee. She pulled up the hem of her pants. Blood trickled down the back of her leg, coating the rim of her brand-new Pendleton socks. Wasting no time, she tugged at the heel of her favorite blue Luccheses.

"Help me get these boots off before I leak all over them."

Levi wrapped his fingers around the heel of her boot, then pulled and slid it off. He gasped when he looked inside. Eyes too wide—showing too much white—stared back at Suzannah. Color drained from his face. She reached for him, pulling him down to her.

"Here, sit down."

She knew he'd pass out otherwise. She clutched Levi to her side with her unaffected arm.

TWO DAYS LATER, she woke up in the hospital in Oklahoma City. Levi and her ex-husband, Frank "The Leech"—'cause he never knew when to let go—Harper, were playing Skip-Bo on her bedside table. Levi tossed his cards down on the table and crossed his arms.

"You're such a cheater, Dad, I swear."

The accusation—not lost on Suzannah—didn't appear to faze her ex. He just laughed, piled the cards up, and shuffled them over and over. Something about the chattering of the cards slapping together or maybe it was just Frank's face—irritated her. Why was he here? She pulled back the scratchy hospital blanket with a groan. Good grief, her throat was sore. Had they intubated her? Her hand reached for a Styrofoam cup filled with ice water sitting on the skinny table straddling her bed. Levi jumped up and rushed to her side.

"Mom! You're awake. Thank God. I was so worried."

She emptied the cup, then gave him a sleepy smile.

"You're not getting rid of me that easy." She held her cup out for a refill. "Pretty please?"

Levi poured more water into her cup. She sucked it down but before she could set the empty cup on the table, Levi leaned over her bed and crushed her face to his chest. He hugged her head, squeezing her face into his zippered Oklahoma State hoodie. After a moment of painful affection, she patted his back—tapping out of the fierce wrestling match.

"Babe, you're smashing my nose and cup."

"Oh, sorry." Levi released her.

"It's fine. My cup took the worst of it."

They looked at her mangled cup—love hurts sometimes—and laughed. Frank moved to the other side of her bed. He touched her blanketed toe. "Hope you don't mind me being here."

Suzannah extended a hand to Frank. "Not at all. Thanks for being here with our boy."

She hated to admit it, but Frank looked good. He'd been working out. His forearms and biceps were never so defined. She allowed her eyes to travel over Frank's rounded shoulders, up the thick muscles in his neck, across his well-defined and whiskered covered jaw to his perfectly shaped mouth—a mouth she knew quite well.

What kind of drugs do they have me on?

Frank smiled down at her. "Just thought Levi needed some company. And I guess I… I was worried about you too."

She watched his lips move as he spoke before looking away.

Stop it! Dead-end street.

Levi clung to his mom, patting the top of her hand with his.

"Goldfinger came by earlier—said your would-be assassin hung himself in his jail cell. Can you believe it? He's dead!"

That particular bit of news could have waited, but Levi knew his mother was a rip-the-Band-Aid-off kind of gal. She took a deep breath and blew it out, allowing the news to settle on her—a freezing, blinding fog. Questions burned in her mind. Questions she wanted and intended to ask the shooter herself. Was he hired to kill her? If so, by whom? Had she done something to him personally? Did he really think shooting her would somehow make him famous?

She shrugged her shoulders at the unanswered questions but immediately regretted it. Pain stabbed her in place. She stared at Levi, not speaking until the pain subsided.

"What else did Goldfinger say?"

"That's it. Sorry, Mom."

Frank ran his thumb over the back of her hand. "That'll save the taxpayers some money, at least." Her spine stiffened at his touch.

"What's with the name Goldfinger, anyway?" Frank's thick eyebrows arched high on his scrunched forehead—furrows like the Golden Arches appeared.

Mickey-D's french fries and ketchup sound amazing right now!

She pulled her hand free from Frank's. "Long story. Basically, Goldfinger is gifted at finding items in inmates' body cavities—contraband."

Frank made a disgusted face, pretending to gag. Levi just laughed—he knew the story well by now. As Suzannah ran her fingers through her hair, she considered telling Frank he should leave. She attempted to comb her hair with her fingers but gave up after feeling just how many tangles there were.

"Ugh! Time to change the oil in this hair. How long have I been here?"

"Two days."

This from Frank. He leaned a hip against her bed. "They had to do surgery to remove a .22 round from your chest.

"The doctor said you're lucky you got shot because...." He stopped talking, his mouth hung open as he exchanged glances with Levi. The muscles in Levi's jaw tensed as he stared back at his father. Suzannah's eyes bounced between them, then stared at Frank.

"It's a good thing I was shot, because... why?"

Frank wouldn't meet her eyes. Instead, he fished around on Suzannah's bed for the remote and the nurse's call button. He found the controller and clicked the button multiple times until Suzannah pulled it out of his hands.

"What the hell is going on? One of you spill it."

Silence. She stared hard at Frank. When he wouldn't meet her eyes, she turned to Levi. She pressed her lips together and squinted her eyes—giving Levi "the look."

"Now!" she demanded.

"May I help you?" The nurse's voice crackled out of the remote, interrupting the tension. Frank leaned over the bed, directing his voice toward the controller Suzannah held.

"Get the doctor, my wife is awake."

Suzannah eyeballed Frank.

We haven't been married in what, ten years?

"Wife?"

He didn't answer. She stared at Levi, but he dropped his eyes to his shoes. So, she squeezed his fingers.

"Tell me. Whatever it is, honey, just tell me."

Another moment passed before Levi choked out the words.

"It's cancer."

Then he crumpled into the chair beside her bed and covered his eyes with his hands. She recalled Frank's words. "...doctor said you're lucky you got shot."

Lucky?

She thought back over the years—all the purchased lottery tickets, raffle tickets, all the times she called trying to win some radio contest. Not once had she ever won. Anything. She couldn't even win auctions where she alone was the deciding factor. *Oh, yeah, I'm lucky all right.*

Her luck was changing—she'd finally won. Hit the jackpot, in fact!

A .22-caliber round changed everything. Fired at close range, piercing her back just below her body armor, the bullet tore through her flesh, went right through her kidney, and broke a rib—slowing it down just enough before it could perforate her intestines.

Talk about lucky.

A four-hour surgery repaired most of the damage and retrieved the mangled but intact ball of lead. Without that small caliber round, and subsequent imaging, she never would have known she had stage three metastatic breast cancer—likely, until it was too late.

THE SURGERIES, AND the chemo which followed, were brutal. A double mastectomy with reconstructive surgery, double breast augmentation, a skillful tattoo artist—known for creating beautiful nipples—five rounds of chemo, and she was back. Back in the saddle. Literally.

Two years and twenty pounds lighter, Suzannah treated herself to a well-deserved, solo vacation in New Mexico—Santa Fe, Ojo Caliente, Angel Fire, Taos. She'd managed her sheriff duties through all of her surgeries and chemo—only taking the minimum amount of time off work. But now, she needed time away. Time to truly recuperate. The sheriff's office was in good hands with Goldfinger. For two weeks she hit her favorite spas, mineral springs, restaurants, shops, and most of all—horseback trail rides.

She rested her hand on the horse's powerful hindquarters as they climbed up and around scraggly sagebrush on the Santa Fe hillside. The rented roan was gentle, lowering her head without hesitation when asked to. Before climbing on, Suzannah, a longtime horsewoman, walked the horse around and around inside the riding stables' sandy pen. She'd never splurged and ridden at Bishop's Lodge before. The posh lodging establishment north of Santa Fe in the Tesuque Valley edged the Santa Fe National Forest, boasting of 450 acres of scenic trails overlooking the Sangre de Cristo Mountain Range.

"That's the grandma horse right there, ma'am. She'll behave for you."

Suzannah smiled at the wrangler in his tight Wranglers, merely nodding her head in reply. She wouldn't climb on a horse if she didn't know—for herself—if the horse was trustworthy. She asked the mare to back, to stand still, to move her hip and shoulder off to the left and right. Willow, the seven-year-old former ranch horse, was a good mount.

Willow's pale face and sky-blue eyes were mysterious, haunting. She led the horse over to the mounting block, climbed the two wooden steps, and waited.

The wrangler's dark eyes met her hazel ones. "Looks like you know your way around horses, ma'am." His callused hands rubbed Willow's forehead.

"I know a little. Willow does appear to be a good mount, thanks."

The wrangler pushed up the brim of his hat with one finger and smiled at Suzannah. He held Willow's reins, motioning to Suzannah with his other hand.

"Go ahead. Mount up."

Suzannah slipped the toe of her new Dan Post boots into the left stirrup and swung her right leg over the back of the horse. The wrangler stepped closer. "Nice boots!" He circled his hands around her left stirrup and bootheel, ensuring its placement in the stirrup. Then he made minor, but likely unnecessary, adjustments to her rigging—tightening the cinch, tucking in the latigo. Suzannah smiled down at him—pink spread across his leathered cheeks.

"There ya go. You're all set."

He shot her a wink before pulling down the brim of his felt hat.

They followed the other horses and riders out of the aged, fir-logged pen, Willow's hoofs clomping a steady rhythm. Suzannah fought the urge to turn in the saddle and look back at the wrangler. She laughed, readjusting her seat in the saddle.

Like I have the time or energy for a man in my life.

Dust floated in the cool mountain air as the trail serpented piñon and ponderosa pines, climbing in elevation. For the next hour, Suzannah's body synced to the swaying of her horse. The high-desert air stung her nostrils, filling her lungs with forest-scented oxygen as she thought back over the last two weeks.

It's been a good trip. Especially Ojo Caliente Spa. So rejuvenating—the mineral springs, massages, meditating.

Eyes closed, she gripped the saddlehorn—trusting Willow. Trusting herself.

Tomorrow, it was back to the grindstone, back to major headaches—a detention officer in the jail stood accused of having sex with an inmate.

When the cat's away....

Goldfinger wrote up the paperwork, but Sheriff Harper would formally file with the Logan County district attorney. Then there were staff meetings, budget shortfalls to face, the Sheriff & Peace Officer Association meeting next week—she hadn't even started on her presentation. Not to mention the hundreds of nonemergency emails and phone calls she had to return. The weight of her position steadily climbed up her arm and rested on her shoulders—an ape with a bad attitude.

Back in Oklahoma, she stepped from her air-conditioned Tacoma into 105 degrees of scorching stickiness. Her emerald blouse melted to her skin. She pulled the poly-cotton blend—matching her eyes—away from her skin, wishing she were back in Santa Fe. She surveyed her beloved home and 160 acres just east of Guthrie—land her great-grandfather claimed in the 1889 land run. The late afternoon sun dipped toward the horizon, its summer rays—a hot haze—discolored everything. Off toward the east, white cumulous clouds churned higher and higher teasing of rain. Unseen cicadas clicked loud, their high-pitched shrills synchronizing with her tinnitus. A harvester team had come while she was away, leaving her wheat fields nothing but rows of tan stubble. Her pond, nearly evaporated, lay still as death. Not a breath of air moved over its calm surface. Still, her heart was light. She was home.

Home. What a weird word—emotion, physicality, memories.

She stretched, grateful to have the nine-hour drive behind her. Levi's Mustang sat in the driveway, but he hadn't greeted her. Neither had her dogs. Her heart flip-flopped in her chest. Had something happened to them? All her senses on high alert—she touched the butt of the .357 on her hip—reassurance. Where were Levi and her hounds?

Please, God, let them be okay.

She found them in the living room.

Levi sat in the V-section of her black leather sectional with controller in hand, playing a video game on her ninety-eight-inch television set—the volume at a ridiculously high level.

No wonder the dogs hadn't heard the gravel pop on my tires announcing my arrival.

Pete and RePete were also on the couch—they knew better. The German shepherds came to life when she swung the front door open.

"Hello, hello!"

Her three wayward loves bounced from their perches and surrounded her at once—two of them wagging their tails.

"Mom!"

"You didn't lock the door, Levi, and you know I don't like the dogs on the couch. Why I ought to...." She slid her arm around his neck, wrapping his head in a mock neck restraint. "As punishment, you have to unload the truck."

Levi made fake choking sounds until she slid her arm from his neck and encircled him in a bear hug. Outside, he pushed his arm through as many shopping bag handles as he could carry at one time.

"What'd you buy me?"

Suzannah smiled at him. "Jewelry!"

THE NEXT MORNING, suited up in her Class-A Logan County Sheriff's Office uniform—complete with brown slacks, taupe shirt, and a black baseball cap with the word *Sheriff* across the front, she walked out the front door of her house. She noted her garden alongside the sidewalk—some needing immediate attention, some beyond help.

She carried her twelve-gauge shotgun in one hand and her AR-15 in the other. As she neared her patrol car just off the concrete pad, she noticed pointy-toed boot prints in the dirt near the trunk of her car. She followed the prints around to the Charger's side doors, as well.

Suzannah surveilled the scene for the trespasser—around her yard, the front of her house, and into the tree line. Nothing. After securing her weapons in her patrol car, she pressed the lock button on the key fob hanging from her gun belt. Then she went back inside to wake Levi. She shook his shoulder until one eyelid raised revealing a cornflower blue peeper. He moaned.

"Levi, wake up. Listen to me. There were fresh boot prints around my patrol car like someone was considering breaking in to my car. You absolutely *have* to keep the doors locked. Do you hear me? And call me if you see anyone."

"Okay, Mom. I will."

She went out through the garage—hit the opener button on the wall and waited. The garage door squeaked as the metal rollers traced the tracks pulling the door up. As the door rose, a pair of legs appeared—someone stood in the driveway facing the garage door. Suzannah cleared leather—pulling her service weapon from its safety holster. She stepped behind the front of her truck for cover. The stranger, a Caucasian male in his mid-thirties, approximately five feet, ten inches and 185 pounds, stood in her driveway. His cowboy boots, knee-torn jeans, and Carhartt tee shirt were covered in what looked like dried blood. Half of the hair on his blond head stood on end—the other half mashed against his skull, bits of grass and dirt throughout. He lifted an arm to shield his eyes against the rising sun, trying to see inside the dark garage. Dried blood covered his face and arms.

"Hey, Sheriff, you in there?"

Suzannah remained silent, sizing him up. Her ire for his intrusion into her personal space a knuckle on a cheese grater.

"Sheriff, I need your help."

Seeing no weapons, Suzannah stepped out from behind the Tacoma, holstered her weapon, and approached him with caution. The thump of her quickened pulse tapping at her temple—a drummer on speed.

"Been in some sort of accident, sir?"

The stranger nodded his head. He slid his hands inside the front pocket of his jeans, his eyes ticking from side to side uncontrollably.

Resting nystagmus. *Drunk. Way drunk.*

"Go ahead and take your hands out of your pockets for me, please."

He jerked his hands free and stuck them high in the air. "Oh, sorry."

He stepped back three or four steps, his hands still in the air.

Not too unsteady on his feet. *Professional drunk?*

"No worries, you can put your hands down. Are you hurt? Do you need an ambulance?"

He lowered his hands. "No, I'm fine." But his hands seemed unwilling to rest at his sides—they rubbed his face, his belly, his arms—then he pointed off toward the highway.

"Had a little fender bender."

"Someone else hurt?"

"No." He turned his body away, staring off in the direction he pointed. Suzannah sidestepped to face him again. The hair on the back of her neck rising. Using her handheld radio she'd pulled off her gun belt, she called dispatch.

"County, I've been approached at my residence about a crash on the highway—party involved will be with me in my vehicle. If you will, send a deputy to meet us at highway one-oh-five and Douglas Boulevard."

The scratchy voice on the radio replied, a deputy was en route. Suzannah's hands clasped together in front of her body at her waistline—the stranger throwing danger vibes like daggers.

"Sir, whose blood is all over you?"

He looked down at his hands and arms—down at his clothes. His shoulders lifted in a shrug. "Don't know." He turned again—still angling away from her.

"Let's go find your car. Hop in. Have any ID on you?"

The stranger turned toward her patrol car—no blood on his backside, no gun in his waistband. He slid a wallet out of his back pocket and fumbled for his license.

"You wouldn't have any weapons on you, would you, Mister Hobbs?" She smiled at the name on his Oklahoma driver's license. David Crockett Hobbs—Davy Crockett.

"...no guns, knives, bombs...?"

Davy Crockett laughed, patting himself down by touching the front pockets and then the back pockets of his jeans. "No. You can search me if you're afraid."

Suzannah laughed, closing the distance between them.

"We ask everyone the same thing before we allow them into our patrol cars. We also pat them down—standard procedure."

His lips pulled crooked across his teeth as his mouth attempted a smile. She motioned for him to turn around by spinning her index finger around in a circle.

"Interlace your fingers behind your head and spread your legs for me."

He complied but turned his head to look at Suzannah.

"You *are* afraid, aren't you?"

Bloodshot, watery eyes.

"Don't move." With one hand, she grabbed his interlaced fingers, squeezing them hard as she patted him down.

Nothing.

She patted him on the back like they were long lost friends.

"Go ahead and get in."

They drove her gravel lane in silence. At the highway, she stopped and cracked her window. Her passenger, odiferous.

Strong odor associated with an alcoholic beverage on his breath and person.

"Which way is your car?"

"Uh, that way." He pointed left.

Suzannah looked left, right, left, pressed on the accelerator, and turned left. When she did, Davy Crockett lunged across her center console, gripping the butt of her holstered pistol and yanked. But the stage-two security holster held the pistol in place. Simultaneously, Suzannah stomped on the brake and scrunched her body into a ball, head tucked toward him, wedging her elbow over the outside of the holster.

"Stop!"

He fought for a better grip on her pistol, grunting with effort. He ripped at her elbow and hands that she'd wrapped around the holstered pistol. Her scream part battle cry, part command.

"Stop!"

Suzannah clamped down tighter on her holster using her head and torso as a shield.

"Stop or I'll shoot you."

He loosened his grip momentarily to draw his fist back. Then he punched away at her skull—*ONE, TWO*—the blows temporarily stunning her. As adrenaline stampeded through her veins, she knew what she must do. With her left hand, she fumbled for her backup weapon stored in the side door pocket. Once her fingers wrapped around the pistol grip, she shoved the .380 up under his chin with a gratifying clunk as his teeth crashed together.

"Stop now or I'll kill you."

HE WAS HANDCUFFED, Mirandized, and seat-belted in the front passenger seat of her patrol car by the time her deputy arrived to work the crash. Under Miranda, Davy Crockett Hobbs admitted that he tried to take her weapon because he thought she was going to take him to jail. He really didn't want to go to jail.

The deputy found the wreckage about a quarter of a mile down the highway—a hefty six-point buck still lodged in the windshield. As the deputy worked the collision, Suzannah transported the prisoner to jail. As usual, she drove the back roads. As they passed the Scottish Rite Temple, her prisoner glared at her stoic profile.

"Women shouldn't be in law enforcement."

Suzannah threw her head back and laughed—a hard, full belly laugh. She gave her passenger a brief sideways glance.

Dumbass.

"You probably think you're the first person to tell me that. Don't you?"

—Betsy Randolph holds degrees in journalism, organizational leadership, horticulture, and a master of fine arts in creative writing. She served twelve years in the U.S. Army Reserves as a military police and drill sergeant. She retired in 2020 from the Oklahoma Department of Public Safety after twenty-seven

years in law enforcement. Her writing has appeared in Southern Literary Review, The Journal Record, Woods Reader Magazine—*among others. She is the author of three adult novels and two middle-grade readers. Betsy lives near Guthrie, Oklahoma, with her husband, George. Together they have two grown children and seven grandchildren.*

RIVER OF RETRIBUTION

VICKY J. ROSE

THE WARDEN IN his way had been a kind man. There were only a handful of women prisoners in the Walls Unit—in for infanticide or, like me, murder. We were housed with the men, with complete lack of privacy and subjected to daily threats of rape that were sometimes followed through. When the warden found out I could cook and had no propensity for violence, he put me in the kitchen. It meant constant hot, steady work and heavy lifting of huge pots and gunnysacks of foodstuffs seven days a week, but it came with special privileges. I got to sleep on a cot in an equally stifling broom closet under the watchful eye of a bent little man with corded muscles like steel ropes by the name of Chancy. He was a local man, and although he cursed me continuously, he never let anyone get close enough to harm me. I was going to miss Chancy.

The warden's words brought me out of my reverie.

"The state apologizes deeply for this grave miscarriage of justice, Missus Fowler."

I nodded and stood up.

"Am I free to go?"

"Yes, dear," the warden said, surprising me with his sympathy. He stood, walked around his desk, and took my hand.

"Evie, don't go back to Carp Town. Go somewhere else and start your life anew."

I nodded again, still in shock.

"Say goodbye to Mister Chancy for me, will you?"

The warden nodded and reached inside his coat pocket.

"I almost forgot to give this to you. Chancy wanted to write you a reference in his own hand."

I took the soiled folded paper and opened it.

Miss Evie, she r a fine cook.
Signed, Chancy Gilhooly

Filled with emotion, I nodded again and turned to the guard who would lead me out of the prison unit. We walked across the yard and out the gate in silence. When I was on free soil, the guard spoke.

"Goodbye, Evie. I know you made do with what you had, and you cooked the best you could. We all appreciated it."

My mouth opened, but no words came out. I nodded and watched as he shut the gate and disappeared inside. I stared at the red brick walls one last time before turning. A carriage rode by, the horses clippety-clopping so loudly I jumped. A big spotted hound sniffed my shoe. I had not seen a dog in three years. I wanted to put my hand out to pet it, but drew back. I did not realize being set free would cause so much fear in me.

I took a deep breath and set out to find the nearest stagecoach station. The settlement I got from the state for wrongful imprisonment was pitifully small, but it would get me, if not to Carp Town, close to it. For I had every intention of going back. The killer, who on his deathbed had confessed to the murder I had been incarcerated for, had died before he could name the person who had hired him. But I knew who she was, and if it was the last thing I did, I would make sure she suffered for it every day of her life until one of us died.

The square around Huntsville buzzed with activity. I tried not to shy at every sound and to ignore the curious stares of people who must have heard of my release. Passing by store windows seemed unreal, especially when I caught a glimpse of my reflection. At first, I wondered who that slight woman was. She looked about to blow away. When I realized I was seeing myself, I stopped to stare. The hair that had once been so thick and luxurious was now dry, thinning, and beginning to streak with gray. I looked down at my red and roughened hands, covered in burn marks. I closed my eyes for a moment, thought about my mission, took a deep breath, and continued onward.

The stationmaster informed me the next stage would arrive first thing in the morning. It would get me within ten miles of Carp Town, but that was close enough. He assured me I would be able to rent a horse from there. I sat down to wait, having no desire to seek out a room and face more stares and questions. The stationmaster kindly let me spend the night sleeping on the bench. He fussed over me a little, and there seemed to be no way I could make him understand that the thought of sleeping in a soft hotel bed after what I had been through was at this point, overwhelming. To be told, "You are free now," and be thrown out into the world alone, with no prior notice, was almost too much for me. Only the desire for retribution motivated me to keep going.

The four-horse coach leaving Huntsville the next morning contained three drummers, two lawyers, and myself, the only woman. I seemed to have lost the ability to make small talk and could barely put two words together. One of the drummers refused to be discouraged and began a line of smooth sweet talk that would have made a grandma swoon. But I had learned the sugary ones could turn on a Liberty dime to become the meanest and foulest of men, so his patter was wasted on me. It disgusted one of the lawyers to no end, and when he and the other attorney figured out who I was, they were full of questions that I demurred from answering. I was grateful I had retained some manners, but I saw no reason to open my life to them.

We stopped at swing stations and once at a home station for food, but this coach traveled all night, which suited me. As the coach swayed back and forth, the men expelled gas and snored, but I was used to that.

I spent most of the night trying to move a sleeping drummer off my shoulder. Compared to the nightmare of prison with its threat of violence and rape, it was like a hayride in the countryside on a moonlit night.

I rolled the canvas up that covered the window and looked out, my arm on the edge, and breathed deeply. It felt so good to be free, but I could not shake the anger and hatred that burned within my heart.

Despite being cut off from the outside world in so many ways, gossip ran rife in the prison. I knew Rafe's parents had encouraged him to divorce me. They had pushed for an annulment, hoping to erase my very existence, I suppose, but the judge had told them not to be ridiculous and granted a divorce without comment. Rafe had waited a barely respectable six months before marrying Eldora. A baby had been born three months later, which meant Rafe and Eldora had wasted no time crying over me. She had claimed it was premature, but it is hard to justify a seven-pound baby as early. The baby had died, nevertheless. I was sorry about that, but my prison cynicism kicked in, and I wondered if Eldora had found a way to get rid of an embarrassingly large premature baby.

She had found a way to get rid of me. Me, married to the incredibly handsome son of a wealthy planter. There were fine horses, champagne and oysters at Christmas, and wonderful balls that were attended by every important politician in the state. I had been giddy with love and excitement.

It started with gossip. Someone claimed that somebody said I had been seen kissing Rafe's best friend. It was always "so and so said he heard it," and it could never be traced back to the original talebearer. And then Rafe's friend had been found murdered with a pair of my sewing scissors. A witness, who later turned out to be the real killer, had claimed to see me running away from the scene of the crime. The theory had been the friend threatened to tell Rafe about us, and I had stabbed him to keep him quiet. Someone had made sure that theory had made the rounds, too. The picture sharpened in my brain, perhaps by the night air, and I realized Eldora had also gotten rid of a friend of Rafe's who disliked her at the same time.

"Madam," one of the attorneys sitting across from me said in a low tone. I jumped.

"Yes?"

"Do you know who hired the man to incriminate you?"

I thought for a moment before answering.

"Yes."

He was silent for several seconds, weighing his next words.

"Did you know your ex-father-in-law died last year?"

"I had heard that. Is… is my ex-husband living in his father's house now?"

It had been worrying me, how to escape detection from their myriads of servants.

"No, they were forced to sell it. He still lives in the same house he lived in when he was married to you. Things are not going so well for him financially."

It was hard for me to digest that. There had been so much money….

"Thank you for telling me." I turned and looked back at the darkened landscape as the stagecoach jostled by trees and cacti on its rough and lonely road.

He drew me back into the conversation.

"If you will allow me, please take my card in case you should need assistance. I feel you were badly represented before."

He handed the card over. I could not read it in the dark, but I thanked him and put it in my pocket. I had no intention of killing Eldora or Rafe. Only to make their lives as miserable as mine had been the last three years.

The liveryman did not want to rent me a horse. I had arrived that afternoon and gone straight there, not wishing to see anyone who might recognize me. He did not know who I was, however. His complaints were about females in general.

"Women have no sense about horses. They ride and ride them without rest, neglecting to give them food and water."

It was only after I bought a large amount of oats to carry with me

and made multiple promises that he allowed me an old horse that had
seen many better days, but I was not in a race. He was dark with no
distinguishing marks, and that was all I cared about. That would be all
I needed, for someone to catch a flash of a blazing white star.

I knew every back trail there was to the house that had once been
my home. The landscape had changed little. I worried about the dogs
barking. Would they still recognize me? But I remembered Eldora had
despised dogs, and she might have made Rafe get rid of them.

The sun was sinking low when I neared the house. This time, clouds
covered the sky, but still I waited, hiding in the woods. As it grew later,
I drew closer. Rafe rode up to the house, dismounting and taking his
horse into the barn. As I looked at his fine figure, so different from the
scarecrows I had been around in the prison, I felt a lump come into
my throat. He had not believed me. He thought I was a murderess.
Why, Rafe? Why?

It dawned on me no dogs had barked in greeting. That made the
reconnaissance I was on tonight much easier. Rafe and his mother had
been deeply superstitious, and I would easily be able to frighten him
with ghostly apparitions and eerie sounds. Eldora was sharper and would
be harder to scare, but if I wanted, I could start a gossip campaign that
would put hers to shame. But tonight, I would do nothing but scope out
the territory and get as close to the house as I could without detection.

Rafe walked back into the house. In a little while, matches were
set to lamps. Figures crossed back and forth in front of the windows. I
waited until it was fully dark before creeping forward.

I tripped over a log and lay in the dirt for several minutes, taking
deep breaths and trying to slow my pounding heart. Getting up on all
fours, I felt a burr stick into my hand and had to stop to pull it out.
On my feet at last, I made my way to one of the opened windows. Just
as I approached, the clouds let loose a rain shower. Eldora walked to
the window to shut it, and I threw myself against the side of the house
to escape detection.

Even with the window closed, I could hear their raised voices. I crept underneath the window and lifted my head enough to peek into the parlor Rafe had carried me into on our wedding night.

It contained more lace and knickknacks than it had then, and it seemed to be crammed with more furniture. Expensive furniture. Rafe and Eldora were not sitting comfortably on it, but were pacing about, having an argument.

"Why can't you have my supper ready when I come in?" Rafe snapped. It shocked me to see what had once been a smooth face was now filled with deep lines.

"Because you won't let me have any servants except that stupid, slatternly girl who won't do anything unless I threaten to slap her."

Eldora did not look so good either. She had grown heavy, and her face looked puffy and blotchy.

They continued back and forth, bickering about money. She spent too much. He did not make enough. He was stupid. Why couldn't he be more like his father? He began to criticize her cooking, her looks, her irresponsible spending. A river of spite and loathing poured from each of them.

Crouching in the rain, listening, water dripped from my eyelashes and ran in rivulets off my nose and down my face. I felt the rainwater coursing down my body, soaking my skin, penetrating all the way to my heart. It and the angry words inside the house began washing three years of hatred away.

I stood upright, not caring if they saw me but sure they were too involved in berating one another to notice anything else, anyway. Turning, I walked back to where I had tied the rented horse. He would be glad to get back to the stable.

The livery owner was pleased to see me and even more happy when I did not demand he buy back the unused oats. I left, walking down the wooden sidewalk. To my relief, the stagecoach station was still open. I walked in, conscious of dripping all over the floor. The stationmaster looked at me with shock but did not complain about the water.

"I want to buy a ticket."

"Where to, ma'am?"

"The farthest place the stage will take me where you think I might get a job as a cook."

I lifted my chin and raised myself up.

"I have references."

—Vicky J. Rose also writes under the names of V.J. Rose and Easy Jackson. Having grown up in a small Texas town with a Wild West past, she strives to impart the excitement of the Old West to her readers.

DEATH & SINGULAR OBLIGATIONS

RANDI SAMUELSON-BROWN

DEATH ENTERED THE room. A presence in the corner, lurking by the door, could be felt, if not seen. I leaned forward and lifted one of her hands as she lay in her deathbed and wondered, not for the first time, how much she understood and whether she cared. Did she feel the presence of death, or even the pressure of my warm hands? The blood cooled in her veins despite the layer of blankets on top of her.

Maybe, by this point, nothing mattered so much, anyhow.

SHE'D FALLEN FROM her horse—and only by the slimmest of odds someone passed by her spread and found her and didn't abandon her to fate. No, the stranger rode to our stage stop and found me carrying water from the well to the station. He waited for me to near—didn't even bother to dismount but stayed in the saddle. The belly and legs of his horse were snow-caked, whiskers coated by frost. Bundled up against the weather, the rider's beard hid most of his features, but a pair of beady dark eyes locked into mine.

"Found an old woman due east laying in a heap. Looked like she tried to mount her horse and fell. I carried her into the house and got her in bed, started a fire so she didn't damn well freeze to death, and took care of the horse. That woman needs tending to, and I ain't the one to do it."

I set the bucket down and stared back. "And because I'm female, somehow I am?"

He shifted, the saddle creaking from the cold and his weight. He spat off to the side, halfway toward bothered. "You're a neighbor, ain't you? The choice is yours. But she'll die if left alone. Hell, she might go ahead and die anyhow."

The wind blew from the north, and I tightened my father's heavy coat around me knowing full well who he spoke about. "Her name is Marybeth McCarthy."

I hadn't uttered her name in years and memories stabbed deep, but it made no odds to the stranger on the horse. He tipped his hat and rode off leaving turmoil in his wake—abandoning me in a severe quandary.

In the mournful cold wind bearing down and bending the pines I struggled—the bucket of water abandoned at my feet, surface rippling. The stranger's back diminished in size, but his words loomed large. For that moment I almost didn't heed the cutting wind but stalled instead, frozen, like the landscape, in place. Wondering when old debts were ever truly repaid—debts, that deep down, might not have even been mine to pay in the first place.

I didn't owe her a damned thing, but she owed me fifty dollars for work I'd done for her. A fifty dollars agreed to. A fifty dollars she never paid. To make matters worse, she showed no signs of making good. At first, she recognized the debt, but always offered one excuse after another as to why she couldn't pay. Later, she refused to acknowledge the debt existed at all, and it drove a wedge between us. A person was only as good as their word, and we all knew as much.

Hers had proven worthless.

"Hellfire," I cursed aloud, although the bleak winter day didn't give a damn. Stronger words were required to sum up the grievances that filled the territory, but in the end, I shrugged knowing the answer I didn't exactly welcome.

Marybeth's solitary fate might one day well be my own. That was the part that caught me and held fast.

>······ ⇒⁄⇐ ······<

THE STEEL BANDS of the plank door groaned as I pushed through and abandoned the bucket upon the table. My father glanced over at me as he tended to the fire which never fully heated the room in the deep winter months, leaving the cold to linger around the edges. "Problems?"

"A rider said Marybeth McCarthy is in a bad way." I pulled off his coat and hung it on its peg.

He threw the wood into the flames and straightened, knowing where the conversation headed. "It's pretty cold outside."

I offered a half shrug, internally debating. "Guess I'll go. You can manage everything here, can't you?"

He nodded, reserved in manner. "Doubt she'd do same for you, you know."

His words cut deep because they held more than a fair amount of truth.

Yet, I rose to her defense, although my words sounded small. "Once she might have. Would have, even. When she was younger."

"Mebbe. You'd better pack some food just in case." Bothered, he scratched the back of his neck, ruffling his hair like bird feathers. "What are you going to do if she dies? You can't dig a grave into frozen ground, you know."

That practicality pulled me up short. "I... I hadn't thought that far."

He shook his head. "You'd better. I guess we could go back for her in the spring with a wagon, after the thaw. Bring back her horse, or horses, in the event she can't take care of them. I don't know what she's got out there anymore."

That was just the thing. None of us ventured out to her claim anymore. We'd all quit trying somewhere along the line. I stopped after I'd worked for two months at the struggling miner's boardinghouse she'd once run. When the claim ran dry, so did they.

Nevertheless, I'd take along a pencil and paper. Just in case I needed to leave a note alongside her frozen, stiff body. A solitary corpse left waiting for the thaw.

Then again, she was mean enough to go on living.

GOD KNOWS I didn't want to do it, but in the end, I rode—the horse's breath forming clouds into the gray day, the wind rushing through the pines and sounding like water. With only the wind for company, the abandoned mine tailings provided stark testament of when their veins ran dry. In truth, riches seldom came, and if they did, they proved but fleeting. This gulch once heaved and teemed with all that accompanied mining, but that time had since passed. All that remained were the listing structures and the mountains turned inside out in the search for gold. The old winding mine road climbed and snaked to the next valley over. Despite the hard lessons that hit the district wholesale, my father and I were better off than most because we served a need—people needed to tend to their horses and often required a place to stay. But we both knew that our stage stop would come to an end one day as the traffic already dwindled. People rushed off to follow the next big strike as with the nature of all mining camps and districts.

None of us blamed them, but it didn't make things easy.

The bleak mountains mocked in silent judgment of the follies of man… and woman. Towering, they would outlast us all, but the thought didn't make me feel any better as I argued with myself the entire five bone-chilling miles to Marybeth's spread. Reluctant, and riding face into the wind, I fought my way through the winter to sit watch over an ungrateful soul.

And despite my bitterness… I rode.

She'd turned mean and quarrelsome in the most recent of years, and that was saying something. Those in the area who dealt with her knew as much—and eventually they left her alone. She remained steadfast and stubborn in the old mining district that had dwindled away to little more than dust. Well-meaning people once tried to convince her to move along into the next town, but that old stubborn biddy held firm and flat-out refused. That was one thing about her. She always thought she knew better than everyone else. Time spent with only ghosts for company had worsened her temperament and clouded her judgment. Everyone knew that solitary people went crazy in the mountains. It was all just a matter of time.

None of which I wanted to happen to me—twenty-seven years old and no prospects in sight. But the dilemma staring me down felt plenty uncomfortable.

Upon reaching the ridge overlooking her spread, I paused the horse to gain my bearings and composure. Smoke rose from the boardinghouse's far chimney, although it trailed off into wisps and ribbons. She lived in the back part of the large structure, leaving the rest of the building to rot. Her corral, located between the house and the barn, appeared unused, although in good enough condition. A few old outbuildings bore down against the wind and the snow.

Easing my mount down the slope, we rode straight into the yard and stopped in front of the barn. I was determined that before tending to another blessed thing, I would take care of my horse. The barn door squealed opened loud enough to alert her if she were still conscious.

But her door never opened to check up on the sound.

Glancing around the barn's interior, I led my horse into the barn to find her horse put away and awaiting in its stall, just like the stranger claimed. The barn held plenty of hay—enough to last the winter. I unsaddled my horse and led him into an empty stall—clean enough—thinking how once upon a time they all had been full. I fetched some hay and checked on Marybeth's horse before grabbing a couple of nearby buckets and an ax and headed to the river.

She never had managed to get a well dug.

Or to be more exact, she hadn't managed to connive someone else into digging it for her.

Thankfully, beneath the frozen gray surface of the creek, rushing water still flowed and the ice bankside provided a wide enough opening to tip the pail into the frigid water. When finished, I delivered the first bucket into the stable to water both horses. Then I lugged the remaining bucket over to the old boardinghouse and pounded twice.

"Marybeth? It's me. Lenora. I'm coming on in."

No response as such, but a faint moan sounded. Either that, or it was the wind. Careful upon entering and using the door as something of a shield, the last thing anyone wanted was to find themselves staring down a rifle barrel aimed at the door. But on that day, no such thing happened. Instead, a lump stirred ever so slightly in the bed—Marybeth underneath a mound of quilts and surrounded by an overflow of debris.

The stench of urine and feces strong.

"Marybeth," I said again, setting the bucket down, catching my breath, and edging farther into the room and toward the bed.

One watery blue eye fluttered open like a fish. "Oh. It's you." Her words came out as an accusation.

Well, hell. At least she was still alive and as ungrateful as ever.

"A man rode by and said you fell off your horse. Claimed you were in a bad way, and I can see that you are."

"I was going for provisions. At least he bothered to help," she grumbled. "People used to do more for others."

Averting my face and holding not only my tongue but my breath, I snatched away the night pot and flung its contents out the door.

CARING FOR AN invalid, any invalid it must be admitted, has never been my strong point, no matter my sex. Yet I managed to do my best, using the ingredients brought along to cook a broth, hoping it might do her some good if I could get at least some of it down her.

Bracing her back, I lifted her into a half-reclining position, wedging my body behind hers. Although gaunt, she remained sturdy and still weighed plenty. I certainly hadn't meant to get this close to her, but it was the only way I could position her upright enough, so she didn't choke on the liquid. Her hair smelled something fierce. I managed to get a spoonful or three into her mouth—enough so that she rallied.

"I didn't figure you'd come," she accused, sounding, it must be admitted, strong considering her circumstance.

"Someone had to." My voice sounded cross to my own ears, but she never noticed. Or if she did, she couldn't have cared less. Feeling a trace of guilt, I tried again with another concerted effort. "How are you feeling now?"

"Like I got the piss beat out of me."

Stiffening, I persevered. "I meant, do you think any bones are broken or are you in pain?"

"Of course I'm in pain," she snapped. "Getting old is nothing but pain. You'll soon learn that for yourself."

Now, I wasn't going to take that. "Oh, you have thirty years on me. Maybe even more."

"Huh. I just took a hard fall when I got dizzy. Nothing's broken. Now get away from me and let me be."

Relieved to be released from her proximity and stench, I slipped out from behind and lowered her onto the bed, her eyes closed. "I'm staying the night. We'll see how you are in the morning," I informed, hoping like hell to be well shot of her come daybreak.

"I'll bet you think you'll get money off of me," she quarreled, eyes still closed and a voice that came out thin but laced with steel and fight.

My spine stiffened and a chill squeezed my stomach. "You know you'll die if you're left alone like this."

"And you'd like that, wouldn't you?"

"No." I was somewhat surprised that I actually meant it. "Not particularly. But most people would thank me—not give me grief. It's not like there's a line of people beating on the door to help you, you know."

To that she grumbled something undecipherable, before falling silent.

Of course, I wouldn't have been human if I hadn't wondered where she kept her money. Or at least the money she owed me, and whether she had any at all.

HER BREATH GREW ragged and shallow.

I sat watch by the crackling fire that evening as the shadows lengthened and drew in, feeling certain that death entered the room. A tin box sat upon the mantle over the fire and most likely contained anything important... like money and deeds. I left it where it rested, undisturbed.

A person kinder than myself would have cleaned or tried to organize the emptied tin cans, tattered papers with notes jotted down, scraps of cloth and clothing, and heaven only knew what else could be found in the detritus. A person with common sense would ask for her last wishes in the next lucid spell, but should I attempt that route, it would only saddle me with more responsibilities that truly weren't mine to shoulder. I'd given enough as it was. I had no obligation to do her bidding—as mean-spirited as that might strike. I knew women weren't supposed to say things like that or think in that way. But the Colorado mountains drove such niceties and replaced them with practicalities.

In the depths of the night, a moan and whimper roused me. Awaking with a start, the fire had dwindled.

"I'm still here, Marybeth."

"Water."

I brought her a cup and felt her forehead. Fever....

"How are you feeling now?" I cursed myself for asking such a stupid question.

"Not good. Worse."

It was possibly now or never. "I don't mean to pry, but do you have papers or anything in case... well. Just in case." The words came out as gentle as I could make them.

Her eyes snapped open, and her voice came out convicted and strong for a woman on her deathbed. "Hoping to see your name on them?"

"Don't be like that," I murmured, but had that been what I hoped? Probably so. Maybe I held on to the hope she might make matters right between us. I tried again. "This is your one chance to get your affairs in order, unless you figure someone else will be stopping by anytime soon."

"If I'd had children, they would do it."

"Well, you didn't." And that was the crux of it. Neither had I.

AFTER THAT SPARRING match I moved away, unwilling to offer more comfort. Judging by the strength of her voice, maybe she would get well, but that fever had me worried. Perhaps I should have ridden back to our stage stop and sent my father onward for a doctor. But in all likelihood, there was little anyone could do beyond that which I already offered. As the hours advanced, her breath took on a different hue and cry. Maybe that was what people called the death rattle. When that sound emerged, I moved my chair away from the fire to sit by her side... a dirty, smelly quilt wrapped around my shoulders to ward off the chill.

Taking one of her cold hands in mine, I sat and waited. Watching. Watching as I felt certain that death entered the room.

Her breath became even more labored and ragged. I squeezed her hand. Although weakened, she squeezed back.

"I'm here, Marybeth. Can you hear me?"

No response.

Her breath rattled more and more... until it didn't.

"Marybeth?"

No response. I felt her wrist for the pulse that wasn't.

Marybeth had passed over to the other side.

I released her hand, crossed both arms over her chest, and drew her quilt over her face, covering her from head to toe. Through the window glass, I noted the morning's cold light rose in the sky. I scanned the horizon and at the sky already turning blue. I thought the date was February 20th, but I might have been wrong on that count. Whatever the case, it would be close enough. Removing the paper and pencil from my bag, I wrote out the words,

Marybeth McCarthy died February 20, 1872.
Will return for the body, once the ground thaws and weather allows.

Signed,
Lenora Wolfe

Pinning the note to the quilt, I was loath to leave a dead body lying in a bed—but she wouldn't be the first—nor the last. Squatters would most likely find the cabin—but whether or not they chose to stay was none of my concern. My eyes traveled back to her strongbox. Surely it wouldn't hurt to look inside instead of leaving it all for any squatters to raid.

Grasping the box, I lifted it down and set it on the table and un-latched the lid. There was her claim and land title, and five gold coins with a paper wrapped around them.

For my funeral and burial

Words written in ink in a scraggy hand.

Fifty dollars in gold stood on the table before me.

I sighed and pocketed the coins.

Debt paid. Whether I carried out her last wishes for a funeral that no one would attend, I'd still purchase a pine box. Somehow, that seemed the least a body could do. Then I put on my coat and went to get her horse and mine.

I had plenty of time to think on the way back to the stage stop. Plenty of time to think of what to do with those fifty dollars and what they truly meant. The only thing I knew for certain was that the mountains we carved lives from remained just as firm and unyielding as ever. True, there were mining structures and dumps—some wagons and carts discarded where they stood—but the result remained the same. Death. Death came for us all in one fashion or another.

Of course, whether I wanted to or not, I'd come back in the spring for Marybeth's body.

Until then, I could only wonder what I'd find when the time came—knowing that I myself might suffer that same fate.

And of course, that was the part that got to me.

⊱┈┈┈⋅⧽⧼⋅┈┈┈⊰

—Randi Samuelson-Brown is originally from Golden, Colorado, but now lives in the rollicking city of Denver. A passion for Colorado history was instilled by her father from childhood, and to this day she feels haunted by the West's lesser-known histories—the dark side—and their long reach into the present. The Bad Old Days of Colorado: Untold Stories of the Wild West *(Two Dot, 2020), her first nonfiction, was a finalist in the 2021 Colorado Book Awards in History and was featured on C-SPAN.* The Western Horse: A Popular History of the Wild and Working Animal *is a 2025 Finalist for the Western Writers of America's prestigious Spur Award. She especially loves writing Western fiction—both historical and contemporary—with a nod to our roots. When not writing, in her free time Randi can be found riding horses and traveling around Colorado and the West, finding inspiration from people, places, and whispers from the past.*

WITS OVER WEAPONS

BILLIE HOLLADAY SKELLEY

IT WAS ALMOST evening when U.S. Deputy Marshal Bret Sharp halted his stallion beside a small cliff and stopped to look around. Experience had taught him to check out every site where his team camped. A few pines provided cover to the south, a thicket of shrubs stood to the west, and a small stream ran toward the east. They were near the Red River Valley, not far from the Texas border, and this was as close as he wanted to be.

Turning his broad shoulders to look behind, Sharp saw his young cook, Jed Cooper, approaching in the supply wagon. U.S. Deputy Marshal Ada Curnutt was riding alongside, and her Colt pistol and belt full of cartridges glinted in the sunlight.

Watching Curnutt approach, Sharp wondered for the hundredth time why this woman, the daughter of a Methodist minister, had decided to undertake the dangerous job of being a deputy marshal—an occupation that required so much commitment, courage, and resourcefulness. In Indian Territory, there weren't many female marshals, but Sharp knew Curnutt was up to the job. She had proven her worth several times when she had accompanied him on trips to bring in felons and fugitives, but he also knew her glistening gun wasn't even loaded. Curnutt didn't believe in carrying a gun—even in the line of duty. Her weapon, worn at his request, was more for show than anything else.

When Cooper and Curnutt were in range, Sharp called out to them.

"This will do for camp. Pull the wagon up beside this cliff."

Once in position, Sharp told Curnutt to get the prisoners out of the wagon.

Still mounted on his horse, Sharp watched as Curnutt took four men, one at a time, out of the wagon. He didn't anticipate any trouble from the young fellow charged with stealing horses or the old man wanted for bootlegging. It was the two redheaded cousins, James and Charles Gentry, that concerned him. Both men had a long history of crimes, ranging from cattle rustling and robbery to arson and murder. They made no effort to hide their hatred of all lawmen, but they were especially riled that a woman had been involved in their capture.

The four prisoners stared at Sharp. Tall and muscular, the deputy marshal was an imposing figure with his wide-brimmed white hat shading his blue eyes, the silver star shining on his chest, and the loaded Colt revolvers strapped at his sides.

The prisoners also studied Curnutt as she directed them toward a large log Cooper was positioning behind the wagon. Curls of long, dark hair and gray-green eyes were visible beneath her black hat. She wore a leather vest over her white shirt and a calf-length, divided skirt. Light from the fading sun reflected off her badge and the pistol at her side.

Curnutt instructed two of the men to sit on one side of the log, and then she placed the other two on the opposite end. Once all four men were seated, she shackled their feet together.

Sharp dismounted, gathered up another chain, and ran it through the shackles of the four prisoners. Then, he secured the chain to the rear axle of the wagon with a padlock.

"Who's next on the list?" Curnutt asked Sharp.

"Sam and Jack Hart. Two brothers wanted for forgery, bank robbery, and murder. They're the last ones we have warrants for... and when we take care of them, we can head back to Fort Smith."

"Are we going after them tomorrow?"

"That's the idea. I'm still thinking on a plan, but the Harts grew up in a house about six or seven miles south of here. Their mother still lives there."

Sharp grabbed the reins of Curnutt's horse and continued.

"If you fetch some water, I'll tie up the horses."

Curnutt went to get a bucket from the wagon. As she passed the prisoners, she heard James Gentry talking.

"It ain't right they let a woman arrest a man. Females should wear petticoats, not pistols."

"Listen, Gentry," Curnutt responded, "I was appointed to the marshal's service by U.S. Marshal William Grimes in 1893—more than two years ago. I can arrest any fugitive or felon, man or woman, I've got a warrant for—so just let it be."

Grabbing the bucket, she headed toward the stream.

"I don't care what she says," Charles Gentry told his cousin. "It just don't seem right for women to have authority... *legal* authority over men."

Sharp, who'd returned from settling the horses, overheard the remark.

"Shut your mouth, Gentry. Curnutt was hired because she can do the job. She believes in the law, and she's on friendly terms with the Cherokee, Chickasaw, and Choctaw. She even speaks some of their languages... and woman or not, I wouldn't advise you to test her."

"I know she's a marshal, but that still don't make it right."

"We'll be in Fort Smith soon," responded Sharp. "You'll have your day in court, and you can tell Judge Isaac Parker all your feelings about women."

"I ain't got nothing to lose," said Charles Gentry. "I might as well speak my mind. After all, the Hanging Judge is just as liable to hang me as not."

Sharp walked away, hoping the two cousins would settle down.

About an hour later, as Sharp and Curnutt watched, Cooper brought four bowls of soup, some bread, and tin cups full of water to the prisoners. As the young cook bent down to help the old bootlegger reach his food, Charles Gentry grabbed the cooking knife in Cooper's belt and tossed it, quick as lightning, at Sharp's chest.

The knife missed Sharp's torso, but lodged deep in his thigh.

As Sharp fell to the ground, Charles Gentry grabbed Cooper and started punching the young cook. From the ground, Sharp pulled his pistol, but didn't fire out of fear of hitting Cooper. The young cook managed to strike Gentry with one of the metal cups. He hit him so hard, Charles Gentry slumped over unconscious.

Then, James Gentry grabbed Cooper from behind and started choking him. As Cooper struggled to breathe, Sharp fired. He hit the prisoner's right arm. Screaming in pain, James Gentry released Cooper, and the cook scrambled away.

It all happened in a matter of seconds.

Flustered and alarmed, Cooper made his way to Sharp.

"I'm sorry, boss. I totally forgot about that knife."

Sharp had removed the blade. He was trying to stop the bleeding by pressing hard on his leg with his hands.

"Get me a rag or something."

Cooper ran toward the wagon, while Curnutt checked that all four prisoners remained securely shackled. Charles was still unconscious, but his breathing was regular, so she left him alone. James's wound appeared superficial, so she went back to check on Sharp.

"How deep is it?" she asked.

"Not too bad," he answered, "but I can't get the bleeding to stop."

Cooper returned with a bundle of rags. When he and Curnutt examined the wound, they realized it was quite deep. Cooper washed the wound with water, applied a clean rag, and wrapped his longest length of fabric tightly around Sharp's leg to apply pressure.

"I'm so sorry. I was cutting a carrot for the soup and forgot about the knife."

"It's all right, Cooper," answered Sharp. "I didn't see it, either, till it was too late. Don't worry, I'll live... but it sure wrecks my plans for tomorrow."

"What do you mean?" asked Curnutt.

"I was thinking I'd walk to the Hart's house and hide out nearby. Maybe try to get the jump on them when they came to visit their mother. The brothers supposedly visit her every other month... near the middle of the month. That's why I saved them till last. It being August thirteenth today, I figured they might arrive soon, but the problem... is that it's flat prairie south of here. If the Harts are hiding out somewhere, checking to see if the coast is clear, they'll see any rider on horseback miles away. That's why I was going to walk—to sneak up on them somehow."

"We'll worry about that tomorrow," said Curnutt. "For now, let's get you to bed so you can rest."

Working together, Cooper and Curnutt got Sharp to his bedroll. Cooper grabbed a wool blanket from the wagon to cover him. They watched over Sharp till his eyes closed.

"That wound is deep," Cooper told Curnutt. "I think we better head back tomorrow in case he needs a doctor."

"Let's see how he does tonight... and if the bleeding stops. He won't be happy letting the Hart brothers get away. I know him. He'll want to bring them in."

"I'll check his dressing during the night," Cooper promised, "and change it if need be."

"Give me a rag for Gentry's flesh wound, but wake me if there's any change in Sharp. I'll think... regarding what to do about the Harts."

CURNUTT WOKE EARLY the next morning. She dressed quickly and found Cooper kneeling over Sharp's leg.

"He's still sleeping. The bleeding stopped around two, but he's lost a lot of blood. I gave him whiskey for the pain."

"Have you talked to him?" asked Curnutt.

"No, he's been sleeping soundly."

"Well, I've decided about the Hart brothers. I'm going after them."

"No," said Cooper, for the first time really looking at her. "What on earth are you wearing?"

Curnutt had put on a shabby, gray dress. She had ripped one sleeve and torn a hole in the skirt near the hem.

"I have a plan," she said, patting the front of her dress. "I've got my gun, badge, and handcuffs hidden in here, and I want you to slap me on the cheek."

"Are you crazy?" responded Cooper. "I'm not doing that."

"Listen, there's more than one way to skin a cat. Sharp had his plan, and I've got mine. If I can get the Hart brothers back here in a few days, maybe Sharp can ride by then, and we can head home."

"You'll be outnumbered. Sharp wouldn't want you going alone."

"He was planning to go alone."

"That's different. He actually shoots his gun!"

"No, it's not," stressed Curnutt. "I have a plan, and I'm your boss. Now, slap me hard!"

Cooper hesitated. Then, closing his eyes, he swung his right hand toward Curnutt's cheek.

The blow caused Curnutt to take a couple of steps back, but she remained standing.

"That... will do, Cooper. I'll be back in a few days, but if I haven't returned in a week, assume I missed the Harts or something went wrong... and head back to Arkansas. Try to give me at least four days, but if Sharp gets worse, head back. Do you understand?"

"Yes... no, I'm not sure."

"You'll have a lot to do between caring for Sharp and watching the prisoners, but I'll be back as soon as I can."

With that, she turned and started walking south.

>······ ⇒⇐ ······◄

THERE WERE FEWER and fewer trees with every step Curnutt took. Soon, she was in open prairie. Here and there, she saw clumps of switch grass, but the ground was too dry for much else. She did see evidence of past storms, where lightning had struck and started a fire. In places, the flames had turned every shrub, sapling, and bit of grass into black ash.

Curnutt remembered an elderly Chickasaw friend telling her that this area was overrun with bison years ago, but when settlers started moving west, the animals began disappearing. Surveying the area now, she saw nothing larger than an occasional rattlesnake.

When the sun was directly overhead, Curnutt began questioning the wisdom of not bringing any water. She was thirsty, but she consoled herself with the thought that looking parched would add to her credibility.

With each step she took in the afternoon, Curnutt went over her plan. Everything hinged on timing and a little luck. If the Hart brothers usually visited around the middle of the month, she needed to arrive today. She considered that they might already be holed up in their mother's house. If they were, it would just affect how she played her arrival.

With the sun bearing down, Curnutt continued walking. Around half past six, she saw a few trees in the distance. As she drew closer, she could make out a house beneath the trees.

Hoping it was the right place, Curnutt walked toward the house and stopped twenty feet from the front door.

She'd hardly caught her breath when an old woman with gray hair and a rifle in her hands opened the door and called out.

"What do you want, missy?"

"I'm thirsty, ma'am. My feet hurt. I've been walking all day."

Curnutt had trouble getting the words out. Her lips really were swollen and cracked.

The woman didn't respond, but she noted Curnutt's swollen, bruised cheek and torn dress. After several minutes, she spoke again.

"What are you doing in these parts?"

"I'm... I'm running away... from my husband. He beats me... and I can't take it anymore."

The woman studied Curnutt again, from head to toe—but finally, she relented.

"I guess you can come in and have some food and water."

The old woman held the door open, and Curnutt walked inside. It was a relief to get out of the sun and sit in a real chair. The woman handed Curnutt a cup of water, which she grabbed gratefully. Gulping down the cup's contents loudly, Curnutt watched as the old woman began warming a pot of beans on a small stove. As the woman stoked the fire and stirred the beans, Curnutt engaged her in conversation. Being so isolated, the woman was eager to talk.

Curnutt told the woman her name was Ada. She was relieved when the woman said to call her Mrs. Hart.

As they ate at a wooden table, Curnutt learned Mrs. Hart had two boys who were also on the run—but they were running from the law. She said when her boys came home, they might be able to give Ada a ride to the nearest town.

Curnutt thanked her, and noticing a set of bunk beds, she asked if she could stay the night. The woman said yes, but she pointed Curnutt toward a small cot beside the stove.

"Those bunk beds are for my boys. They might be home any day now."

Curnutt lay down on the cot, and Mrs. Hart went in the back room to sleep. The old woman had left her rifle propped up against the wall. Curnutt waited till she heard Mrs. Hart snoring, but then she got up and emptied a single bullet from the rifle. If Mrs. Hart had additional ammunition, Curnutt couldn't find it, so she dropped the bullet down a crack in the floor and went back to bed.

During the following day, Curnutt did small jobs around the property, trying to make herself useful. That evening, as they were once again sitting around the table, Curnutt heard a long, loud whistle. She got up and looked out the window, but the sun had gone down and there was no one to be seen. Curnutt tried to look anxious, like she was worried it might be her husband, but Mrs. Hart just smiled. The old woman got up from her chair, opened the front door, and gave a loud whistle herself.

Suddenly, from out of the darkness, Curnutt saw two men approaching on horseback. They were riding rapidly toward the house.

"It's all clear," Mrs. Hart called out. "Come on in."

Two tall, heavyset boys dismounted and entered the house. Looking warily at Curnutt, they repeatedly hugged Mrs. Hart.

For her part, Curnutt tried to look nervous, weak, and uncertain.

"Don't look so worried, Ada," Mrs. Hart finally said. "These are my boys I told you about, Sam and Jack."

Mrs. Hart told them to sit down, and she placed beans, salt pork, bread, and water on the wooden table. Sam produced two bottles of whiskey, and they all ate and talked.

After hearing about a bank robbery and a shootout in Arkansas, Curnutt acted amazed and impressed. She didn't drink any whiskey, so there would be more for the two boys and Mrs. Hart.

It was late when they all finally went to bed. Jack and Sam fell asleep almost immediately, but Curnutt waited till she heard Mrs. Hart snoring before taking the handcuffs from beneath her dress. She got up from her cot and quietly handcuffed the two brothers while they slept. She was careful to do this without waking them up.

Early the next morning, however, Curnutt woke the two boys and forced them outside at gunpoint—with her unloaded pistol. She had fastened her badge to the front of her torn dress, and it was only when the badge glinted in the sunlight that the two outlaws realized they had been captured by the law.

Mrs. Hart was furious. She tried to shoot Curnutt with her rifle, but it wouldn't fire.

With her prisoners in front of her, Curnutt began walking the handcuffed brothers across the prairie. From her front door, Mrs. Hart cursed at Curnutt, but the deputy marshal kept striding north, frequently reminding the Hart brothers that her gun was aimed at their heads.

"Step lively, boys," Curnutt told Sam and Jack. "We've got miles to cover."

It was another long trek, but by nightfall, Curnutt was chaining the Hart brothers to the other four prisoners.

"How'd you get them?" Cooper cried out.

"Never fired a shot," answered Curnutt. "I told you there's more than one way to skin a cat."

"I don't believe it," marveled Cooper.

"You should never doubt a U.S. deputy marshal," said Sharp, coming around the wagon and leaning on a walking stick for support.

Curnutt smiled at him.

"I'm glad to see you're up and walking. Tomorrow we head to Fort Smith, right? We'll collect the rewards, get paid, and then head out again with our saddlebags full of new warrants. Like they say, if you're going to be a lawman, you must be devoted to the law, committed to getting your man, and willing to do whatever it takes. I just like to use my wits instead of a weapon."

>····· ≫⊱⊰≪ ·····<

—*Billie Holladay Skelley earned her bachelor's and master's degrees at the University of Wisconsin-Madison. She has written several health-related articles for both professional and lay journals, but her writing crosses different genres and has appeared in various journals, magazines, and anthologies in print and online—ranging from the* American Journal of Nursing *to* Chicken Soup for the Soul. *An award-winning author, she has written thirteen books for children and teens. Her book,* Ruth Law: The Queen of the Air, *was selected to receive the 2021 American Institute of Aeronautics and Astronautics Children's Literature Award, and her book,* Bass Reeves: Legendary Lawman of the Wild West, *received a 2024 Will Rogers Medallion Award and a 2024 Spur Award.*

Look Beyond

ALICE D. TREGO

NEBRASKA TERRITORY
SPRING 1879

GOOSEBUMPS TINGLED LARGE on Adelaide Wilkes's arms and alerted her to a strong feeling of misfortune. She gripped the steamboat's railing, clenched her jaws, and expected the worst. Speckles of ginger-colored dust dotted the air. Snorting and grunting heard at a distance became a thunderous roar within seconds. Waves of muddy water sloshed against the vessel that rocked against the tide.

The *Montana* steamboat's shrill whistle blasted, pierced her ears, and a sudden stop jolted her to the wooden deck.

Adelaide fell to her hands and knees in a most unladylike fashion. She sucked air back into her lungs a few times to catch her breath. *I can't be drowning,* she thought. Her hands suffered from prickled sensations like she had grasped a rose stem with its thorns stabbing her bare hand. She shook her fingers to bring them back to life.

Within seconds, strong hands assisted her by her elbow as she clumsily stood amid a jumble of crinolines, winter dress, and a long woolen coat.

"Are you all right, miss?" A deep, masculine voice brought an unexpected flush from her neck to her cheeks. To avoid any embarrassment, she straightened her rounded corner hat that had been sent askew during her fall.

"Yes, I... I'm fine, thank you. I need to get to my mother," she wheezed, and continued to hold onto his arm while she steadied. Adelaide realized the inappropriateness of leaning on a stranger's arm, so she busied herself by pressing down her long woolen coat to remove any unseen wrinkles.

Other passengers on the steamboat exclaimed their surprise to one another but quieted as Captain Aloysius McCall bounded down the steps from the pilothouse to the passenger deck. Witnessing an array of people, tall and small, being helped to standing positions, the captain came to the aid of a few stragglers still splayed on the deck. In doing so, he glanced around and noticed a shamble of boxed goods of dishes, foodstuffs, tack, and other supplies that had shifted from where they were placed. He would make sure his men inspected the goods in short order.

He removed his pipe and cleared his throat.

"I apologize for tha sudden stoppin' of this here vessel on such short notice, folks," he announced in his lilted Irish brogue. "The buffalo crossin' the Big Muddy happens from time ta time. So we'll have ta wait til the beasts finish their business ta git from one side ta the other."

He placed his hands behind his back, rocked on his feet, and carefully weighed his next words.

"In order ta give these animals a wide berth and not hit any o' them, I steered the *Montana* toward the edge of the nearest riverbank so's not ta cause any collisions. Me men are disembarkin' now to check for damages, but I usually don't damage any vessel I pilot."

Adelaide paused the smoothing of her overcoat as she straightened, wrung her gloved hands, and interrupted the captain. "How long will we have to wait, sir?"

"Now dontcha worry none, lass. We'll reach our destination in good time. We just need ta wait for the miles-long buffalo herd ta swim the water."

"We'll reach Fort Benton in a timely manner, won't we? My brother is waiting for me and our mother, and I'm expected at the fort as the children's new schoolmarm." The rush of her concerns resulted in a high-pitched sound she barely knew.

"Well now, lucky ya are bein' the new schoolmarm there. Yer ta be congratulated on the new position as the young'uns are in need of some schoolin' there at the fort. I'll make sure we sail on in good time."

Adelaide harrumphed and refused to resign to her predicament. *Maybe I should help the captain?* Turning, she noticed her immediate unsteadiness, walking like a drunkard in a back alley. She proceeded to her cabin to check on her mother who had become ill shortly after they left the dock in St. Louis. She hadn't realized the young man followed her, placing his warm hand close to her back to guide her.

"There'll be some swayin' of this passenger vessel so hang on tight when walkin' back ta yer cabins," the captain called out as if an admonishment needed to be given to his passengers.

A buzz of voices sounded as Captain McCall clicked his pipe in his mouth, took a puff, and sauntered back upstairs to the pilothouse. As he climbed the wooden steps, he thought of the many times he'd seen buffalo crossing rivers, but this herd stretched for miles. The length of the *Montana* and then some. His vessel and passengers were going to be sitting for hours to come. He wasn't looking forward to explaining about some of the ghastly sights that might be left behind in the muddy Missouri River.

No need to tell 'em there might be some carnage of beasts along the quicksands on the banks of the river when we finally move along. Some buffalo wouldna be so lucky as they sink and go out of sight, others comin' on top of 'em. In all me days as a river captain, I ain't seen the likes of so many buffalo crossin' at one time.

Adelaide now managed a brisk pace despite the constant rocking. She was in a hurry and anxiety overwhelmed her as she moved toward her cabin to check on her mother. After two previous steamboat trips from Halifax, Nova Scotia, that would take them to Montana Territory, this was the last leg of their journey before their feet were once more planted on solid ground. She hoped her mother would be well enough to continue on.

"What's happened, Adelaide?" her mother shrieked as she met Adelaide at the door that opened out into a long hallway, now littered here and there with shifted crates of goods. "Why has the steamboat suddenly stopped? I fell out of my berth most unceremoniously!"

Adelaide encircled her mother's waist and led her to one of the two chairs that occupied their small room, along with a three-drawer dresser and their two single beds. "It's all right, Mother. Captain McCall has explained that a large herd of buffalo is crossing the river, so he took instant precautions against hitting them and forced the steamboat to the edge of the riverbank. Unfortunately, the passengers were not given enough time to prepare for this small incident."

"Oh, my word," Mrs. Wilkes said, grabbing her linen handkerchief from her dress pocket and dabbing her forehead. "Our trip so far on two other steamboats has been so smooth. How long do we have to wait? Do you know?"

"The captain didn't say but I presume waiting will take a long while for all the buffalo to cross the river. He has his men checking the outside of the steamboat for any damages, too, and he suspects there won't be any."

"I'm beginning to feel a headache coming on," her mother said as she rose from her chair. "In spite of all this clatter, I may be able to rest some more."

"Yes, that would be best, Mother. We won't be going anywhere for a good while. You need sleep."

Adelaide made her mother comfortable before she slipped from the room. As she clicked the door shut, she startled at the sight of the young man who had assisted her. She had supposed he would go his own way, not follow her like a lost puppy.

"Is everything fine with your mother?" he asked, twirling his felt hat in his large hands. "I thought I would stay and escort you back to the bow so we might watch the buffalo pass by?"

"She's trying to nap again, which is best for her and no doubt will help with her malaise." A heavy sigh escaped from inside her. "This journey has been an arduous one for her in many ways. And I would like your company again, thank you."

He nodded, as if he understood, and replaced his hat on his head as they crept at a slow pace along the deck toward the bow.

They coincided their steps with the rhythm of the rocking steamship caused by the buffalo making waves as they moved through the water. *Walk slowly, Addie, otherwise you'll be staring at the wood flooring again.*

A difficult feat for them to keep their balance so he was ready with his arm in case she needed to grab hold.

A sideways glance by Adelaide revealed his tall stature and muscular build. Offhandedly, he reminded her of her brother Edmund, who was the main reason she and her mother had traveled for months, toward a new life in Fort Benton.

Once Edmund made the journey West and had settled into clerking at the R.H. Sutton Goods store in Fort Benton, he wrote letters home giving Adelaide instructions for boarding the three steamboats needed to bring them West. He also made sure to include enough money for their passages and other expenses. Adelaide smiled as she recalled that there was extra money so she could purchase her new hat in St. Louis. How thoughtful of Edmund to be aware of her fashion sense. He had regaled her in his fine handwriting tales of the children she would be teaching, suggesting he knew every one of them.

"My name's Finn. Finn Anderson," he said, clearing his throat and interrupting Adelaide's reverie.

"I'm Adelaide Wilkes. Thank you so much for your kindness before and walking with me now."

"No trouble at all. We have nothing but time, so we might as well converse with one another."

He grinned down at her. His fine white teeth accentuated his tanned face and made him more handsome.

"We do have some time, don't we? Depends on the buffalo, but I wish they'd hurry and get to the other side of the river."

They both chuckled as they reached the bow. Grasping the railing, Adelaide admired the western sun that had turned white that afternoon. As it lowered toward the horizon since their sudden stop, hues of orange and red began to fill the blue sky. The nighttime would soon be upon them.

Luckily many passengers had no doubt been offended by the odors of the beasts and made decisions to return to their cabins. She and Finn were able to stand by the railing alone except for a few passersby awkwardly avoiding scattered supplies.

From her vantage point at the bow of the steamboat, the buffalo were a mesmerizing sight. Despite their huge size, Adelaide's fascination with the animal's adeptness at swimming mesmerized her. The brown fur-topped clumps bobbed in the water as they made their way across the Missouri River, treading water with a graceful ease.

She had become used to the constant chug-chugging as the steamboat clocked five miles an hour past the town of Omaha. Sometimes she could hear the piercing song of crickets on the passing riverbanks. But not today. The swishing waters would become a balm for at least a few more hours.

"These animals are truly amazing, aren't they, Finn? It's a wonder that their massive bodies can carry them across the water like… like feathers."

"They are a wonder. In Montana Territory they roam wild and free. I've seen them from time to time, but I give them room and walk way around them. You'll see once you've lived in the wilderness that surrounds Fort Benton."

I wonder if he's joshing me or telling me the truth?

"I'm headed back to Fort Benton." Finn broke the silence. "I've been in St. Louis for a couple of weeks, trading with some businessmen on behalf of R.H. Sutton." He didn't want to tell her that he'd noticed her when she and her mother boarded in St. Louis.

"You work at R.H. Sutton?"

"Yes, I'm a trader for them and travel often, bringing goods back and forth down the Missouri River."

"Then you must know my brother Edmund?"

Finn rubbed his chin and shook his head. "Not that he sounds familiar. Nope, can't say as I do know him. R.H. Sutton has quite a few men working for them. Most of the men are off with wagons loaded with supplies to Spokane, Washington, and places in between."

"Oh, I see."

He sensed her disappointment and quickly added, "But since you'll be living in Fort Benton, you'll have to introduce us."

"I'll have to do that."

The sun reached the horizon, causing the colors in the sky to dissipate. The daytime would soon become night.

"Looks like we'd better head to our cabins before it gets too dark. I wouldn't want to hear about you falling over barrels or crates that wandered away from their resting places."

There was that gentle smile again. Adelaide had to agree with him, though. She began to tire from the eventful day.

He offered her his arm, she wrapped her arm around his, and they walked toward their cabins. Once he was satisfied that Adelaide would be all right in her small room with her mother, he sauntered to his cabin down the hallway.

Despite the splashing against the steamboat sides and the noises of the crew finishing their chores of moving goods back to where they belonged, Adelaide was finally able to fall asleep.

BY THE NEXT morning, the familiar chugging of the steamboat awakened her, and the loud blast of the whistle announced they were on their way once again.

Another month and a half of travel brought Adelaide and her mother to their destination. As she packed her valise, she thought back on the last miles on the Missouri River and realized they were without any more obstacles blocking their way. She was thankful for this. And thankful that her mother had received lots of tender care and recouped from her short illness. Frequent dotings by Finn helped too.

The *Montana* made its way to the dock at Fort Benton. Captain McCall sidled the vessel with a sea captain's expertise that Adelaide had come to appreciate during the last leg of their journey. The shrill of the two smokestack whistles announced the final arrival. The plank lowered and freighters off-loaded their wares.

Adelaide, her mother, and Finn waited their turn to disembark.

Finn doffed his hat and smiled his best smile. "It was my pleasure to meet you, Missus Wilkes," he said as he gently shook her hand. Then he turned toward Adelaide. "No doubt we'll be seeing each other from time to time here at the fort. It would be my misfortune if we didn't meet up once in a while."

"Most definitely we'll see each other, Finn," Adelaide replied. "I look forward to it."

When Adelaide and her mother walked down the plank along with the other passengers, they steadied themselves to regain their balances after so many days on the water. At once they picked Edmund out from the crowd gathered at the riverbank and stopped to wave at him. He waved back, his hat high in the air, and then he began making his way to the edge of the river.

"Haalloo," he called. When he finally met with his mother and sister after such a long absence, he gave them both tight squeezes. "I'm so glad you're here!"

>····· ⇒⋗⋐ ·····◄

—Alice D. Trego began writing people's stories in the late 1980s for a column called "Conversations" for Missouri's Suburban Journal *newspapers. During the 1990s, her focus expanded to include historical nonfiction and fiction. A few of her works garnered placement in various writing competitions. She currently serves as administrator and member of Women Writing the West, an international writing organization known for its rediscovery of women in*

the West, and she is also a member of Western Writers of America. Alice can be found on LinkedIn – www.linkedin.com/pub/alice-d-trego/1b/3b5/8b3/ and Facebook–https://www.facebook.com/alice.trego

Not the White Man's Vengeance

KIMBERLY VERNON

"I NEED A FRESH horse," the dusty stranger barked as he rode up. He raked hard eyes over me, then dismissed me, addressing Chester. "And some supplies."

I was helping Chester fix the corral fence, but I turned and slipped inside so they could talk business. I'd learned some men are funny about talking business in front of a woman, especially a half-breed like me.

The buckskin colt I'd been working stood tied to the fence, and he called out to me as I disappeared, probably thinking I was leaving him for good. I still had a few more lessons for him before I fed and turned him out. I could already tell he was going to be a good one.

The stranger's gruff voice was louder now. I heard Chester answer him, low and slow, but couldn't make out the words.

A shot split the air.

I dashed out the door in time to see Chester crumple to the dust. A scream exploded from my chest. "No!" My knife hurtled through the air, slicing deep into the stranger's gun hand before I realized I'd drawn it.

The stranger bellowed, dropping his pistol in the dirt. Blood slung from his hand. Seeing me rushing toward him with another long blade, still shrieking, he grabbed the colt's rope and jumped on his own horse. His hat fell from his head, revealing a tangle of orange hair.

Dust billowed as they bolted away. I sank to the ground beside Chester, sobbing. His blood soaked into the dirt as his life ebbed away. My life might as well have been soaking into that dirt along with his.

My wails and screams carried to the heavens as I mourned the kindest man I'd ever known. What would I do without Chester?

Sometime later, when I couldn't scream or cry any more, I retrieved the shovel from the barn. I clenched my teeth, knowing what had to be done, both here and down the trail.

I don't put much stock in the white man's God, but Chester did. So I did things as I knew he'd want.

I picked the spot under the big cottonwood, where the shade was deepest. One autumn night, we'd spread a quilt in that very spot and watched shooting stars streak over the mountains. My people believed the streaking stars were spirits on their way to the afterlife.

Chester was a big man, but my grief and rage gave me extra strength to move him. I tucked turquoise stones and arrowheads into his pockets, then wrapped him in that same quilt. My tears dampened the quilt before I finished.

My voice was harsh and scratchy as I said the only thing I knew to say. "Chester's God, if you're listening, he's yours to take care of now. Give him a good horse and plenty of open range to ride. And he likes rabbit stew every Sunday. He's a good man." My voice broke on the last words.

I wept as I filled the hole. Chester had been the first man who had showed me gentleness instead of inflicting pain. We'd built a good life out here in the middle of the plains, trading supplies and solid horses to travelers. Bitter gall rose in the back of my throat, and I choked it back. I finished piling rocks on Chester's grave.

I returned to the house and stoked up the fire. From the barn, I retrieved Chester's branding iron, with the letters *C* and *T* joined. When the iron was glowing red-hot, I pressed it into a fresh wood slab

Chester had planed, burning the image deep into the wood. When it quit smoking, I drove the wood into the soil at the head of Chester's grave. I don't know enough letters to spell out his whole name—Chester Tanner. But I marked his grave as best I could, with his signature, the brand he'd used on every cow and horse he raised. Even the horses he shod bore a miniature of his brand on their shoes. I think he'd be proud.

As daylight faded, I heard horses coming. I slipped into the shadow of the barn door and leveled Chester's rifle toward the approaching riders. When they came into view, I recognized one as Marshal Bates, who'd traded with Chester several times. Lowering the rifle, I walked out to meet them.

"What's happened? Where's Chester?" The marshal's eyes swept over my swollen eyes and the rifle I was toting.

"A Wasi'chu killed him!" I tried not to, but I began to cry again, the story pouring out in a mixture of English and Lakota.

Marshal Bates slid from his horse and led me to the porch. He sat beside me on the stoop, anger in his eyes. "Do you need help? With the burial, I mean?"

"It is done," I said.

"What did he look like?"

"He was nearly as tall as Chester, but scrawny. With hair the color of pumpkins."

"That sounds like Red Monroe. That's the man we're trailing."

"Well, he's got a nasty cut on his gun hand," I said. "And he'll be bleeding a lot more when I catch up with him."

"No, Missus Tanner. You need to leave this to the law. When we catch up with him, he's going before the judge, then he's gonna hang."

Marshal Bates was one of the few white men—hell, one of the few men—I trusted to keep his word. But I didn't want the white man's vengeance. I'd rather see Chester's killer bleed and die a slow death than hang. I stared at the ground, not wanting to agree with him.

"Monroe is a dangerous man, Missus Tanner. He won't hesitate to kill a woman. Please let the law take care of him."

I finally met his eyes. "When you find him, I want my colt back. And I want to be there when he meets the judge. I want to see him hang. Will you give me that?"

He stood and offered his hand to shake. "Yes, ma'am. You have my word."

After the marshal and his posse rode off, I put away the tools and fed the animals. I missed the colt fussing at me to hurry, as he always did. But the colt was smart and resilient. I believed he'd be okay.

In near darkness, I built a small fire behind the cabin and sat on a blanket beside it. I sprinkled sage on the fire, held my beads in my hands, and stared into the dancing flames until the images began to take shape. In words handed down from my ancestors, words I couldn't explain in English if I wanted to, I chanted and sang, calling on spirits both named and unnamed. I begged them to escort Chester on the journey, to help me know what to do without him, and lastly, I asked them to guide the buckskin colt back home.

When I woke, the fire was a bed of red coals and the night sky was still dark. Events of the day slammed into me, stealing my breath.

RED MONROE LED the horses through the narrow opening between the rocks and up a steep incline. He needed to secure them so he could take care of the wound where that crazy squaw had knifed him. It hurt like the devil. And he'd lost his pistol. All he'd wanted was a fresh horse. But the old trader could tell he was running from trouble and had refused to help him. It all went to hell after that.

He cleaned the wound as well as he could with the water from his canteen and his spare shirt. Then he tied it as tight as he could stand. He'd just rest a bit, then get back on the trail. He'd find supplies at the next settlement. The sooner he got to the border, the better he'd like it.

He woke with a start, surprised he'd dozed off. It took a minute to realize the sound he heard was horses' hooves clattering over rock. He scrambled over to the two horses he'd tied. They were alert and staring back the way they'd come, but thankfully, making no sound.

Red crept to a ledge and looked down to the main trail. He recognized the riders as a lawman and posse who'd been on his trail when he'd left Mill's Crossing. He'd had a good lead until his horse had worn down. That's why he'd stopped at the old trader's place. If he could've just got a horse and some ammo and got on down the trail, he'd be far from here already.

Sweat trickled down his neck as he waited. He gripped the rifle and considered opening fire. If they spotted him, or even turned this direction, he'd have no choice but to shoot. But he was low on shells, and what he really wanted was to let them pass, then head south. There were places he could stock up along the way.

He breathed a sigh when the riders disappeared without a glance in his direction. Once he was sure the posse wasn't coming back, he led the horses back down to level ground. He stripped the tack from his worn-out bay and saddled the buckskin. The horse was young and strong and seemed calm and surefooted. After tightening the cinch, he slipped the bridle over the colt's head. As soon as the bit touched the horse's lips, the animal exploded. He reared and spun, knocking Red off his feet. The animal then took off, galloping out of sight.

Red cursed as he scrambled to his feet. He was stuck with a rifle and only a handful of shells, a worn-out horse with no tack, and a posse looking for him. On foot, the closest place to remedy his situation was back at the trader's place.

He'd have to watch out for that crazy squaw, but he might enjoy making her pay for throwing a knife at him. Teach her a lesson about hospitality, then use her own knife on her. That might not be so bad after all.

Without at least a bridle, the bay was useless. He turned him loose and started off walking back the way he'd come from yesterday. Thinking about shooting the buckskin and the many ways he could make the squaw pay made the long trail bearable.

THE HORSES IN the corral heard the approach before I did. They snorted and blew restlessly, then one gave a whinny. A distant whinny answered, and my blood ran cold. Soon I heard galloping hoofbeats. I slipped inside the barn door, the rifle ready.

The hoofbeats grew closer, and I saw my buckskin colt racing toward me, riderless. The colt wore a heavy leather saddle. An empty scabbard flopped against his side. A leather bridle hung over his neck, the bit dangling under his chin.

I pictured the outlaw saddling up the strong young horse, tightening the cinch, preparing for a long ride. Things would have gone fine until he tried to shove the big, curved bit into the animal's mouth. I train all my horses to hackamore, only graduating to the bit in the finishing stages of horses we planned to sell. And only after I've established a deep trust between horse and rider.

I stepped from the doorway and reached for him as he skidded to a halt in front of me. But where is the murdering thief who'd taken him?

As glad as I was to have the colt home, my skin prickled. I knew the man was out there, and I knew he was coming back. I just didn't know when.

As darkness started to fall, I hurried through the chores, knives in the pouch at my waist and the rifle never far from my hand. I put the horses inside the barn and shut it up, knowing that's the thing he needed. But my bet was he'd go for the house first. He will want to punish me for cutting him. I don't know how I knew this, but I had no doubt.

Not wanting to waste a minute as I prepared, I ate a quick supper of cold biscuits and jam. I rolled and piled quilts in the rocking chair near the stove, then turned it facing away from the window. From outside, I hoped it looked as if someone was sitting there. There was just enough light from the stove to see shapes inside the room. I left the window open.

I retreated to the back room and waited. Several times, I doubted myself, worrying that he'd hit the barn, grab some horses, and be gone.

But the images I'd seen in the flames made me believe this was the path to my vengeance.

Wood creaked at the window. I tensed and gripped the weapon in my hand, holding my breath. The orange-haired man crawled in through the window. He crept across the room toward the chair, where he thought I was dozing.

Holding my breath, I slipped behind him. I slammed the hammer down on his skull with a satisfying thud. His knees buckled and he slumped to the floor. He was out cold, maybe dead. In case he wasn't, I wrapped thin leather strips around his wrists and secured them, then did the same with his ankles.

As soon as he was secured, I hoisted his feet and dragged him to the door. I didn't want this monster in my home. I didn't stop until he was lying in the dust halfway between the cabin and the barn.

I grasped his hair and lifted his head. With quick movements, I sliced along the hairline. Not dead, he screamed as I removed a large strip of scalp and orange curly hair. I dropped his head in the dirt and walked to the pump, hanging the scalp on the fence before washing my hands.

By sunrise, I'd dug a deep hole out behind the chicken coop. I was tired, so I saddled the buckskin. I threw a rope around the murderer's feet and tied it to the saddle horn. Sometime while I was working, the man had stopped screaming and cursing, but he started again as I dragged him to the edge of the hole.

"You should have wished for the white man's vengeance instead of mine."

I removed the rope from his boots, slit his throat, and rolled him into the hole. I left his feet and hands bound, to make sure he was identified as dangerous in the next life. Once it was level, I shoveled manure from the chicken coop and tossed it over the area, disguising the disturbed earth.

Returning to the yard, I carried the scalp to Chester's grave. Placing the scalp under a rock, I said, "I made sure he won't hurt anyone else."

I knew the white man's law did not approve. But I felt no more regret at taking his life than I felt for killing the skunk that got into my hens or the rattler near the well. That man killed Chester and meant to kill me. His death was kinder than deserved.

A few days later, Marshal Bates and his posse rode back through.

"Did you catch him?" I asked, meeting them in front of the barn.

"No, we were thinking he might have circled back."

"My colt came home three days ago wearing a strange saddle, so I expected him to show up. Maybe he's buzzard bait by now."

The marshal stared at me a minute, then tipped his hat. "You keep an eye open. There's lots of bad hombres out here."

"Yes, sir, I will."

The men rode on, but I could feel the marshal's eyes on me long after they were out of sight. He seemed to know I'd gotten my vengeance.

—Kimberly Vernon grew up watching the old Western TV shows like Gunsmoke, The Big Valley, *and* Bonanza. *Though she writes in many genres, she has a special place in her heart for all things Old West. She has won many local and regional awards for her short stories, essays, and poetry. Her work has appeared in several anthologies and magazines. She writes a monthly nonfiction feature for* Life in Chenal *Magazine. She is the author of a children's book,* Toolshed Surprise, *and a collection of poetry,* A Rhyme for Every Season. *Kim lives in central Arkansas with her husband, award-winning writer Gary Rodgers. The couple published a collection of award-winning stories titled* Favorite Animal Stories. *They share their home with several spoiled rescue pets. The two enjoy traveling, reading, and competing in writing contests. Her website is www.kimberlyvernon.net.*

ℬLUE ℐHADES

JULIE WESTON

NOT THE YELLOWED high-collared shirt, not the pink hose with runs, not the silk ties her customers had left behind, not the torn slip with lace on the hem. Ah, there it was. The blue silk sash, as blue as cornflowers. Octavia Cash drew it out of the box and sat back on her haunches, shoving the other scraps to the back of the closet.

This sash had wrapped her mother's waist. It came off the white robe her mother had worn when she died in the hall of the sanitarium. If Octavia closed her eyes, she could smell again the sharp, sweet odor of medicine and see the lime green walls. She could feel the hand that touched her cheeks.

Her own hands and her knees, both swollen in damp weather, ached. She crawled from under the hanging clothes and stood in her sitting room. The sash shone in the afternoon sun angling through her window.

Octavia began to sew a quilt on those nights when few customers called for one of her girls. She had intended merely to occupy her hands. Bits of material were easy to take up and put down when she answered the door or poured a drink or accepted the wrinkled bills and silver dollars proffered by customers or called a girl to entertain in the waiting parlor.

A double wedding ring was her pattern choice, an intricate inter-locking of eight patched circles. As with a compass, Octavia always knew where she was—at one end or the other. The idea of two wedding rings pleased her since she had never had one. Sewing gave her hands new life. She sought the texture of thread and cloth, stitching together pieces of cotton, silk, chenille, wool, and corduroy—all the fabrics she could find in shades of blue, fragments that seemed alive.

A patch of blue the color of sky reminded Octavia of the day she had escaped the house of prostitution in Seattle. With all her savings—her tips and the nickels and dimes and occasional dollars she'd stolen from men's clothes while they slept, change they wouldn't notice was gone —she had built a cache of over a thousand dollars. She knew just where she was going—away from the water by train, over the mountains, and across the desert to Idaho. There, the skies would not rain all the time, drizzling away hope, drowning plans, depressing the customers and making them mean.

The mining towns of Idaho were ripe for a new madam. Prohibition reached that far, but from gossip she'd heard, no one paid attention to it. Hundreds of men came in from the forests and out of the mines looking for women. She could make her fortune and leave the whole dreary business in a few years.

Just before she boarded the train, the sun had broken clear and a small patch of blue smiled at her. That was her omen. She had made the right decision.

Up a winding road in Bitterroot, Idaho, stood a three-story build-ing—an old boardinghouse—nailed shut. Octavia walked around it, counting the broken windows, smelling sweet orange from the white-flowered bushes growing wild along the hillside, hearing the groans from the steps when she climbed to the railed porch. Next door at a bar with dusty windows and double doors thrown open to catch wandering drinkers, she inquired.

"Who owns the boardinghouse?"

"Who wants to know?" The barkeep removed chairs from the tops of tables, swabbing each table with a dingy cloth. He stopped and studied Octavia.

"I do. I want to buy it." Octavia sat on a stool, making certain her dress crawled up her thigh, swinging her leg, studying the barkeep back. Men liked a woman who looked at them square. His eyes were the same seaweed green as the waters around Seattle.

"Pretty lady, I'd like you as a neighbor, but you don't want that house. It's haunted."

"Haunted? How?"

"Dead miners. Ones that died in a fire underground. They used to live there. At night, in winter, you can hear the flames crackle and the moans." Then he winked at Octavia. "But only if you sleep alone."

She did want the house, and she bought it cheap. On opening night, the new pine wood stairs, the oak banister leading up to the rooms with secondhand brass beds and clean sheets, the freshly waxed furniture in the parlor, the art-deco lamps on side tables, and the oriental blue carpet on the floor dispelled all rumors of ghosts. Men spruced up before they came to Octavia's house. Octavia found the shapeliest girls, the prettiest girls, even some ugly girls, but they knew how to please.

After one of her sporting girls died of opium poisoning, Octavia arranged for the burial. She dressed the body in a red dress and paid ten dollars to the undertaker to bury her in a churchyard, not the pauper's plot. She tried to parcel out the dead girl's clothes to the others in the house. As superstitious as the barkeep, they refused them, so Octavia cut squares from a worn blue gown to add to her quilt and threw away the rest.

Word spread through the brothels in northern Idaho and neighboring Spokane that Octavia had paid for a burial plot. More girls came to her looking for work. A wan, skinny girl, not much over sixteen although her eyes bagged like she was thirty, slouched against the railing when Octavia opened the door.

"Please, Missus Cash. Men like me, they do. I'll make money for you. It don't take much to keep me and I can turn 'em around three to an hour."

"We have no rooms." Octavia liked plump girls, even if they cost more in food. Girls with a little fat had more resilience. They didn't mope around and then kill themselves.

"Starr said you did, now that Tina died." Perspiration blistered the skin above the girl's mouth.

"No rooms." Octavia was afraid the pale thing would die on her stoop. "Go away." She began to inch the door closed, unwilling to pinch the girl's fingers in it. Then she noticed the cloche hat clutched in the girl's hand. It was more purple than blue, the intense violet color found in fall blooming salvia. She reached for the girl's arm and gently pulled her inside. "Come in and sit a spell."

Relief softened the girl's features, sharp with hunger or perhaps pain. "You'll take me?"

"We'll talk. I'll give you a spot of tea. You look like you need something to warm you up."

While the girl sat in the kitchen, it happened. She lifted the teacup with one hand and held the toast with jam in the other, as if uncertain which to put to her mouth first. "You're so kind, Missus Cash, not like I… oh—" The tea spilled over the side of the cup, and the toast fell from her fingers and landed jam side down in her lap. She slumped over the table. Her hat slid to the floor. Octavia retrieved the blue hat and called the doctor, annoyed with herself for ignoring her intuition.

The Girl: That old madam was going to take me in. When I passed out on her table, I was sure she'd send me to the workhouse even though I'd already been kicked out for being sick. Seems like I was always too sick and too tired and too skinny for other people's tastes. Not for some men, though. Sometimes I'd get paid and sometimes I wouldn't. I tried getting a job, but then I'd take sick again and there wouldn't be no job left. Slacker, they said.

She stuck me in a bed in the attic. There must have been a hundred steps to get there but the other girls helped. A doctor poked me and put that hard cold thing on my chest and listened to me breathe. He knew I was dying. So did Missus Cash. They talked over me, and then he put me in the hospital.

While I was laying there waiting to die, I had this dream. My uncle and aunt, who took care of me after my mama couldn't, sat on the railing of my bed and cried about how they didn't treat me better. They said if I'd come home, I could sleep upstairs instead of in the basement where spiders crawled across my face at night. My teacher said if I'd just get well, she'd keep me forever, and I could do my letters and read any book I wanted. I wouldn't have to walk the streets no more. They were all sorry. When I woke up, I fixed my hair as best I could. I pinched my cheeks and lifted the corners of my mouth to look like I was smiling even though I was dying. Maybe a visitor would come.

I never did leave there. Funny thing, Missus Cash kept my hat.

⇀·····⇌·····↽

SATURDAY NIGHTS WERE always the busiest. Miners with Sundays off, loggers in from the woods, a few farmers from the Washington valley—they all knew where the best sport was. Octavia juggled rooms and girls like a casting director for a Hollywood film. As often as not, a lovesick swain would arrive and claim to Octavia that one of the girls was his and he wanted her right then.

Abby, who had curly black hair, a dimple in her chin, thread-thin brows painted over eyes a little too close-set, and a way of circling a man's arm like he was the only man for her ever, never mind what she did, attracted more beaus than most girls. Octavia exerted some effort to keep Abby's boys mollified because they were willing to pay extra. She poured whiskey and brought in other girls to entertain them. Then she sent someone to knock on Abby's door and say, "Time's up."

If Octavia hadn't reaped another shade of blue for her quilt, she might have dumped Abby one Saturday night. Her latest regular beau, Johnny Applecakes she called him, came off duty from a fire crew in the woods. He smelled like burnt cedar and pushed by Octavia at the front door, treating her house like a cheap boarding place. He stomped up the stairs and pounded on Abby's door, crashed it open and pulled a customer out by his ear, hammering on the man's face with his other hand.

Naked Abby dashed out with a high-heeled boot in her hand and pounded at Johnny. The heel broke skin on his cheek. When he hit Abby, Octavia brought out her pearl-handled gun and shot it into the ceiling. All the people who had congregated to watch quieted. The naked man who had been with Abby cowered with his hands covering his private parts as if he thought his were different. Johnny scowled and Abby picked herself off the floor, using the high heel as a crutch to roll over. The stretch marks on her large bottom bloomed white under the hall lamp.

"That's enough." Octavia prided herself on never raising her voice, although she had been tested often. The sapphire blue of the material covering the boot had caught her attention and she coveted it. She held out her hand to Abby. "Give the boot to me."

Abby: "It's not my fault," I told the old lady. But I handed over my boot. I knew I'd never see it again, so I went back into my room to get its mate. She was one madam who didn't like nonsense going on in her house. But she never cheated us, and she let us keep our tips, not like other places on the line. I didn't want to get thrown out on my bum.

When I turned to go back to my room, I realized everyone in the hallway—including Johnny and Dirk, my customers—could see my stretch marks. I usually hid them either by sitting a lot or wrapping silk around my fanny. If Johnny knew I'd had a baby, I'd lose him for sure. He didn't mind me being a sporting girl and all, but a kid! That would rip it.

Just in case, I turned again and backed into my room, slammed the door, and scrambled around in the dust bunnies under the bed for my other boot. Then I opened the door wide enough to hand it out to the old lady. I flopped on my bed and sobbed. Maybe my heart would break and I'd die. I didn't care who heard me, but I guess all those feet shuffling around and doors slamming covered it up because no one came to comfort me.

When it got all quiet again, I blew my nose and fluffed my sheet and blanket to get the smells out. I waded through my closet and pulled down a clean robe—the green one that looked like emeralds and my eyes—splashed some Evening in Paris on my neck and arms, brushed my curls, and licked my fingers to wipe off two smudges by my nose. There was still time for another customer or two.

Later, I wrote Johnny. I told him how Dirk had promised me a feather boa, something I'd never had before. Otherwise, he didn't mean a thing to me. I was still stuck on Johnny, and he'd always be my favorite.

Something about that letter must have struck Johnny because he came back for me, all smiles and with a bouquet of flowers—daisies, I think they were. He told the old lady how he wanted to marry me, turn me into an honest woman. He told me to pack my things—he was taking me away from that life. The old lady thought I was making a mistake, but she let me go. At the hotel room, looking into the black bore of the gun Johnny pointed at me, I knew the old lady was right. There's only one way to leave the sporting life.

⊱┈┈•═ ⇌ ═•┈┈⊰

OCTAVIA MISSED ABBY. Girls like her were hard to come by. She had been cheerful and willing to do anything a customer asked and still kept her beau on the side. When Johnny came and took her away, Octavia had half believed his story. Although it was rare, some girls did marry. Later, when the newspaper reported Johnny had shot Abby in a hotel room in Spokane, Octavia almost cried.

While Octavia sewed one scrap of blue to the next, she allowed herself memories. If her hands were busy, the images that blew through her mind didn't haunt her. When she awoke during the night, or dreamed, the same pictures became nightmares.

Baby blue flannel brought a sadder time to mind of her own child, a girl with the bluest eyes of all the babies in the world and skin silky as a mink muff. Before her baby died, Octavia had found purpose in her life, knew that turning tricks was the fastest and maybe the only way to bring in enough money for the two of them. They could make it. Ten, as in Octavia's own family, couldn't. Her mother and father ran out of names on their eighth child. They ran out of money and out of love and patience and out of health and happiness. Her mother had died not long after Diaz was born. He was the one everyone in the family took care of and held and cuddled until he turned blue and died. Octavia wondered if her baby and her brother had known how the love that wrapped around them had failed them.

Her father didn't sell Octavia. He would never have done that. A man with slick hair and a fancy suit promised her father that Octavia would be a movie star. With her eyelashes and her legs both so long, and her bee-sting mouth like Clara Bow, she would wow everyone in the movie business. She could have a home in Hollywood. Her picture would appear on a silver screen and in magazines. Enough money for the whole family would flow like water. And it was the family her father worried about, along with Octavia's own future. How could he refuse her the chance? Octavia took her mother's sash with her for luck.

At first, Octavia wrote letters home, telling her family about the people she'd seen. Names everyone knew like Douglas Fairbanks, the sweetheart of the movies, Mary Pickford, and the dashing John Barrymore. She didn't mention Fancy Suit's demand and her compliance, or the less-than-famous names she had been passed around to, or the money paid not to her but to Fancy Suit. Instead, she described her expensive clothes, her makeup artist, and her hairdresser as if they really existed. When Fancy Suit sold her into the circuit, Octavia didn't write anymore, not that it mattered. Her last letter home had come back marked "unknown," a word she could easily have used to describe herself. So many siblings, scattered and lost to her.

>⸺ ⸺≈⸺ ⸺⸱⸱⸱◄

IF IT HADN'T been for Lily, Octavia would never have discovered the silk pictures of women in cigarette packages, a come-on to entice men to smoke. Lily pulled up her skirt, drew a pack of Chesterfields from a garter around her leg, carefully pulled out a cigarette with red lacquered nails, fitted the cigarette to a long holder which she swore came from Delmonico's in New York City. She lit up, inhaling deeply. Blue smoke, smelling of evenings in lounges full of people in formal clothes, obscured the cold linoleum floor and barren walls of Octavia's kitchen.

"You've never seen someone like me, have you?" Lily always talked like she was poking whoever listened to her in the chest.

Sometimes the other girls answered. Sometimes not.

"You don't even know what I am, do you? I'm a call girl, not just a whore like you girls. Rich men called for me."

One of the girls might begin a story about a rich miner, but Lily always interrupted.

"Not a workingman!" Lily would wrinkle her nose like she'd been presented with a dead beetle on a stick. "Do you know what a rich man is? He's beaver coats and clear pomade and alligator shoes and twenty-dollar bills lighting his cigar. You haven't lived until you've had a champagne bubble bath, let me tell you. And I killed a man, don't you know?"

Octavia didn't like to ask her girls for things, especially something as trivial as a used cigarette pack, so she watched Lily, counted the cigarettes, and waited for the pack to empty. Sometimes, the crumpled paper with its cellophane wrap ended up in the woodstove in the kitchen, still used to heat the room on winter days. Usually, Lily could be relied upon to save the silk scraps. She practiced the glamorous poses before losing interest.

After a while, Octavia's ear was tuned to the sound. She hurried to wherever the crackle came from, watched Lily from around a corner or through a door, and pounced on the picture as soon as Lily left the room. If Lily knew Octavia wanted the pieces of colored silk with their images of scantily clad actresses, she didn't let on. She simply saved them from extinction and left them around.

If only, Octavia thought, she had refused Fancy Suit. She might have been one of the actresses on the silk scraps, although most of the actresses were nothing but prostitutes anyway. She knew, finally, that Fancy Suit had never intended to get her a part. He made his money seducing young girls and then sending them around to different brothels. The more girls, the more "royalties," as he had called them.

Lily resembled the pictures—pearl-like skin and glossy hair, bosoms pushing against low-cut gowns of silk. Octavia didn't question her about the killing-a-man story. It probably wasn't true, but then again, things like that happened in New York City.

Octavia added the silk pictures to the circles in her quilt, stitching a shade of blue on either side. As she completed each circle, she hung it on her four-poster bed with the draped canopy, one of the luxuries she permitted herself, along with a cashmere dressing gown, satin sheets, and silk hose. She finished the circles about the same time Lily finished her life.

$$\rightarrow\!\cdots\!\!-\!\!\approx\!\!\sim\!\!-\cdots\!\leftarrow$$

Lily: You could fool everyone. Whenever I lit up a cigarette, I could see myself in their eyes—a fancy call girl from New York City, strutting and smiling with their teeth showing. In the Plaza, the girls come in the door on a man's arm, all made up with vamping eyes and dressed in short satin dresses, rolled up stockings, and floor-length furs. Jewels hang in their ears and around their necks.

Louise wasn't any name for a call girl, so I changed to Lily. The movie magazines said if you used enough lemon juice your hair turns blonde. The sun works better, but it roughens up your skin. Vinegar doesn't do so bad either. I wasn't a dishwater blonde, more like honey chestnut. I thought about calling myself Honey, but that was too cheap sounding.

Before I ran away from the farm in South Dakota, I figured out how to make money. If you read enough magazines, you knew that gold diggers were beautiful. My ma and pa would have croaked if they'd known what I was planning. They probably never even had sex except twice, once for me and once for my sister. Ma nearly fainted when I said the dog was pregnant. But you can find out things. Bobby Lee showed me. After that I knew what to do. You have to leave the farm if you want clothes and nightclubs—gin mills they were then—and handsome men and adventure. I was Sheba, not yet anyway, but I knew I could be. If you had the basics, like slick hair, no pimples, fairly straight teeth—although mine were bucked a little—and eyes that weren't too close together, and you acted glamorous, then men thought you were.

Things didn't turn out quite like I planned. For one thing, you couldn't just walk into a club and say, "Here I am." Even if you got all spiffed up, the stuff you wore couldn't be chintzy. And some men could be real mean and not even give you money. Then I tried sitting in a hotel lobby like a paying guest, reading a book. Not too many ladies just hang around, so you sit next to an old man and pretend to be with him. If he notices, then you make up to him, string him a line. If you're hot, you can make some money.

A better plan is to follow a call girl to a room and talk to her when she comes out. It worked for me. She took me along to a man in a nightclub— Jake was his name. He said he'd get you dates. But you had to give him all the money and then he'd buy you dresses and furs and jewels and things. I wasn't a dumb Dora, I told him. I wanted my own money. He smiled like I'd caught him out and said sure you'd need spending money, but he'd manage the rest—invest it for me and see I got my fair share.

Maybe I wasn't a dumb Dora, but I sure was a dumb Lily. Jake taught me to walk and act like a vamp, to like ritzy things, to talk up a john, to snort snow. The first time you didn't do exactly what he wanted, he'd beat you up. Then he'd make love to you and give you more snow. I almost died. Instead, I stuck him with a knife, stole all the money in his apartment, and ran away. Maybe I bumped him off, but I didn't care. Out West, you could make a pile and no one would find you.

It didn't take long to figure the old lady wanted the pictures from my cigarettes. Someone said she was an actress once. She thought she had a pretty high-class house there in Idaho. For Idaho you could say it was okay.

It was the boonies if you were from New York, but it was safe. Then one night a swell-looking Eastern dude came in. I should have known he was from Jake. Or maybe he wasn't. He brought snow with him, and we snorted some. He said he had something better. He shot it into my arm. "You won't want cocaine anymore," he said. He was right. You were dead.

BY THE TIME Prohibition ended, times in the mining town were skinny, but not as desperate as most places. The mines stayed open, but the dollars didn't flow as fast. Fewer girls came looking for work. When Octavia grew tired of the smelter smoke and the snap of grasshoppers in summer weeds, or the snow that crept up to the eaves before melting in sludge rivers in the street, or when she thought she heard flames licking at night, she slept with the barkeep and let his eyes remind her of the spring flowers in Seattle—yellow daffodils and red tulips and purple crocus—and the breezes licking along the water.

Four times, Octavia intended to sell, but the mining stock she bought collapsed, or she lent money to the barkeep and he went broke, or the local minister preached against her, and she wouldn't give him the satisfaction. No one was going to chase her out of business. Maybe when the quilt was finished.

After a while, Octavia spent more time on her quilt than she did on her house, searching for more blues—turquoise, aqua, cobalt, ultramarine, navy. She forgot to keep her eye on the business. The chandelier in the hallway, with its missing pieces of colored glass and half its candle-shaped lights gone out, murmured to customers that they could chip away at the prices. The antimacassars on the chairs and davenports in the parlor no longer covered all the threadbare spots. The oriental carpet, bright and lush when new, faded until it seemed all one color—muddy brown. In her room, Octavia wove her circles together on white summer cotton, tying a back on with blue yarn, filling the insides with goose down.

Not long after she completed the quilt, Octavia didn't come to the kitchen at noon. No one thought too much about it, but when she didn't show up for evening inspection, one of the girls checked her room. She found Octavia still in bed, plucking at her quilt. Her head looked old and crumpled, unlike the stern dowager whose bony cheeks and eyes like still water reminded everyone she was beautiful once.

"Come in, girls," her weak voice called. "I must tell you about my quilt." Octavia patted it. All night, her head had filled with visions of blue—her dead daughter's eyes, Abby with sapphire feet, a stick of a girl with violet-blue skin and a skull with strings of blue hair, and a trainload of smoking actresses.

"This blue is my mother." Her finger, shaking with palsy, outlined a piece of silk.

"This blue is my brother," she said, and then changed her mind. "No, it's my baby."

"This blue is the sky above the train." On each shade of blue, Octavia attached a new label. Her voice droned on, and she didn't lift her head. Sometimes, she thought for a minute and her voice faded. "This blue is Abby, sweet Abby. No, not sweet." She shook her head and moved to the next scrap.

The girls looked at each other. Had the old lady gone round the bend? Was she dying? Overnight she had become a crone. The wind blew around the house, pushing at the dark panes of glass, and rain spattered on the roof. It had been the worst fall anyone could remember, wet and sad. The quilt rippled on the bed.

"And all these pictures. They're Lily."

>----- ⇒⇐ -----◄

BEFORE MORNING, OCTAVIA died. The girls collected money and paid the undertaker ten dollars to bury her in the churchyard. The night before her burial, the girls divided up her belongings. No one wanted the box of scraps in the closet, or the sheets she died in, or her shoes, or her underwear, except for the lace camisoles that had never been worn. They packed up the leftovers to give to the church poor box, although the preacher wasn't sure he wanted them.

"Who wants the quilt?" one of the girls asked.

"It's full of dead people," another whispered. "Didn't you hear her tell the stories?"

"It smells like smoke and old ladies."

"Let's give it to the funeral man. He can wrap her in it."

Octavia: No one wanted my quilt. No one, that is, except the undertaker. The girls brought it in and said to bury me in it. He didn't. He kept it for himself.

I couldn't sleep under it when I was alive. The ghosts slipped in and out. They weighed on my head like stones on my eyes. I wonder if the undertaker is haunted by my blue shades and if Lily still looks out from all the silk pictures.

—Julie Weston grew up in Idaho and practiced law for many years in Seattle. She is the author of the Nellie Burns and Moonshine Mystery series, all taking place in 1920s Idaho: Moonshadows *(finalist for the May Sarton Historical Fiction Award),* Basque Moon *(winner of the 2017 WILLA Award for historical fiction),* Moonscape *(Bronze Winner of the Foreword Award for mystery),* Miners' Moon *(Bronze Will Rogers Medallion Award for mystery),* Moon Bones, *and* Salmon Moon: River of No Return. *Her nonfiction memoir of place won honorable mention in the Idaho Book of the Year Award. Her short stories and essays have been published in several journals and magazines. She and her husband live in central Idaho where they ski, write, photograph, and enjoy the outdoors. Visit www.julieweston. com for more information.*

BIG SKIES. BOLD FLAVORS.
REAL RANCH COOKING.

Will Rogers Medallion Award-winning author **Sherry Monahan** takes you on a delicious ride through the kitchens of America's most iconic dude and guest ranches in the first volume of her new Culinary Treasures cookbook series. From sun-up sourdough flapjacks to sundown skillet suppers, *Dude & Guest Ranches of America* delivers recipes straight from the trail, the chuckwagon, and the family table—each served with a side of Western heritage and hospitality. Learn the secrets of perfect cowboy steaks, campfire beans, and flaky ranch pies, all while exploring the untold stories of the families who keep these living legends alive. Fire up your range and rediscover the spirit of the West—one unforgettable bite at a time.

"A man only learns in two ways, one by reading, and the other by association with smarter people."
—Will Rogers

WILL ROGERS
MEDALLION

RECOGNIZING EXCELLENCE IN WESTERN MEDIA AND STORYTELLING AND COWBOY POETRY

www.willrogersmedallionaward.net